Best Wishes,
Mark

The
I Can't
Get Enough
Club

A Novel

The
I Can't Get Enough
Club

A Novel

Mark B. Weiss

Benjamin Mandel Publishing Company
2442 N. Lincoln Avenue
Chicago, IL 60614
www.benjaminmandel.com

ISBN: 0-5780-6340-9
ISBN-13: 978-0-578-063409

Dedication

I write with passion. Often anxiety and emotion fuel the ability for me
to think and create. I dedicate this to those who embrace passion, find
sensuality in life and in ideas and have no fear to explore and do for
others. Live while you are alive!

Advance Praise

"Chicago real estate entrepreneur Mark B. Weiss has already established himself as the author of five highly acclaimed books on buying, selling, renovating, developing, flipping and maintaining real estate properties. Now, Weiss has ventured into the world of fiction with a stunningly good page turner. *The I Can't Get Enough Club* is loosely based on his personal experiences with the banking institutions that finance his projects and the characters that inhabit that milieu.

The all-too-real storyline takes readers inside a world of high finance, where nobility of character comes with a price tag, and greed and changing fortunes dictate the creation and dissolution of alliances. Along the way, the book's characters provide the uninitiated with a primer on real estate and banking practices, City Hall bureaucracy and the pulse of Chicago's ethnic neighborhoods.

I grew up in one of those ethnic Chicago neighborhoods with lifelong pal Mark B. Weiss. We took different paths. He immersed himself in the world of business. It is from this informed-insider perspective that he was able to pen this fictional tale. I immersed myself in the world of letters and continue working as a long-time reporter and feature writer at the *Albuquerque Journal*. It is from this perspective that I've honed something of an ability to detect the heart and truth of things.

The I Can't Get Enough Club is Mark B. Weiss to the core. It has heart, it has truth, and it is alive with the ironies, absurdities, oddities and hypocrisies of living and doing business in Chicago. These are the very things that drive Weiss, the businessman, crazy in real life; but these are also the very things that give Weiss, the observer of humanity and the author, an opportunity to showcase his distinct voice and wit."

--Rick Nathanson, *feature writer at the Albuquerque Journal*

"It was a pleasure to read a book that is right on the money about why this financial world is in such turmoil. The story kept my interest from start to finish. The characters gave me a personal insight on how a long line of abuse and the dishonest quest for money and greed change one's integrity. This story should be required reading for the average citizen who wants answers to why I can't refinance my home and what happened to the credit markets.

Every author covets timing of current events and this story has the catchy cast of characters and events to keep a reader's interest. Let's hope Mr. Weiss, your story gets published and readers can be informed and enjoy a brilliant piece of storytelling."

--David Glassman, *Comptroller Universal Steel*

"*The I Can't Get Enough Club* is an ambitious and gutsy novel that takes a very straightforward and unnerving look at greed and corruption. This book is a well observed study of the business practices that take place in today's world and it is impossible to put down. I loved the characters and the out of kilter world in which they live...Mark B. Weiss writes in a strikingly honest and straightforward manner. Bring on the sequel!"

--Marilyn Egel, *MCSW*

"In *The I Can't Get Enough Club*, Mark Weiss has not only made a challenging subject (banking and finance) understandable, he has also made it readable in an engrossing way that keeps the reader happily turning his pages. Weiss has crafted a work that is as informative as it is entertaining. And it is very entertaining."

--Dan Baldwin, *Author and Editor*

"Greed is greed and it doesn't much matter where it happens. *The I Can't Get Enough* Club is as relevant in London, Moscow or Sydney as in the Chicago that the action within it takes place. Further, it is especially relevant at this time of global credit squeeze and junk mortgage bonds. If you (like me) do not really understand how our current banking crisis has come about, after reading this book it will be clearer.

'But,' I hear you say, 'surely you are not going to tell me that all international bankers are corrupt and greedy, surely some of them are honest.' Well maybe, but as the reader will discover as the engrossing story unravels, the bad and powerful get the bad and weak to do their dirty work and within their plots, the good and weak become ensnared leaving the good and powerful too few in number to have any effective impact. As the old adage goes, 'power corrupts and absolute power corrupts absolutely.'

The story features two anti-heroes. The first and present throughout the whole book is Fran Kontopolus. To be blunt, she is a nasty piece of work who only 'just' knows how to behave within the norms required to get along. But get along she does and makes a habit of doing it at everyone else's expense. The second, who appears about halfway is Sonny Vulich. He is Fran's mentor. But only because it serves his current purpose. He is an arch manipulator who can bide his time, waiting for the right moment to appear. But more than that, with prescience he plans his game. As time moves on his real nature becomes revealed as those whom he controls play the part he orchestrates and the weak get pushed aside until he is ready to make his play for endgame.

Ultimately the book questions the reader's own moral compass. Most ordinary people like to consider themselves as their 'own man' aloof and immune from the corrupting effects of the seven deadly sins. But this story will cause you to question your own moral fabric as it becomes apparent that very few are safe when presented with the opportunity to profit.

Mark Weiss has crafted this tale from a mixture of personal experiences and the events with which we are all too familiar. The story is told in an 'easy to read' style where the more complex financial aspects are explained clearly and easily for the lay reader and are not allowed to interfere with the narrative. This is entertaining and events flow easily from one chapter to the next.

The biggest criticism I found was that like the protagonists, I wanted more. The book made me 'greedy' to know what happens next. So, Mr. Weiss, roll out a sequel so that we can find out how Mr. Vulich gets his kumupence!"

--David Sherwood, *Businessman United Kingdom*

Acknowledgments

I want to acknowledge those who supported my effort to tell you a story. Over the three years from concept to completion the following people read, heard my narratives, re-read, and read again my ideas typos and varieties of this tale.

To my friends and family who supported this effort, I thank you. You have shown me your continued support and I appreciate it. Marilyn Egel, Daniel Egel-Weiss, Charlie Egel-Weiss, Rick Nathanson, Clyde Millman, Fred Rudin, David Sherwood, David Glassman, Dan Baldwin, Janie Stiller, Joel Paine, Ivana Egel, and Kathy Welton. Your support was what I needed.

PROLOGUE

"Corporate America consists of two types of people. The first perform well looking for recognition. The second undermine their fellow employees in order to succeed by making others look bad!"
— Adam Berg

Hell blazed above Chicago. As he rushed south on Lake Shore Drive, Fire Commissioner Patterson saw the fire devastating the forty-ninth floor of the luxurious Wacker Tower Apartments. The clock in his car read only 6:18 p.m., yet the blaze lit up the night like a torch. Daylight Savings Time had just ended and darkness covered Chicago earlier than he was used to. For an instant, his mind flashed to those horror movies from the thirties, the films with angry, torch-bearing villagers raging to burn some monster in the night. *Not a bad image for Chicago these days*, he thought.

In his eight years as commissioner, Patterson had never been pulled from *60 Minutes* and dinner with his family. He was a dutiful man. Lives and property were at stake. And his pension. News, police, and fire department helicopters hovered above the building as he arrived, their spotlights probing the burning apartments. The police and firefighters searched for someone alive and in need of rescue. The news reporters just wanted a bit of gore as a lead in to the late news. The noise of the vehicles, sirens, chopper blades, and traffic became a heat blast of confusion as he stepped out of his car.

A high-rise fire was unusual. One preceded by an explosion forty-nine stories above ground reminded him of 9/11, but he could see no indication of a plane crash, and his gut told him this was not a terrorist act. *Terror? No, not a high rise,* thought Patterson. *There are too many choice targets in Chicago. Far too many.*

He was immediately greeted by Captain O'Malley of the Chicago Avenue fire station. Located on the Gold Coast across from the old Water Tower, the building had survived the Chicago Fire of 1871 and still served the public welfare. "What gives, Tom?"

"Well, Commissioner, best as we can tell it was a gas explosion."

"Do we know how many apartments got hit?"

"One. Belonged to a woman named Kontopolus, Fran Kontopolus."

Patterson knew the name. "Was anyone injured in the blast?"

"Well, we don't know. The fire is still in charge up there. If she were home this would have been a hard one to live through. May the Lord have mercy on her soul."

"Not everybody would agree, Tom." He looked up. Hell on the forty-ninth floor.

✫ ✫ ✫

A nervous young man named Kent Shem scratched a few lines on a notepad. The paper, like his well-chewed pencil, carried the bank's logo. He drew a line of stick men, the same number as the men in the board room. Off to the side he sketched another figure holding a stick rifle. Flame shot out of the barrel and little dots of gray lead shot across the page. One by one, he crossed off the men in the line. Little puffs of air popped out of his mouth as he drew an X through each little man.

The other board members were sullen. Their consciences were weighing heavily. They had been set up. Worse, they had gleefully participated in their own subjugation. They waited with a sense of dread for their new chairman to arrive and begin the meeting. This was a serious day for Sunrise Bank. They had an obligation to be civil to the chairman, but they all felt like a shadow of themselves. Hollow men, they shared more now than ever before. They were truly one. The young board member felt like some Mexican peon from the past. Facing the officer with the bright uniform and shining sword, he had been given a choice: slavery in the mines or "up against the wall."

The news on the local radio and television stations repeated the story about Wacker Tower all morning. It was on the front pages of the *Sun Times* and the *Chicago Tribune*. The fiery shooting star of Chicago banking had fallen to earth, blazing, but not in glory. No, her crash and burn was far, far from glorious. That kind of news was not what the board needed, not at all. The federal investigation, the gossip about her sudden downfall, and now this was just too much to handle. They were pawns and they realized it was too late to do anything about it. Regardless of their feelings for that woman, their new leader was worse. And they had supported him all the way.

Part of life is not realizing you have made a mistake until after the mistake is made. Hindsight, what a bitch. They looked at each other as if they were all going to hang for the crime. That would never happen even though each carried the weight of guilt. Each man wanted what was promised and each would certainly get what was coming to him. They had all come out on top in a sense, but there was only one real winner, Sonny Vulich. They could take their place in the mines or go stand against the wall. The board had pulled back the sheets, seen the devil, and jumped in bed with him anyway. Their own greed had set them up and now it was time for payback. Another bitch. This nightmare wasn't in the plan, at least not their plan. The sentence they were to serve was predestined and they had to live with themselves for the rest of their lives. Kent Shem looked around the room and mumbled, "Welcome to the club."

✫ ✫ ✫

"Ten million in the first two weeks, that's more than this bank earned annually in any of its previous years. That key man insurance is sure to pay off too. Now we don't have to raise capital for some time. When the board meeting is over, meet me for lunch at Gibson's, usual table in the back. One sharp and don't be late, Marshall." The chairman snapped his phone shut, disconnecting the call to his lawyer.

At last, all the pieces had fallen together. He grinned in anticipation of the meeting. Even with an ego the size of the Rock of Gibraltar, Sonny Vulich could not believe the rise of his success. The fate of Fran Kontopolus never crossed his mind.

CHAPTER ONE
(The Previous Night)

Her smoking was getting worse. She was already back up to two packs a day. Her clothes, her apartment, and her car reeked of burning tobacco. From the moment she woke until the moment she closed her eyes cigarettes surrounded her. The ashtrays in her apartment were overflowing. Ashes dusted the furniture and carpet like a foul, gray snow, and sometimes the air was as thick as a fog coming off the lake. She used a Zippo lighter as she had early in her career. She liked the sharp, slightly threatening switchblade "ping" of metal when it snapped shut. There was a finality about it. The smell of the lighter fluid brought back her younger days, a time filled with energy, a competitive spirit, and venom.

Nervous all the time, she could not sleep without two Ambien washed down with hard booze. Staggering from the sofa to the bed without falling or spilling the precious vodka on ice became a game. She had stopped eating. Her bulimia had morphed into anorexia. Her body, like her life, was shrinking, dying. And she didn't give a damn. She would often lose her balance, falling sideways. The lack of nutrition, the drugs, and the alcohol made her knees buckle. The truth attacked her when she was alone and her apartment became a prison cell in the sky. Her neighbor was a former governor recently indicted. He was leaving the following week for a six-year sentence in a white-collar prison in Wisconsin. She wished she could go with him, away where she could hide for a few years, but she knew she could not get away from herself.

She had been disliked. Hell, most people hated her. She had worked her entire life to achieve that goal. But Sonny, her Sonny, how could he do this? She had trusted him and he took advantage at a time when she was most vulnerable. Her fall from the top of the world two weeks earlier had been sudden, brutal, and totally unexpected. She had always been the one doling out punishment and reward, the one with the upper hand. Now she was the victim. Her paranoia raged. She gulped the vodka and stumbled again, this time into the stove. She bumped a knob just enough to turn on a burner. Vodka spilled onto the burner and the pilot light. Both flames were extinguished. She didn't notice as her vision blurred. Nor did the smell of the natural gas strike her as being odd. She was determined to get into bed before falling again.

Once under the sheets she opened the Zippo lighter and lit another cigarette. She held it between her fingers, hypnotized by the red glow and the swirling smoke. As it slowly burned, the apartment filled with gas. She closed her eyes and the cigarette fell from her limp fingers onto the bed. The bed cover began to smolder and smoke started to fill the bedroom.

This was the last night any neighbor would stay awake listening to the snoring of Fran Kontopolus.

CHAPTER TWO

A smart businessman like Sonny Vulich looked to other people for one thing—an advantage, preferably a decisive one. Morals and ethics never came into play. His business and his profits were never compromised. A true shark, he always took advantage of everyone and every situation he possibly could, burning bridges with abandon along the way. He had one goal and that was to make as much as he could regardless of the rules. Burn bridges, hell, burn people.

He was born in Hegewisch, an ethnic neighborhood like many in Chicago with one exception, one unusual quality. Located in the Tenth Ward just west of the Indiana border on Lake Michigan, it was invisible. Anyone who found himself there wouldn't notice much difference from most ethnic communities. So why was this typical neighborhood invisible?

Hegewisch was located on a side of Chicago that does not exist for most residents, the east side. Everyone in Chicago knew that Chicago did not have an east side. The lake was the east side, not the quiet, self-contained, blue-collar community. Here men went to work. Women stayed at home and raised the kids. Families came from Eastern Europe, Poland, Serbia, Croatia, Slovakia, and Russia. Most of the men worked in the mills. Independent businessmen owned butcher shops, bakeries, and taverns. Signs for Schlitz, Miller, and Hamms Beer lit up the streets.

The center of social interaction and of course the polling place, where everyone voted Democrat, was the corner tavern. A man's watering hole was a special place. Unlike television's *Cheers* where everyone only knew your name, the local tavern was the place where everyone knew your name, your family, your successes, failures, frustrations, and your problems. Customers attended the same church and worked in the same businesses. The community always chipped in money to help the bereaved family as they always passed the hat when a home burned, a friend required medical care, or to bring friends and family from Europe.

The walls were lined with fading memorials to the neighborhood's fallen—yellow, curling pictures from WWI, small black and white photos from WWII, color snapshots from Korea and Vietnam, and now color computer printouts from Iraq. Death and technology marked the years.

The people of Hegewisch prayed together, worked together, mourned together, and enjoyed drinking together. Women, other than the wife of the barkeeper, were never seen in the taverns. The factory whistles ended the dayshift at 5:00 p.m. and by 5:15, the metal lunch boxes hit the top of the bar with a series of clanks and rattles. The rhythm of the bottle tops popping inspired many snappy tunes from local musicians. The suds of the beer bottles resembled the overflow of lava. Drinking and blowing off steam was an essential part of one's day. Supper was being cooked at home, usually boiled meats and potatoes. The taverns were empty by 7:00 when the men headed for home and the family table.

Residents of Hegewisch were xenophobic. Sons were expected to work in the factories where their fathers and grandfathers worked. That was it. A boy married a girl from his church. Newcomers were relatives of neighbors from the old country. That is how the population increased—marriage, procreation, and immigration. New arrivals began working at the mills on the nightshifts. That was always the entry to work, and English was rarely heard during the nightshifts. Relatives stayed with family. New transplants slept in the A-frame attic of old houses or in the basements, huddling and snuggling in small beds to keep warm. There were no zoning laws to limit the number of people who could live together. Deadly house fires were common in these cheaply constructed frame houses. Someone smoking in bed or a spark from a meager fire would ignite a house and with relatives sleeping in small places with little to no ventilation and no escape route the worst often happened. And once again the hat was passed.

But the United States spelled freedom and work was plentiful after the Great Depression. Hegewisch was a community like many in the Midwest, but it remained an unknown entity to most residents of Chicago. The secret to its invisibility was that it was the lakeshore industrial community that connected the city to Northern Indiana. It couldn't be seen on the highways. One had to get off the main roads and have a reason to go to there. Someone could live an entire life in Chicago and never hear of the place and certainly never visit this very real and vital neighborhood. As with much of life, people don't see what they don't want to see.

In 1938, Sonny, the eldest of four children, was born in Hegewisch, delivered by a midwife in his grandfather's single-story home. No one in Sonny's family worked at the mill or any of its suppliers. They were carpenters and handymen. Sonny's grandfather never learned English, but in the years before technology, when machines and anything mechanical had logic to their proper operation, Mr. Vulich could fix anything.

Throughout his life, old man Vulich was the original Mr. Handyman. When a neighbor had a damaged chest of drawers or a broken radio old man Vulich could fix it. When a sink or toilet was not working, a child would be sent to the Vulich home. Nothing was out of the realm of the old man's capability. He simply knew how things worked. He knew that one gear turned another. He knew that a handle fit something else that was connected to that thing that made the item do the thing it was supposed to do.

Vulich would look slowly and carefully at an appliance or piece of furniture and know that somewhere below the surface was a damaged piece of the whole that was broken, chipped, bent, or loose. Finding that piece of the puzzle and overcoming its challenge kept the old man stimulated and interested in life and was as necessary to the community as the local doctor. The man with the toolbox cured the diseases of the mechanized age. He had one son and five daughters. He paid little attention to the girls, but Sonny's father, Duke, was special. He was a strapping boy. At the age of three Duke went on house calls with his father and handed him tools. Duke was always seen either on his father's shoulders or running quickly behind with a small toolbox of his own. The box wasn't filled with toys. They were real tools, small but functional, and the old man made sure Duke knew how to use each one.

Duke was the oldest of the children and his father's pride and joy. He took naturally to the tools and duties of a handyman and became able to repair or fix anything. As a young man, he decided he wanted more for himself. Duke saw his father walk house to house day and night when the neighbors called and he was proud of his father, but Duke saw that there was never enough money around. Often the old man was paid in trade and that was all right, but frequently payment was deferred, which meant payment never arrived.

Duke decided that he would learn carpentry, build houses, and make something of himself. At any opportunity, he would help neighbors put up four walls to build a house. Duke would pass a construction site and ask the foreman if he could assist the tradesmen. In a short time and while still a very young man, Duke learned all he could about the products, tradesmen, assembly, and coordination of home building. Unlike many apprentices, he knew how to nail properly. Hit the head straight on so you don't create a quarter moon divot in the wood, a task that is a bigger challenge than most think. He impressed the foreman. "You're a good 'nailer,' kid." It was one of the finest compliments he had ever received. Duke started moving up the construction ladder.

He learned the sequence of building. The preparation of the foundation, framing, electric box routing throughout the walls, plumbing locations, how to run water lines and waste hook-ups to the street. Duke would lull himself to sleep at night building houses in his mind. He could do space planning and layouts in his head. He saved every penny and soon created a small but profitable home building company in Hegewisch.

After World War II, with his son, Sonny, at his side, Duke would tell the boy that being a carpenter was a necessary trade. More than that, it was an honorable one. And like father like son, Sonny would hand his father tools and materials as he worked in the booming post-war building business. Duke wanted more for Sonny than simply building houses in the neighborhood. Sonny was of a generation more American than Eastern European. Doors closed to his father and his father's family could be opened for Sonny. Duke wanted the boy to be the first of the Vulich family to go to college.

Duke kept a secret from his family. From the day Sonny was born, Duke deposited five dollars a week into a savings account at the local credit union. This was for Sonny's college education. When Sonny was eighteen and had completed high school, Duke called the family together for Sunday dinner. The family knew something was special that day. One, he had not changed clothes after church as he usually did. Two, he did not join his friends for a beer at the tavern to watch the Chicago White Sox on TV. Three, he came home, sat in the living room, and listened to classical music on the radio. He brought out a bottle of the anise-flavored Slivovitz Liquor, brought to him by a friend from the old country, and sipped it all afternoon.

It was not until dinner, after grace and after he carved the roast beef, that he raised his glass and tapped his fork against it to get everyone's attention. As all eyes turned toward him, he made his announcement. "My family, we are fortunate and blessed to be eating this food together and blessed to be in this wonderful country. We are blessed that we are healthy and blessed that we have been successful and have some money. Sonny, who has a responsibility to the next generation and to this family, well, Sonny, this is an important time for you. You have decisions to make that will affect the rest of your life. My father could not speak English well. He certainly could not read English and yet he worked hard, bless his soul, and we must be thankful to him. But now we look to the future. I have a surprise for the family and you, Sonny. The week you were born, I opened up a savings account at the Hegewisch Credit Union where I deposited five dollars per week for the last eighteen years. This money, which earned interest, is your money to go to college. I want you, as the future patriarch of our family, to be the first to graduate from college and make a good career for yourself and your family."

Mama started to cry. His sisters began to clap. Papa Duke had tears in his eyes and all seemed right with the world in the Vulich house. Sonny was speechless. He had dreamed of going to college and of doing better than his father. He had been a quiet observer over the years. He had worked in construction and watched as the builders and bankers came to evaluate the work. More than that, he paid attention to the negotiating, the wheeling and dealing, the lies and half-truths, and the details of putting deals together. Sonny did not like the calluses on his hands and he did not like jumping whenever a boss shouted an order laced with an obscenity. He wanted to be his own educated man. And Sonny knew that the values of education would lead him to downtown Chicago. He felt his life was just beginning and walked over to Duke and gave him a big hug and kisses on both cheeks. Silently, he said goodbye forever to Hegewisch.

CHAPTER THREE

Fran Kontopolus was the first born in a family of three children. Her parents, immigrants, knew all too well about the risks to children with too little to eat. They had survived the Great Depression. Now living in Post-World War II America, Fran's father, Dimitri, was not going to have his children go hungry. Dimitri Kontopolus opened the DK Fish Store. Having loads of food was a sign of abundance and a symbol of success in a nation of immigrants. The Kontopolus family always provided plenty of food for their kids, especially the eldest.

"Eat up, sweetie."

"Clean your plate."

"Have some more mashed potatoes."

"Remember there are starving children all over the world."

From the time she was a child Fran took to the sport of eating. To hear Fran tell it, her first love affair was with mayonnaise. Being extremely overweight, she was picked on and ridiculed by the neighborhood children. They loved making fun of "Franny Fatty Franny"—for a while. Eventually she realized that she was the biggest kid in her age group, bigger and stronger even than the boys. Fran became a bully, picking on both girls and boys with equal glee.

During her rise to banking fame, reporters would interview her classmates and pre-school teachers from the Lady in Waiting Orthodox Church in the Budlong Woods neighborhood of Chicago's north side. They were surprised that Fran was remembered as a pincher. Her classmates would come home with bruises from bullying. Pinching would startle the children, make them cry, and she could wrangle away the candy bar, soda pop, or bag of peanuts they were enjoying. To distract the teacher from what was really going on she taught herself to cry. At a very young age she spent hours in the basement of her home teaching herself the art of weeping on command.

She would blame her younger brothers for making her cry. She would pinch herself until a welt formed on her arm and blame it on them. This was her skill—distraction. When she hurt a classmate she herself would cry too. The teacher would be confused and, not knowing which child was guilty, both would escape punishment. This technique would be useful to her as an adult in the business world. Fran Kontopolus was a deceptive little bitch. She operated like a master pickpocket or magician, distracting someone with her left hand while her right hand performed all the mischief.

She was not the most popular girl at school. What bully is? She attended the local public school in Budlong Woods. Beginning in first grade, children brought their lunches to school. The bags were filled with corned beef, roast beef, bologna, apples, and homemade desserts. Fran began stealing from her classmate's lunch bags and this only added to her miserable reputation and lack of acceptance. She didn't give a damn. Each day, Fran looked forward to the parade of lunch bags. The food, the wonderful array of food, was on her mind from the moment she woke up. Fran could not wait for school. She associated learning and school with food, a Pavlovian association.

Fran was bright, ready, and willing to learn. An excellent reader and speller, she also had good penmanship. She wrote well. Her stories appeared in the school's newspaper. Her homework was always handed in on time and she was often the first to raise her hand to answer a question. The teachers liked Fran for these traits. She was smart. But on the playground her behavior was off the charts. She was a little angel to the teachers, but the devil incarnate to her classmates.

She was a voracious reader and her reading level was the highest in her class. Her homework, handed in ahead of schedule, would be presented to the teacher with food stains on the paper. The teachers overlooked her sloppy nature because the content of her homework was outstanding.

The unwritten rule of the playground was that a boy could not hit a girl. Fran quickly learned that she could get away with just about any mischief. At home she would torment her younger brothers. If one of the boys struck Fran in retaliation, Mr. Kontopolus would use the strap on their behinds, because boys-*slap*-can-*slap*-never-*slap*-hit-a-girl-*slap*-*slap*-*slap!*

Fran took advantage of that rule and as an adult translated it to, "Men can't fight back." Anti-social behaviors became part of her life.

The little girls in her class wanted nothing to do with her and no little boy ever developed a crush. When a new girl moved into the neighborhood and joined Fran's class, Fran was the first to sidle up to her and pretend to be her friend. She was just sizing up her next mark. Many of the girls' mothers insisted that Fran be invited to their daughters' birthday parties. "It's what we do in this neighborhood," they said. "How can we leave one girl out of a party when all of the other girls are invited? We can't embarrass her mother."

Elaina Rosen was an adorable fourth grader, bright, popular, petite, and pretty with long, dark hair. Fran hated her. Elaina's parents purchased an above ground swimming pool for their back yard, which took days to fill with a garden hose. The pool was to be the focus of a swimming party for their daughter who had the last birthday in the class. This was the middle of June and the weather was delightful. The pink invitations that Elaina's mother mailed to the girls included instructions that the girls bring their swimsuits to school and walk together to Elaina's home when school let out. The girls were invited to change into their swimsuits there, swim for an hour or so, have birthday cake, and watch Elaina open her presents. Parents were given a pick-up time of 5:00 p.m.

The first girl to change into her swimsuit and get in the pool was Fran Kontopolus. She lumbered out just before her classmates jumped into the delightful, cool water. They wondered why Fran sat on the grass laughing and chuckling to herself while they swam and splashed. One girl asked Fran why she was not in the water. "I don't swim in my own pee!"

The kids shrieked and scrambled out of the water. The girls insisted on taking baths before continuing, which delayed the party. The kids barely had time to wolf down a piece of cake before their parents started arriving, and Elaina opened her presents with only her parents to watch. Later that day Mr. Rosen drained and started refilling the pool. Fran knew how to ruin a good time.

As the years went on, Fran became more despised by her classmates. In staff meetings at school, the faculty discussed her unbecoming behavior. Mr. Leitzo, the school psychologist, was consulted. After observing Fran in a variety of environments and situations his diagnosis was that she suffered from a genetic defect. She lacked the gene of refinement.

As a teenager, her jealousy and envy worsened. She would start rumors or make up stories about her classmates. If two high school students were dating, she would spread a rumor that the boyfriend was seen hanging around with another girl. She was entertained by the arguing and fighting that resulted. The rumors and lies became worse and worse. Fran became a mean-spirited young woman and worked hard at becoming the most despised girl in school. The more she bullied the more isolated she became. Her bullying created paranoia. "Who's out to get me now?" Her paranoia led to more bullying, which only increased her level of paranoia. She believed that everyone was out to get her. She vowed to always strike first and never give them the chance.

CHAPTER FOUR

Sonny was not an outstanding college student. He wanted his silent goodbye to Hegewisch to be permanent, so his drive to make money took precedence over study and class work. He studied just enough to get by and four years later received his degree from Roosevelt University in downtown Chicago. The location of Roosevelt University on Michigan Avenue motivated Sonny more than any teacher or text. His daily train ride downtown was a stimulating event. To and from work he watched out the window of the Illinois Central Train, as the skyscrapers grew taller and taller. He walked downtown streets, looking up at the large banks teeming with money to lend to builders. Although skilled in construction, he knew that money, more than men, concrete, or steel, created those skyscrapers. During his college years, Sonny saw the face of Chicago change and grow and he wanted a piece of that action.

After college Sonny received a job with the H-SART home building firm. H-SART Homes were beginning a development of multi-unit buildings on the north side of the city. The north side was new ground for a southeast side boy. The unwritten rules of Chicago were that southsiders didn't go north and northsiders didn't go south. Loyalties in the city were simple. The northsiders were Cubs fans and the southsiders were White Sox fans. The westsiders were free to choose who to cheer for. Being southeast defined Hegewisch as a White Sox town. Having a White Sox jersey, hat, souvenir, or a mug in your office told people far more than just your allegiance to a ball team.

Sonny soon realized the efficiency of building multi-unit properties. One could build more units on less land and the aggregate sales prices were more than a single family home. Someone could make more money by appealing to a lower priced market and selling more units to more people. It was basic math. A plus B equals C, C being cash. Location was crucial to build a successful development. Farmland became a hot commodity and residential units were popping up everywhere in the City of Chicago.

Sonny enjoyed working for H-SART Homes and learned the geography of the city. He wanted to learn as much as he could about building in that potentially rich environment. He may not have been the best student in college, but work was a great teacher and he applied himself with phenomenal energy and drive. He extended himself to his bosses at every opportunity. He began to respect and envy the construction supervisors who wore white shirts, loud ties, and white rather than yellow construction helmets. He wanted to be a man in a white helmet, an inside guy calling the shots. He knew that the supervisors never got hurt, made more money, and helped organize and plan the project. And their hands weren't calloused. He watched, listened, and learned the ins and outs of construction in Chicago.

Within a year of starting with H-SART, Sonny was promoted to work inside a trailer on a job site—no more shivering in winter, sweating like a field hand in summer, dodging lightning and rain, or slogging through snow, ice, and slush. Sonny was quiet, a likable person, and made friends easily. His bosses liked him and knew that he would perform his job thoroughly and efficiently. During the next two years, two things took place. First Sonny was promoted to construction supervisor at an entry level and received his white construction helmet. But most important, he was included in the business meetings that allowed him to listen and learn how to do deals, how to avoid getting screwed, how to screw somebody else and not get caught, and how to make lots of money.

Sonny was a fly on the wall when conversations between the owner of H-SART, Phillip Nacht III, and his banker took place. He could not take in enough information. He found that being friends with a banker was essential to success. The banker shared confidential information about builders who were over-extended or in trouble with their projects. This gave Nacht the opportunity to move in, seize somebody else's troubles, and "buy right." This made him a pile of profits over the years, and Nacht, as a thankful profiteer, kicked back money to his banker for the inside information. One dirty hand washed the other.

As a young and reliable employee, Sonny was often tasked to act as a confidential courier. Often the item being delivered to Nacht was a gift or an envelope. The owner of H-SART would take the banker golfing, buy tickets to many sporting events, and treat him lavishly at expensive bars and restaurants. Occasionally Sonny was told to make deliveries of fat envelopes to the banker.

At first Sonny didn't think anything of the delivery of these items and envelopes. But one day Sonny overheard a conversation between the two men. The banker knew of some land ripe for a large development, but another homebuilder had the deal all but signed. The price for the land was low in comparison to the market. This confidential information would provide Nacht with opportunity to buy the property right out from under this competitor. That was a "double whammy." He made a great deal and got to stick it to the competition at the same time.

The deal was basic Chicago business. The banker wanted the construction and acquisition loan so he could collect his fees. He would receive a large year-end bonus for originating the loan. The banker had collected so much cash over the years from customers such as Nacht that he was running out of confidential space to hide the money. In the tradition of Chicago politicians, he kept the money in shoeboxes at home. But he wanted more money. He knew that he would receive another gift envelope to seal the deal for H-SART.

The banker said that he could persuade the landowner to accept a contract from H-SART because of the banker's assurance that the company could close. He was willing to convey doubt about the first buyer's financial strength and his ability to close. As time passed working in the office of H-SART, Sonny observed many inside deals, envelopes being passed, and much unethical behavior. He recognized that unethical and immoral behavior made more money. Why care about ethics, morals, and people's feelings? Get more money! Sonny could not get enough money for himself and he envied and planned to exceed the success of Phillip Nacht III.

CHAPTER FIVE

Fran's father, like all the fathers in the neighborhood, tried to hold on to the traditions of the old country. He knew exactly how girls should behave and why. Once teenagers, they were never to be left alone. They must be chaperoned. Girls must be taken to school and from school. They must help their mother with the cleaning, cooking, baking, and other household chores. Girls must have their father's permission before going to college and certainly their father's approval as to which college to attend. They must have their father's approval to work, the type of work, and the location of that work. Dates must be approved by their father and the first date must be in the home with her parents present. When it was time for marriage, a girl's father chose the boy from a family of his country of origin.

Fran loved her father, but in adolescence she began to rebel against his strict control. She became bulimic. As she matured and began to lose her baby fat, her father became more and more adamant about her eating habits. If she pushed the plate away, not wanting to eat any more, he told her to clean the plate. She learned to finish every bite even when she was not hungry. She would stuff herself as she did as a child, but as a teenage girl, she began to hate that stuffed feeling. She would excuse herself and go to the bathroom and throw up. She felt good after vomiting. She would flush the toilet and run the water to disguise the sound of purging. She hid a feather in the bathroom that she would use to tickle her throat to trigger her gag reflex. She derived a double pleasure from this act. She could eat to make her papa proud and at the same time defy his authority.

As she grew, she began to be noticed as an attractive young woman, and the prettier she became, the more control her father exerted. Her anger grew and she became increasingly mean to her classmates. The purging continued as she cleaned her plate and ate, and ate, and ate. "This is so good, Mama, I just have to have more" and then back to the bathroom.

As a first child, Fran was held to tradition. Mr. Kontopolus had two younger sons and was always disappointed that his first-born was not a boy. But keeping to tradition, the first-born, although female, would have real responsibility to the family. He would see to that. This old world attitude created conflicts for born-in-the-New-World Fran. She just wanted to be Daddy's little girl. But Mr. Kontopolus, with his finger pointed at her, would sit her on his knee and expound on the responsibilities *she* had as his oldest child.

She nodded her head as he told her how it was up to her to take care of the family when he was gone. Taking responsibility for an entire family was not the kind of bedtime story this little girl wanted to hear. He kept reminding her how she should be distrustful and take what she could from life any time the opportunity presented itself. These speeches made Fran want to prove herself to her father, but the resentment she felt about the eventual responsibility for her family only added to her bullying.

Mr. Kontopolus was a short, heavyset man, with dark skin and a thick mustache and he always had a half-smoked and chewed-up cigar clamped in his teeth. He smelled of old cigars and fish. He drove Fran to school and picked her up each day through the end of high school. Papa was there in the deepest snow and on the hottest day.

Dimitri Kontopolus drove a big American car, a white Oldsmobile Delta 88, with electric windows. During the spring and summer months, he would wash his car by hand each Saturday. He wore a white under-shirt and stood in front of the house with the garden hose running. He had a big bucket of soapy water and a large, round khaki sponge. His sons would play and squirt each other with the hose. The front yard on Gregory Street was a typical Chicago scene in the summer. Dimitri wiped, polished, and shined every bit of that car while the boys laughed, splashed, and continually got in his way. He loved every minute of it.

With high school about to end, Fran asked Papa if she could go to college. "Yes," he replied. He wanted Fran to continue her education, but the school had to be close to home. He thought about it and suggested the local teachers college. Fran felt that the University of Illinois just south of downtown would be a better choice. The school was located on the route to her father's place of business, the DK Fish Store on Seventy-ninth Street. Fran wanted to become an attractive, desired co-ed who could control men, businesses, and the course of her life. That meant she had to break the ties of her father's control.

Dimitri thought about this and realized that taking Fran to school on the way to work would be easy. In fact, after school he could pick her up and she could then work in the fish store with her papa and her brothers. She could learn the fish business and apply her education to keeping it healthy and in family hands.

Fran had other ideas. She wanted her own money and a different kind of job. Fran hated the smell of fish her father carried home and she had no desire to run a fish store. Her grades were excellent and she knew she could get a better job.

She knew what she had to do and on a hot summer's day, in an elder female child's seductive way, Fran approached her father while he was washing his car. She explained her thoughts and feelings, suggesting that she work at the community bank, the one where Papa had his money. "That would be the best place for me to work." Fran explained how her brothers should work with their father, but that she should follow a different career path. She told Papa that she was too smart to work in the fish store, that it was not for a young American girl, and that she could accomplish more in an office setting while attending college. She continued by explaining that he could drive her to school. After school she could take the elevated train to work. He could pick her up after work. "What do you think, Papa?"

He continued sponging the dirt off the car. Fran waited. She looked at Papa as he contemplated her suggestion. Allowing a daughter some independence was a big step for any father. But Mr. Kontopolus knew she was right. "Fran, my dearest, love of my life, on Monday I will call Mr. Eberstark, the president of the bank, and see if he can find a place for my sweet little girl," he said.

When Monday arrived, Mr. Kontopolus called the bank. A job interview was arranged for the following day. As expected, her father picked her up at school, then drove her home and waited while Fran changed from her school clothes to her Sunday best. Her mother was waiting to help Fran get dressed.

Fran's interview went well and she was excited about her prospects. Two days later she was offered a part-time job as a check sorter for State Bank of the Community. She worked afternoons from 4:00–7:00 p.m. and Saturdays 9:00 a.m.–4:00 p.m. She was placed in the basement of the bank in the sorting room with three others. The task was not challenging, but Fran was thrilled to have an opportunity to work and finally get out of the family grip.

Her first boss was Mr. Hecker, an employee for almost twenty years. He lived nearby in a small house with his wife and three children. If the bank was compared to a family, he would have been one of the wise, old, friendly uncles.

Fran worked quietly and quickly, sorting more checks than her fellow employees. Often when she completed her sorting and still had time until her shift ended Fran would go to the employee cafeteria for a doughnut or a nice packaged apple pie. She kept an eye on the refrigerator where employees could leave food brought from home. By the end of her shift the cafeteria was empty, so she began stealing food from her fellow employees. She would grab something, wolf it down quickly, and disappear into the ladies room to purge before heading back to her desk.

Fran soon got the lay of the land. She quietly observed who had power and how they used or abused it. She recognized the weak employees and the weak middle managers, the people who had no ambition and were just collecting a paycheck. Many had "retired on the job." She saw how they put senior management on pedestals. She craved that position and power.

Employees diverted their eyes when Mr. Eberstark walked by. She noticed how secretaries quivered and worked late for the officers. Fran saw the cutthroat attitude of employees trying to get ahead. Over time she did more than sort checks. Fran became aware that her environment was a battlefield for power and she wanted that power and more.

She knew right away that banking was the career path she would follow. The State Bank of the Community was to be her home. Over time, Fran figured how to climb the ladder at the bank one rung at a time, stepping on anyone to get to the top.

CHAPTER SIX

Sonny grew up in a community that valued a man's word as his bond and a man's obligation to support his fellow man in times of need. He was torn between the morality of his upbringing and the immorality of his dreams. He reached a turning point watching his boss take over another company, the company of a friend. King Brothers Construction was a mid-size builder with a good reputation throughout Chicago. The King brothers were friends with Nacht; in fact, they had started in business around the same time he did. The Kings were loved by all. They were happy and they loved each other and loved life. One brother always carried candies in his pocket to hand to children of customers and friends. They were wonderful men, and as competitors go, they could be described as friendly competitors with all the city's builders.

Both firms were members of the Home Builders Association of Chicago. The King brothers were as good as gold in building and warranting their work. They gave homebuyers their home phone numbers, and when a customer had a problem, they were known to respond to requests in person when the customer called. Everyone admired and respected the brothers.

One of the King brothers unexpectedly died of a sudden heart attack. Nacht soon learned that the surviving brother needed money to buy out the partnership interest of the deceased brother's family. The rules of the partnership agreement were written so that if a partner passed away, the surviving partner had 120 days to buy out the family of the deceased. If he could not do so in the allotted time, the company would be put up for sale. The proceeds would be divided equally among the families of the two brothers.

King Brothers Construction's bank was also H-SART's bank. So as one might expect, Nacht knew more than he should. An application for a credit line to the surviving King brother had been made. He desperately needed funds to retain ownership of his company.

A quiet agreement was made between Nacht and his banker. The banker would delay approval of the loan, then as time ran out Nacht would have a golden opportunity to intervene.

H-SART was flush with cash. Nacht waited until the president of King Brothers Construction had only five business days remaining until the deadline. The man was in a tight spot and the financial noose around his neck was getting tight. King Brothers Construction was building many homes at that point and was extended on its credit lines. Any reliable bank would have recognized this situation and stepped in quickly knowing the value of the company and its reputation, but this was not to be the case. King found he could not borrow enough money to buy out the estate of his beloved brother in time. He was going to lose the company.

Nacht waited and waited and then called his friend to a meeting in his office. He told King that it was to his benefit to meet with him, so King rushed right over. Nacht had already secured the financing to act quickly before he called King. This was Monday afternoon and the money had to change hands before Friday. In this meeting, in which Sonny eavesdropped, his boss at first spoke gently. "Look, we've been friends for a long time and I am sorry, deeply sorry at the passing of your brother, but I think you might need my help. King, do you need any money?"

King looked as if he was seeing an oasis in the desert and spoke openly of his dilemma and the Friday deadline. Nacht knew this, but needed to hear it out of King's mouth. He had to put King in the position of a beggar. Nacht's voice and manner then became all business as he presented his ultimatum.

Nacht suggested that King make him a partner and use his money for partnership investments as long as he replaced King as president of the company and had an ownership position of 51 percent. He "nailed" the deal with a threat. If King did not embrace his offer, he might bid a low price for the company on the open market, thus leaving King and his brother's family with very little cash.

"To assure that I'll be the winning bidder at the sale of the company, I've already reached agreements with other potential bidders," he said. King was by this time as white as a ghost. Nacht continued, "I'll be the only bidder and you will essentially get nothing for all your years and hard work building King Brothers Construction. This is a take it now or leave it now offer, King."

With no options remaining, the ultimatum was accepted by King, and by the end of the week Nacht and H-SART had controlling interest in King Brothers Construction. Within sixty days, the new president and majority shareholder of King Brothers Construction fired Mr. King.

King received nothing. Nacht had had his lawyer insert, or rather slip, into the new partnership agreement a paragraph that stated, *"After sixty days of closing, the president has the right to remove from the company any remaining or other shareholders and that in exchange for the salary or compensation paid in the prior sixty days, this consideration will, in fact, be adequate and acceptable compensation for the purchase and exchange of ownership of the shareholders stock in King Brothers Construction."*

Under stress and in haste to save the company, King did not read every line of every page of the agreement Nacht's attorney prepared. King received less than nothing because after he was fired, Nacht sued for not keeping the business of the company confidential. His ultimatum became to shut up, leave quietly without a counter-suit, or experience an expensive court battle that may have resulted in penalties and most certainly expensive legal bills. Nacht and H-SART got their cake and ate it too. Sonny forgot his upbringing, his father and grandfather's traditions, and chose the "acquisition of cash" as his religion.

CHAPTER SEVEN

Through her college years, Fran worked part time at the bank, but during summer break she was able to work full time. After work her fellow employees gathered to have a burger, a beer, and to blow off steam at a local pub called The Clam Bake. Fran never joined her peers as Papa was always waiting to take her directly home. She knew that she was catching the eye of the young male bankers and she hated her father's parochial attitudes more and more for his control over her life. As a defense mechanism, she pretended to her co-workers that she really didn't care about socializing. She convinced herself that the employees at the bank were beneath her and that she really didn't want to join them. They were just worthless, replaceable people. She began to hate her co-workers with displaced anger toward her father.

Four years of college ended and Fran became the first in her family to complete or even attend college. Graduation was a big day and everyone celebrated her achievement. After graduation, the bank offered her a full-time job as a teller. The tellers were single young women who would inevitably get married, become pregnant, and leave their jobs. The teller line had the highest turnover rate of any job in the bank. Fran saw things differently. This was just an entry position, the first step toward the riches and rewards she craved.

Fran trained with the teller she was going to replace, and after two weeks she was handling money. She was very efficient and the highest volume of customers passed through her teller line. She was quick on the adding machine, making deposits, and counting change, faster than any other teller. The customers liked the short wait and the fast-moving line. Fran was soon noticed by management.

But she was brash and impatient with customers, and she lacked the skills and the desire to be social. She was not the most gracious teller, far from it, but the efficiency factor worked in her favor. Customers lined up before Fran's window to get in and out quickly. She would often shout, "Next," while a customer she had just served was still at the window.

As she received recognition, she felt a desire for more responsibility. Her second nature had always been to find a tender underbelly, someone's vulnerable spot to pinch and exploit so as to get the candy bar or the new toy. The toys were bigger these days.

The supervisor of the teller line was Mr. Hudson, a single gay man who, in the days before gay men were openly gay, could never bring up his homosexuality. Hudson was thought of as a perpetual bachelor. He smoked Kent cigarettes, wore nice suits, and his trademark was a folded handkerchief in his breast pocket. He was pudgy in the way men were before exercise and working out became fashionable. He always wore a stiff-collared white shirt with a colorful tie and gold cufflinks on French cuffs. On his desk was a coffee mug with a Chicago Cubs logo. He kept coffee candy in it. He always seemed to have a piece of coffee candy in his mouth, rolling the pieces from cheek to cheek.

Fran wanted to supervise the teller line. She felt the other girls slacked off and did not work as hard or effectively as she did. She could run the teller lines more efficiently than Hudson.

Many nights Fran stayed up tossing and turning in bed. She could not help thinking about what she could do to get Hudson's position. He was to become the first of many targets to be hit in her banking career. The question came in two parts. How could she do it and how could she get away with doing it? How do you take on a quiet man, a stable employee who had been working successfully within the same routine for fifteen years or more? How do you take him out? He was a perfect employee for his job. He was a genteel man and everyone liked him. Fran watched him each day as she stood at her position in the teller cage, wondering and waiting.

Hudson had vacation time coming and he was taking a cruise. By coincidence, another bachelor, Mr. Pizella, assistant to the vice president of real estate loans, happened to be on the same cruise ship.

As bank employees recalled, Hudson and Pizella seemed, by coincidence of course, to always have vacations the same week and by another coincidence to travel to the same vacation destinations year after year. If anyone suspected, and some did, no one ever said a word. Fran was one who suspected. She kept quiet too, but not out of respect. She was waiting for the right time to use the information to her advantage.

A week before his vacation, Fran asked Hudson who would supervise the teller line when he was gone. "Thank you for your concern, Fran, but there's no need for that. Everyone here knows her job." In case there was a situation that required addressing, the bank's vice president, Mr. Wilson, could be called to assist. Fran knew Mr. Wilson. His secretary, Ms. Pico, attended Fran's church.

At church that next Sunday, Fran approached Pico and suggested that she mention to her boss that he might consider having Fran substitute while Hudson was on vacation. The teller line was important and really needed an acting supervisor all the time, she said. "I know how busy Mr. Wilson is and how often he's out of the bank at meetings. My stepping in as supervisor for a week, with no additional pay increase or bonus, will give Mr. Wilson peace of mind," said Fran.

On Monday morning, after taking dictation, Pico made the suggestion. Wilson liked the idea and was impressed with Fran's enthusiasm and her commitment to the bank and its customers. Pico was directed to have Hudson come up to the office. Hudson was a meek man who had no basis for an argument with his boss, so he agreed without comment. He spent the rest of the day training Fran how to act as a supervisor. She was taught to write daily reports and to schedule lunch breaks for the tellers. She was shown the vault where the tellers' cash boxes were kept. She was told to receive a balanced cash drawer from each teller at the end of each day. She was excited as her plan began to unfold. Step one was taking place. She would start her new position on Monday.

On Monday, Fran arrived early to set up Hudson's desk her way. She had an 8½ by 11-inch manila envelope and a bright red file folder. She inserted the envelope into the folder and placed both in the back of the file drawer in Hudson's desk. No one noticed. Satisfied, Fran began to get comfortable sitting at a desk. She sat in the leather chair and swiveled to the left and the right. She quickly got used to the experience of being a manager. Then she reached over to the Chicago Cubs mug filled with coffee candy, unwrapped two pieces, and popped then into her mouth. Better than delicious. She was sitting high.

At the end of the first day, everything had gone well. The tellers did their jobs, balanced out their cash drawers, and it was a seamlessly easy day. But Fran was not satisfied with the performance of "her" new team. Tuesday she decided to become more active by standing behind each teller and checking her work. She looked over their shoulders, seeing that the work was completed satisfactorily. This annoyed the tellers and made them nervous and no one looked forward to returning to work the next day. Who did this little bitch think she was?

On Wednesday, Fran decided to unleash her plan. She knew it would involve a person of influence in the bank, but who? As the day passed, she figured it out. It would have to be the secretary to the president, Mrs. Ethyl Lazar.

Before businesses became nationally franchised, neighborhood stores in Chicago were open late only on Mondays and Thursdays, closing at 9:00 p.m. Thursdays were busy with merchants coming into the bank for extra change and often multiple deposits of cash. By 4:00 p.m. the main floor was crowded and busy. Customers were coming and going. Mrs. Lazar had just returned to her desk where she found a note. It appeared to be from Mr. Eberstark. It was typed and there was no signature. The note read that he needed a file from Hudson's desk. This red file folder contained a manila envelope. In it were Hudson's daily reports from the prior week. The note continued, requesting that Mrs. Lazar please review the contents prior to bringing it to him to make sure it had the reports he needed.

Fran looked up from where she sat and gazed anxiously to the atrium level where Lazar sat as she read the note. When the secretary pushed away from her desk and proceeded to the stairs that led to the main lobby, Fran rose from the leather chair and walked to the teller area. She was standing behind the teller line as Lazar approached the desk, opened the drawer, took out the red file folder, identified the manila envelope, and emptied the contents onto the desk.

To her surprise, two homosexual magazines and a pair of pantyhose fell out. The pictures in the magazine were compelling, and Lazar couldn't keep herself from turning a few pages. Her face turned redder and redder from embarrassment. Lazar could not contain herself any longer; she looked at the other employees sitting at their desks and motioned to them to come look at what she had discovered. A small crowd gathered around the desk. So much clatter was going on and so quickly that customers walked over to see the commotion.

This gathering brought Eberstark out of his office to put an end to the silliness. He had long suspected Hudson, but as the man never brought his sexual preference to work, he had looked the other way. Pornography and worse in the office place was something else.

An impromptu meeting of senior staff met after work the next day, Friday. They reviewed what was found in the desk. It was unacceptable. After the bank closed, the desk was inspected and examined further. Fran hadn't missed a step. Deep in the drawers were rouge, lipstick cylinders, and assorted make up. In the commotion, the fact that Eberstack never asked for the file was overlooked. Whether or not Hudson was gay, which seemed pretty obvious, was irrelevant in those days. The suspicion alone was enough to ruin a career.

Hudson returned to work Monday after a wonderful week at sea. But that day he was met at the entrance by the bank's security officer who escorted him directly to the personnel department where he was immediately fired. This was the last thing he expected. He was shown what was discovered in his desk and he strongly and emotionally denied that those were his things. It was too late.

Employees who knew Hudson doubted those were his items. Employees liked him and felt sorry about his firing. No one knew what really happened, not even Hudson himself. Fran was never suspected. Things were about to change at State Bank of the Community.

After Hudson was fired, personnel informed Fran that she was now the new teller line supervisor, which included a raise and more responsibility. Fran got what she wanted by destroying another person's career and life. *This is easy and I get more money. I like work,* she thought. Fran would have patted herself on the back but her arms could not reach around her. Following Old World tradition, she tendered her paycheck to her father each payday.

CHAPTER EIGHT

As manager of the teller line Fran was front and center. She had risen to management not through ability, but through betrayal. She was proud of that. Rather than manage in a quiet and pleasant style like her predecessor, she fell back on well-established traits. She was loud, brash, and bullying. Fran's choices of words were not what one would expect from a young woman in such a respectable business. She used profanity, often graphic profanity, to make her point. And she made a lot of points.

Fran's management style was to demean and humiliate. The staff and employees of State Bank of the Community were shocked at Hudson's firing. Fran's management style was a greater and ongoing shock. She took pleasure in humiliating tellers in front of customers. Anything could kick off the assault, a run in a stocking, the pile of paperclips too high in the box at a teller cage, even an innocent remark or gesture. Sometimes she picked on one of the girls just for the hell of it. *Keeping those bitches in their place,* she thought.

Although her management was exclusive to the teller line, other employees shivered when she walked by. Fran had power and she loved using it. As long as she did her job well, she could pretty much humiliate anyone who came into her field of fire. Besides, this was a bank run by men and there was not another woman in management. She knew her presence was important for the bank's image.

Fran made her rules clear to the tellers, and there were many rules now. Should a teller need to request time off to attend a wake, funeral, graduation, doctor's appointment, or any event, permission would have to come from Fran. And that permission did not come easily.

Within a few weeks of Fran's promotion, a young woman named Marsh, who had been a full-time teller longer than Fran had worked at the bank, requested an afternoon off to go shopping for bridal dresses for her sister's wedding. Under Hudson a request like this would have been approved easily.

Those who were in the bank when Marsh made her request refer to the event as the eruption of Mount Saint Fran. She was seated at her desk reading a memo and chomping on her morning box of Dunkin' Donuts doughnut holes. Although she loved the power and her ability to misuse it, responsibility was taking its toll. She had begun eating more than ever.

Marsh approached Fran's desk almost on tiptoes. "Excuse me, Ms. Kontopolus, may I speak to you for a moment?"

Fran looked up. "Who said you could leave your cage!"

"There are no customers in my line and I know you're busy, so I placed the Cage Closed sign in my window so I could speak to you." Her voice was low, with a distinct quiver.

"Well, now that you're here, what the hell do you want?" responded Fran.

"My sister is getting married in three months. I would really appreciate you letting me take Friday afternoon off next week to go shopping for bridesmaid dresses with her and my mother."

"What! You want to what!" Fran screamed so loud the employees in the basement down in the closed room where Fran had once sorted checks heard her. They thought the bank was being robbed.

Fran stood up from her chair, her demeanor making her seem like a giant. She towered over the petite, slim, gentle young girl. "Get back to your cage right now!" Fran grabbed the Chicago Cubs mug that Hudson had not had enough time to take with him when he was fired and threw it on the floor, just missing the feet of Marsh. Like a scared rabbit, Marsh ran back to her teller cage, tears streaming down her cheeks. She was embarrassed at being dressed down so publicly. The other tellers wanted to console her but were afraid to leave their cages.

Everyone in the bank was silent. No one had seen anything like this before, especially not within the bank. Even employees who came from homes with alcoholic parents were shocked at the violent temper Fran so openly displayed.

Eberstark's office was located on the second floor and he heard the ruckus. He jumped from his desk to find out what was going on. Mrs. Lazar told him what she had seen. He took a few steps and looked down from the second level of the bank. Everything was quiet, too quiet, and the employees appeared to be "hunkered down."

He immediately sent Lazar to fetch the obvious source of the disruption. She walked slowly and deliberately down the stairs and to Fran's desk. The maintenance man was already cleaning up the broken Cubs mug. Fran followed Lazar up the stairs to Eberstark's office. He was standing behind his desk when Fran entered. Lazar left, closing the door behind her.

"You are Fran Kontopolus," stated Eberstark.

"Yes."

"You are the daughter of Dimitri Kontopolus?"

"Yes, of course."

"Well, Ms. Kontopolus, never in my twenty years of running banks have I ever seen or heard a display so loud and so rude as what I have just heard. It's..." He stumbled for the right word. "Outrageous." Fran started to get red in the face and began trembling.

"In fact, Ms. Kontopolus, I have never–in any bank I have ever worked in–heard of anyone throwing anything either." Fran turned on her well-rehearsed tears, the mascara running down her face. She really turned on the water works.

Eberstark continued, "Ms. Kontopolus, I don't know what happened in your area, but all of our management people are examples to others and to our customers." He could not help noticing the heaving, coughing, and waterfall of tears in his office. He picked up his phone and called Lazar to come in with a box of tissues. She promptly knocked, entered, and exited, leaving the box in front of Fran. "Now calm down, Ms. Kontopolus. Just calm down." The more Fran cried the more the big, tough president backed down. Fran was going for the Oscar that morning.

By the time Fran left his office, Eberstark was apologizing to her. He had not anticipated the tears and rehearsed suffering that Fran displayed. Fran walked back to her desk, picked up a fresh doughnut hole, and popped it in her mouth. *Oh, this is sweet,* she thought. She swallowed it down with a couple of fast chews. No one from the teller line ever asked for time off from Fran again.

Fran had the tellers hopping. She had a desk, business cards, phone, and authority. Better still, she was proud of herself for taking the first step up the ladder.

As time passed, she created more ideas on how to move up even higher.

Having a desk in the public area of the bank meant Fran was expected to dress professionally like the other ladies at the bank. She had never worn high heels, as her father did not think this type of shoe was proper attire for his daughter. Times and circumstances had changed and the family went on an outing after church to help Fran find high heels. Wearing heels made her feel tall and important, but she never walked gracefully. It was not unusual to see her stumble and catch herself from falling as she entered the bank building.

Once on a winter morning, with snow on the ground, Fran entered the bank and slipped on the terrazzo floor. She began to fall and landed on her left knee. If the incident with Marsh sounded like a volcano erupting, this fall was like an earthquake with a yowl the likes of which no one has ever heard since.

Fran's uniform always was a black dress or black skirt suits. She thought that black made her look thin. Her nickname at the bank became "The Dragon Lady." Some employees never knew her real name.

Eberstark let her be, even with her rude and unbecoming behavior, because men don't know what to do with a woman who starts crying hysterically, especially in a corporate setting. He never knew that after the tears she would dash into the bathroom and laugh herself silly. She had him and the other male managers right where she wanted them.

CHAPTER NINE

Fran was comfortably established in her position as manger of the teller line and she decided to begin acting like a manger. She started smoking cigarettes since it seemed that this was a common trait of others in management. She noticed that women chose a thin cigarette and Fran wanted a woman's brand. She chose Virginia Slims and began smoking a pack and a half a day.

Her parents were not happy seeing Fran begin this habit, but she told them that smoking would help her lose weight and she could stay thin. "It's about image too," she said. She needed to fit in with the other managers, all of whom smoked. Her parents backed off their objection. Papa bought her a Zippo cigarette lighter at the neighborhood drug store. It was a wonderful gift. Her eating disorder remained a secret and the purging continued. Not eating resulted in weight loss. And although she began to smoke, Fran, who could afford to miss a meal once in a while, never missed a meal.

Fran walked clumsily in her black high heels with a cigarette in her hand and her handbag in her fist. She could never find the right balance. She never saw herself as anything other than a fat little girl. When Fran Kontopolus was seen, employees behaved like privates in the army when the sergeant called, "Attention!"

As spiteful and frightful as Fran Kontopolus was, upper management liked her accomplishments in the teller line. She ran the tellers in military fashion. She viewed them as her soldiers. She insisted all the tellers wear white blouses and black or navy skirts. Hose were required. The only approved make up was lipstick, no eye shadow or rouge. Hair must be pulled back. The only jewelry other than a ring could be a gold or silver necklace. Earrings were to be hoops, gold or silver only. To the amazement of the teller line, she would occasionally hold inspection.

No one challenged the dress code. An unwritten and humiliating law came into effect. Before a teller could wear her engagement ring at work, she first had to show it to Fran and get her approval. Fran never denied any girls wearing an engagement ring, but she enjoyed making each and every one of the engaged tellers kowtow to her before they could enjoy and share their excitement. With every new engagement of "her girls," Fran became more jealous and her hatred of each girl, engaged or not, grew.

Her paranoia grew with her power. She just knew the girls were fomenting plots. Her defense was to keep them too busy to scheme. Like the wicked stepmother in Cinderella, Fran worked these girls as hard as she could. Efficiency was the rule of the day. Fran knew that customers wanted to get in and out quickly. She reorganized the teller system and designated certain lines for change counting only, cashier's checks, money orders, or American Express Travelers Checks, deposits of checks only in another line, and deposits of cash only in yet another line. Sitting when customers were absent was not allowed. Talking was prohibited. Everyone was designated a bathroom break time. One either took their designated time or lost it.

It was not easy working in the teller line and for many of the girls it was a challenge. Fran found ways to eliminate every teller who had worked for Hudson. She knew that if she did not have the loyalty of employees who knew only her as a boss, she could not rule strongly.

Fran let it be known to the tellers that she enjoyed home cooking. Not a surprise, of course, but each day a different teller brought Fran home-cooked food. Ida Lupio would bring her mother's meatball stew. Catherine Tsiopolus would bring fresh gyros her father made. Olive Pipick brought Fran raspberry and chocolate cake baked by her grandfather who had been a baker in Austria. Fran was in heaven. Food, glorious food! Then off to the ladies room.

Fran came to realize early that as long as she had the power to control the employees' pay, over-time hours, and bonuses, the tellers kissed her ass and bent over backwards for Fran even if they hated her. She had power and could bully whomever she wanted when she wanted. Fran had it good.

CHAPTER TEN

S onny's first independent business venture was home repair and remodeling on Chicago's north side. After working for H-SART, he saved enough money to leave the company and start his own business, Venture Inc. Although a mature adult of twenty-six years, he was still living at home, saving every penny possible to invest into his business. He wasn't motivated so much by greed as by a driving need to become a "player" in Chicago real estate and banking.

He had never seen employment at H-SART as a long-term move. Despite his continual coddling up to management, he had always planned to leave the company after a couple of years. He always looked ahead and planned every move with incredible attention to detail. First he had to create an edge for himself, an advantage, which assured him of needing little to no money to start his business. To Sonny, that meant one thing—theft. To begin a business to remodel, renovate, fix, and repair new homes and apartments, a large outlay of cash went to buying tools and materials. From his first day at H-SART, Sonny lifted or stole a tool here and a tool there. He collected hammers, levels, screwdrivers, and more expensive power tools such as drills, saws, and a wide selection of essential hardware. He was crafty and clever, slowly stealing enough to build up an inventory, but not so obvious as to be noticed.

Within a couple of years he had all the tools he needed. He was a genius at making things disappear and at covering his tracks. A few employees suspected what was going on and one or two even tried to catch him in the act. He was too slick. "I know he's doing it, but I'll be damned if I know how he's doing it," they'd say.

In addition to tools, Sonny pilfered reams of paper, stamps, and office supplies. When he was responsible to close a job site at the end of the day, other, more valuable, supplies disappeared. Copper pipe, two-by-fours, conduit, and assorted building material walked into his pick-up truck and mysteriously appeared in a small warehouse Sonny rented in the back-of-the-yards neighborhood near Chicago's stockyards. By the time he left H-SART, he had stolen hundreds of thousands of dollars worth of tools and materials.

In establishing himself as a north-side home remodeler, Sonny knew that he could squeeze homeowners to pay him more than the contract amount. He would bid a job lower than his competitors, then begin the work, open a wall or two, and then "discover" a more serious problem or even a series of costly problems. He would claim that the homeowner needed more work than originally represented. The initial repair or remodeling damage to the existing home would result in the home owner having little choice but to increase the contract amount and pay Sonny more money just to have his workmen return to complete the job. Extortion, blackmail, remodeling, they were pretty much all the same thing when Sonny was on the job. He knew making people miserable enough and forcing customers to beg for completion of their home would create significant additional profits for Venture.

Sonny maintained a business checking and savings account at State Bank of the Community. He came to the bank every Friday to make his deposits. Although he did not have a relationship with Fran, he knew her, as every customer did. No one could enter the bank without noticing the shrill dictator of the teller line. Sonny prided himself on his looks and appearance, and he would shake his head as he waited in line and observed this disgusting girl with the vulgar mouth. *She must have something on somebody*, he thought.

Within a year of being out on his own, Sonny heard of a neighborhood three-flat apartment building being foreclosed by the bank. As a customer, Sonny made an inquiry to the loan department about the pending foreclosure. The loan officer referred him to the attorney representing the estate of the seller who had died just a few months earlier.

Sonny called the attorney and learned that although no mortgage payment was delinquent, the bank had decided to exercise a little-known clause referred to as a "due on death" clause. This clause, common in many mortgages, required that a mortgage be paid in full upon the death of a property owner. Smart home buyers have had this clause deleted from their mortgage contract for an obvious reason: It is a financial trap for the surviving heirs who may have to come up with an extraordinary amount of money with little or no warning.

The attorney told Sonny that the property had a good cash flow, but the heirs were scattered around the country and had no interest in managing the property. The bank had given the attorney an alternative that he could not comply with. The loan officer wanted the heirs to personally sign and guarantee the mortgage, but they had refused. The bank had moved ahead and was pressing on with the foreclosure. If the foreclosure took place and the bank ended up owning the real estate, the heirs stood to gain nothing.

Sonny knew the property had value. If he stepped in and closed the deal before the foreclosure, he would stand to gain the property and the guaranteed cash flow. He needed to move fast. After the foreclosure, anyone could compete to buy the property from the bank and Sonny liked competition when he was the only competitor.

Upon finding out the mortgage loan balance the bank was owed, he realized there was a nice profit as soon as he bought the building. It was like buying a dollar for 55 cents. This was the opportunity Sonny had been looking for. He figured that if he could offer the estate some money over the debt before the foreclosure deadline, they would sell eagerly. He could make more money by re-selling, or flipping, the deal after he closed and owned the property. He also had the attractive option of holding on to the property and enjoying the benefits of a good cash flow. It was a win/win situation.

When working at H-SART, Sonny had learned about making a bank work for the customer. He had deposits at the State Bank of the Community, and knowing that banks liked to loan money to their customers, he took the bank officer out to lunch and proposed buying the property from the estate by borrowing the money from the bank. He would pay off the existing loan from the borrowed funds, thus avoiding foreclosure proceedings and legal fees by the bank, restore the loan to the bank under his name, and pay the bank interest on the loan, thus restoring profit to the bank.

The loan officer embraced his suggestion. It was a win/win situation for the bank and for his banking reputation. Sonny contacted the attorney for the estate and offered $500 to each heir over the amount owed.

With eight heirs, Sonny could easily pay $4,000 over the outstanding mortgage balance. He told the attorney that if his offer was not accepted he would ultimately buy the property from the bank post-foreclosure, and when the foreclosure was complete, the heirs would get nothing.

The heirs had no choice. They unanimously decided to sell the property to Sonny and get something rather than nothing. Within a few months, Sonny sold the property, paid off the bank, made a nice profit, and developed a relationship as a borrower. He had succeeded and was well on his way to becoming a "player."

CHAPTER ELEVEN

The efficiency of the teller line was never better. Customers, residential and commercial, large and small, commented to their account representatives and loan officers how easy it was to get in and out of the bank. Although Fran lacked any social graces, she insisted that her tellers use them to full advantage with every customer. They were courteous, efficient, friendly, and thorough. The single customer with just a small checking account was treated just as well as the business owner with multiple million-dollar accounts.

No one even remembered Hudson, but this is often the case in corporations where "out with the old, in with the new" is standard operating procedure. In fact, the incident Fran had so cleverly created was so startling that many of his former friends and admirers in the bank began to look back on his days with distaste. Such is the power of prejudice and the weakness of memory. Fran had not only cost the man his job, she had cost him his reputation. He wasn't officially blackballed in the Chicago banking community, but the word was out and he couldn't find a decent job in his chosen field. When Fran read the small notice of his suicide in the newspaper she sniffed, wolfed down a glazed donut, and never gave him another thought.

Upper management liked Fran's ability to make the bank look good. Her tellers were often the bank's first contact with its customers. Happy customers meant more customers. Many people didn't like the way they interacted with their bank or, more accurately, the way their bank interacted with them. They often felt they were being processed rather than served—and rightly so. Individuals, families, and small businesspeople, after hearing of the great service their friends were experiencing at State Bank of the Community, began to transfer deposits, opening checking and savings accounts, and applying for loans. They often mentioned Fran or her tellers as the primary reason for the change. Frans's stock with the bank management continued to rise.

The bank, like all banks, made money by taking in deposits and paying customers an interest rate. The monies were then loaned out at a higher rate, generating the bank's profit. For example, a retired couple deposited $100,000 and received five percent interest on their deposit. A local business borrowed $100,000 and was charged nine percent in interest. In addition to the four percent difference, the borrower might be required to pay a $250 fee for document preparation and $1,500 annually as a fee to process the loan. The bank earned $9,000 a year in interest plus $1,750 for additional fees, or $10,750, which is equal to 10.75 percent. The bank paid $4,000 to the depositor, but earned $6,750 on the depositor's money. Not bad work if you could get it. Multiply this transaction by thousands or millions of dollars and multiple transactions and you realize how banks made loads of dough.

Lee Ryan was vice president of the State Bank of the Community Real Estate Loan Department. He began his career as a teller at the bank's original location in a small storefront in Chicago's Ravenswood neighborhood. He worked hard and soon began building a good reputation and a solid career.

Ravenswood was a working-class neighborhood with doctors and dentists in offices above the little retail stores on the streets. Streetcars rumbled by, their antennas sparking off the electric lines hanging above the main streets. The local families shopped exclusively at the little shops in the neighborhood. The concept of a mega-store such as Wal-Mart was inconceivable. Everyone knew the butcher, the dressmaker, the poultry shop owner, the corner pharmacist, and of course the banker. The bank was an essential element in building the community and holding it together. State Bank of the Community was started right after World War II by a local political leader, a Chicago alderman named Hogan who raised the money from friends, relatives, and a few connections. "Yes, I am starting a business to make a profit, but my business will be to help others earn and keep their profits too," he said. He was committed to Ravenswood.

Hogan felt the community needed a bank, and if the alderman began the bank, the voters and residents he took care of would deposit their money in his bank and take care of him. Contractors who wanted city or ward contracts would borrow money to fund those jobs and life would be good. So Hogan began looking for the right people to staff his new bank. Lee Ryan's mother worked in the ward office of the alderman, and back in the old country, Lee's family and Hogan's family were cousins. Loyalty in politics and business is often a function of nepotism and nepotism is often good for business.

Hogan did not take an active role in the bank's day-to-day activity, but he was chairman of the board of directors. He believed in hiring the best people possible and then letting them do what they did best. A German man by the name of Eberstark was hired as president when the bank opened its doors in 1947. He was well known and an accepted member of the community, as his father had been one of the doctors from the small neighborhood hospital. Dr. Eberstark had delivered hundreds of babies in Ravenswood during his active years. These were the days when house calls were the norm. The working poor might not have the two dollars to pay the doctor for the house call, but that didn't matter. The doctor took care of people because he cared about the community.

If a plate of cookies was offered, the doctor took that as his compensation. He knew it was given from the heart. All Dr. Eberstark really ever wanted was a sincere "thank you." Eberstark often took his son on house calls and he was soon known as "the doctor's boy." He knew and was known and liked by almost everyone in the neighborhood by the time he graduated from high school. The young man attended college and received a degree in finance. He was immediately employed at the Exchange Bank downtown. Alderman Hogan was a smart man. He knew that having a bank president that everyone in the neighborhood knew and trusted would be good business for the bank. Eberstark was given stock and a minor ownership interest in the storefront bank. He was a serious young man and made a good president.

Knowing the neighborhood had a large German population that voted in large numbers, Eberstark's appeal to these Germans was simply good business. Although the community was mixed Irish and German and the two cultures had their favorite ethnic shops and taverns, both were Catholic. The people may have come from different countries and cultures, but they prayed together. Hogan wanted them to vote together and deposit together too. They willingly complied.

Ryan began working at the bank when he was just twenty-one. There were only two tellers and a minimal staff in those early years. He was promoted to real estate lending when the bank required two lenders, one for commercial real estate and one for commercial business loans. Hogan never micro-managed his business. He let his managers manage, but he always directed the course of the bank's progress. In the early 1960s, an old factory was demolished after a fire. This large piece of land was located across from a Sears Department Store in a convenient and high-traffic area. Hogan used his connections and considerable powers of persuasion to have the land condemned by the City of Chicago. The bank bought the property for a very low price. His objective was to build a large, glass, contemporary building and expand the State Bank of the Community. "It is important to be successful, but it is also important to look successful," he said.

This was an exciting time for State Bank of the Community. The new building was a two-story structure with a large lobby and offices on a surrounding terrace. There were drive-through tellers, an innovation in banking services. Other modern conveniences and technologies were incorporated as they were introduced to the markets. The bank started a trust department and installed a large vault with safe deposit boxes. To say that everyone from the neighborhood came to the ribbon cutting and grand opening is not an exaggeration. After all, this was *their* bank.

Ryan headed up the real estate loan department as the other lender, a Mr. Jones, took on commercial business lending. The bank was growing faster than ever before and Ryan needed an assistant to help process the real estate loans. "I want someone with 'balls,' someone who knows the neighborhood and who can get the money out onto the street," he said. The culture of the bank dictated hiring from within. Outside employees were only brought in as entry-level employees. Promotions were given to employees who understood and worked well within the State Bank of the Community culture.

When reviewing who would perform well from current management, one name rose above the rest, Fran Kontopolus. Fran had balls all right. Some said she pissed standing up. No one knew just how poorly she treated her staff. They were too intimidated to complain.

All management ever saw was the statistics showing her outstanding success as a manager.

Fran had built a reputation as a team player and Ryan knew that he could train her to take his orders. He had confidence she could do the job. Fran wasn't ready to meet customers yet, but his assistant would have very little customer contact. She would oversee the loan-processing department and that meant paperwork, deadlines, and lots of tasks and challenges. She would be too busy to cause trouble.

Before she was offered the job, Ryan had to consult with the personnel department and Eberstark. He was reminded of the incident of the shattered mug, the tears in the president's office, and the demeanor or the so-called misdemeanor of Fran Kontopolus. They asked him how he would deal with a hysterical outbreak. Ryan listened but did not speak. He knew he could break Fran Kontopolus the way a cowboy breaks in a wild horse. Ryan was a flaming queen and was a lot smarter, tougher, and harsher. And he was a bigger, angrier bitch than Fran Kontopolus could ever imagine. He knew what had taken place with his friend Hudson and had his own ways of getting even.

Fran was on her way up again, but she had also stepped into the center of a corporate bull's eye.

CHAPTER TWELVE

Lee Ryan called Fran to his office after lunch on Friday. He was confident in his decision and, despite the reservations of personnel and Eberstark, knew Fran was a good candidate for the position and that he could control her. She was bright, she knew banking, and, as he had told his friend Bud when they were out for drinks the previous evening, "If I can teach a monkey to make loans, I can surely teach a Dragon to run an office."

The next day Ryan called Fran to his office, asking her to close the door and sit down. She started to speak, but he just said "wait" as he slowly closed the drapes on the floor-to-ceiling windows. Unlike her tellers and many other bank employees, he was not afraid of Fran. A queen and a female bully in a fight? The queen would win every time.

He sat down in a blue velvet easy chair. Few people ever realized it, but his chair was purposely set several inches higher to give him a psychological advantage. No matter how tall the people on the other side of the desk, he always looked down on them. He opened an expensive walnut cigarette box that sat on a small table next to his chair and put a cigarette in his mouth. He reached in his pocket, retrieved a gold cigarette lighter, and lit a Benson and Hedges 100, the long cigarettes. Like the height of his chair, the walnut box, gold lighter, and the ceremony he made of lighting up was staged for effect.

Fran wondered and waited. Ryan took a couple of puffs. He held the cigarette in his fingers the way one pictures a movie Nazi to hold a cigarette during an interrogation scene. The office was filling with blue smoke. Fran wondered why she was not offered a cigarette. Ryan blew smoke in Fran's direction. She ignored the insult.

"Fran, or should we say, Ms. Kontopolus, I don't like you. In fact, I don't like anything about you. But I admire your smarts, sweetie." She did not expect this behavior from Lee Ryan. "Franny, you have served enough time in the teller line. You are coming to work for me." Fran was quite surprised at the announcement. It was a command, not a question or request. "I need someone tough and resourceful. I need you to process the real estate loans. I may despise you, especially the clumsy way you walk in heels, but you're very bright and know how to get things done. I need that in my department."

She started to say something, her face beginning to turn red, but he waved her off. "This bank is growing and that means more deposits and that means more money must get out on the street as loans. I am busy getting that money out there with lenders. I need someone to tend to the office while I work with the important people."

He continued to explain the job, her duties, and her limits. He said he had already obtained Eberstark's blessing, which was something of a stretch, as Ebersark had really said, "Well, you've named your own poison." Ryan also explained that refusing the opportunity would not look good to Eberstark and the others who were in the know and who controlled promotion and pay scales.

Fran was not sure if she wanted to give up her power as manager of the teller line. That was until he told her of her salary and increased benefit package. That bit of information changed her whole perspective. *To hell with this bastard's attitude, just bring me the money,* she thought. This immigrant's daughter would be making more money than she ever dreamed possible so early in her career.

In lending, someone not only had a salary as a bank employee, but a lender received bonuses on loan production too. When a customer paid points for a loan, typically three percent of the gross amount of the loan, those points were paid to the bank as loan origination fees. That money was divided between the bank and the loan officer who originated the loan. Ryan assured Fran that he would share some of that money, those points and origination fees, with her for handling the processing of his loans. She couldn't believe it. Fran would be earning more money than her father. How much more could she make? A veteran at the bank and a student of greed, she had long realized that the real money and power was not in the teller line. It was "upstairs," and now she had been invited to step up. For the first time in her life, she was not thinking about food. She was thinking about money. For an instant, Fran lost her appetite.

In that same instant her ego inflated. Fran stood and held her chest out proudly like a rooster in the yard. She knew who would be under her command in the loan department. She knew every employee in the bank quite well by now. Even if she had never had a conversation with a specific person, they all knew Fran Kontopolus, Dragon Lady. Fran knew she could handle the job and she felt she could handle Ryan. She had gotten rid of Hudson and she could get rid of this pompous bastard too.

Before Fran carried the thought about taking Ryan's job any further, he interrupted her train of thought. "Ms. Kontopolus, I am not afraid of you. In fact, I'll keep you in shape, dearie! I laughed the day Eberstark didn't fire your little ass right on the spot when you cried in his office. I'll have none of that. In fact, I like making bitches like you cry. You want to cry go ahead, cry now. I'll just laugh. Don't pull that shit on me. I can offer you a nice deal here, darling, so what do you say? Come on. Quick-quick!" He snapped his fingers.

Fran accepted the position with the understanding that she could have the weekend to think about it and consult with her father. The delay was a feeble attempt at gamesmanship and Ryan saw right through it. He knew he had her. Fran knew that during her term at this position she would have access to Ryan at any time she needed help. She had seen how people fail and become scapegoats without the proper training and she did not want to be set up to fail and be fired. As she thought about what she was just offered, she wondered what was really happening. She knew she was not the most popular person at the bank and that her bullying was just an expression of insecurity.

Over the weekend Fran thought about the new position. She would have a private office, access to a semi-private ladies room, and she would make the physical and equally psychological move upstairs with the senior officers of the bank. She would learn the business of banking from experienced experts in the field. The education would be better than free. They'd be paying her for it. More people would eventually come under her thumb too. This was a huge step up for the daughter of a fishmonger.

Fran's younger brothers worked with their father in the store. Each day they would wake before the sun came up. They would dress in jeans and t-shirts with white coats over their clothing. Then the boys would take the family truck, a white Ford van with "DK Fish" printed on the sides, and drive while Papa drove his fancy car to the Randolph Street Market to choose the right amount of fish and the proper mix of fish to sell that day. The selection was an art more than a science.

The Randolph Street Market was always teeming with merchants buying produce, flowers, meat, and fish for their neighborhood shops throughout the growing city of Chicago. The Kontopolus boys wore rubber knee-high boots so they could walk through piles of crushed fishy-smelling ice on the ground, which overflowed from the crates of fresh fish. There they would choose Lake Superior whitefish, catfish, and orange roughy, trout, salmon, shrimp, cod and many more fish of the day. The rule was to take less than you can sell. You were better off running out than have to throw out fish you have paid for but couldn't sell. They would ask for seven pounds of this, ten pounds of that, and twenty pounds of something else and so on until their order of the day was completed.

Catfish was always a staple, as the store was located in the Afro-American shopping district of Seventy-ninth Street. The store had occupied the same location for twenty years, and the local residents were loyal customers. The boys always smelled of fish and so did Papa. Fran was glad she did not face the life of running a fish store. She hated the smell, but worse, there was no chance to obtain real power and real wealth in a neighborhood shop. Even if she stayed around and eventually ran the store, the profits would be shared with the family. That just wasn't enough for Fran. By now she was twenty-eight years old and ready for advancement. While other young women at the bank and in the community were set on catching a man and getting married, she had other, more ambitious, plans. Fran's father would suggest that he fix her up with the son of an old family friend and have the young man and his parents over for dinner. Fran would politely decline, saying she was too involved with work at the bank.

Fran was now focused on money, money, money and power, power, and power. She seemed more excited than she used to get at the all-you-can-eat Friday fish fry at the local Swedish smorgasbord near her home. She was at last getting a taste of the real goodies. Fran was ready, but was this opportunity too good to be true? Was there another motive pushing Ryan and maybe even Eberstark? Who was out to get her in the bank? Who wanted her to fail to purge her from the bank? Who could it be? Fran never verbalized these thoughts and ideas to anyone. She was too paranoid to expose herself that way. Over and over and over again, Fran thought, obsessed, and found enemies where none existed. She even went to church that weekend and as difficult as it was physically, she got down on her knees, lit a candle, and said a prayer—a selfish one.

Even after she took the job, moved into the new office, and had her photo placed in the bank's monthly newsletter, paranoia was a motivating factor in everything she did. The more insecure she felt, the harder she worked. She worked people below her even harder. She worked them harder than those ingrates in the teller line. Ryan's new hire studied loan processing and began to break her team up to develop specialties for the loan customers: loans $500,000 and below, loans above $1 million, home loans, investment property loans, commercial property loans, special business loans all became separated to process loans more quickly. Compartmentalization also gave her more control.

When borrowers wanted and needed capital, they wanted it quickly. Fran's department's objective was to get the money out on the streets as fast as they could. In ninety days, the department was set up and running exactly the way she wanted. Fran was still in the background and was not yet a lender herself, but she understood how to make a department hop. As with the teller line, she was a hero to management but a villain to those below her.

When Fran arrived at work one day, she found a bullwhip on her office chair. A note read "Giddy Up and Get in Line." Fran was not insulted. She laughed and tried to crack the whip. Cracking a whip properly takes lot of practice and she only succeeded in a few weak "whifffts." In the process she knocked a pencil holder, a stapler, and a hand calculator off her desk. Later that afternoon she had someone from maintenance hang the whip on a nail on the wall. This was Fran's first trophy. It hung there the entire time she worked at State Bank of the Community. She would show it off to customers and staff. She was proud of this prize. "It's true. I 'crack a mean whip,' but my staff gave me this as an award for making them so successful," she said.

As part of her training for this new position, Fran attended a citywide seminar with other lenders from banks located all over Northern Illinois. This gave her not only the opportunity to learn the business of lending from professionals with experience, but to meet competitors working in other banks. All of those attending the class were men, of course, college graduates, many just out of school who wanted a career in banking. The seminar discussed and reviewed the proper lending guidelines and techniques allowed by the Fed and that organization's crucial role in banking and the national economy. Topics included mezzanine lending, debt-to-equity ratio, cap rates, appraisals, and what percentage of loan-to-value the bank could lend to a borrower.

Fran learned how to run credit reports and interpret the credit information. She learned that banks, depending on their gross assets, could lend a percentage of that number to a single borrower. She learned about participation loans with other banks. There were many things to learn in a system that was regulated and always changing. Fran loved learning and took in all the information. It was ammunition. At night, she read additional books borrowed from employees in her department. There were books on economics, lending, and business related to banking and the history of lending. She learned quickly and was more than ready to get the department moving in the direction she wanted. She was thrilled.

Miss Marsh replaced Fran as teller supervisor and a dark cloud was lifted on the main floor of the bank. During lunch hour in the cafeteria one day, Marsh hosted a shower for one of the tellers who was expecting her first baby in a few weeks. The girls were gleeful and cheerful and they all shared the feeling of relief that their former tormentor was now someone else's demon. Some hummed "Ding Dong the Witch Is Dead" from *The Wizard of Oz*.

At the end of the party, one girl lit a candle on a cupcake and called everyone together. "This happy occasion could not be a finer time to wave a fond, and I do mean fond, farewell to the old Dragon Lady herself. May she go down in flames and blow her flames up someone else's skirt. My young ass has been burning for toooooooooooooo long."

The girls said, "Right on," gave each other high-fives, and returned to the teller line. One girl chuckled, blew out the candle, and tossed the cupcake in the trash.

Later that afternoon Fran was walking through the cafeteria and saw the fresh cupcake on top of the trash. She looked both ways and when she was sure no one was looking, she grabbed it and wolfed it down. As she walked toward the ladies room the cupcake wrapper was stuck to her shoe.

CHAPTER THIRTEEN

Fran got the loan department up and kept it churning. Her new job was not like the teller line in which everyone arrived at a specific time and left work at a specific time. The processing department did not close when the bank closed and she expected her employees to work half-days, twelve hours. If they didn't like it, well, they could quit, find another bank in another neighborhood, and spend half their day commuting.

Those who could not keep up knew that they would not be keeping their jobs for long. The others, almost all college graduates who majored in finance or businesses, decided to stick it out and hope for the best. They expected to work hard, learn from real-world experience, and move up to senior management in the organization. Fran did not disappoint them in terms of hard work. They kept their "eyes on the prize," but paid a terrible price for the effort. Fran's employees may not have had calluses on their hands but they developed calluses on their souls.

Ryan was true to his word and Fran did make more money. He shared a fair percentage of what he earned. But because she was who she was, Fran always wanted more. She just couldn't get enough. More and more she became intoxicated with money, power, and the ability to control someone else's life.

Fran continued to live at home and turned in her paycheck to her father as she always did. But she decided that someone her age and in her position should have her own money without having to ask Papa for it. She decided not to tell him about the additional money she was earning, the increased salary and her bonus money. One afternoon she ducked out of the bank and took a taxi to a nearby neighborhood where a branch of a big downtown bank was located. She opened her own savings account, using a post office box to receive her monthly account statement. Fran began depositing her bonuses and watched her money grow. Ryan was good at his job and the department quickly expanded its customer base.

Fran's extra money followed. She had never had her own money before and it showed. She began dining out at the most expensive restaurants, buying expensive jewelry, clothes, and shoes. When she first received a credit card, she almost could not believe her eyes. Fran went through money like piss through a cocaine addict. The habit of spending large stayed with her the rest of her life.

Ryan was a tough loan officer with a tough loan procedure. He taught Fran that a loan was only as good as the person who could repay it. Forget reputation or friendship and look always at the bottom line. He wanted to know of each loan application and exactly when the loan was ready to disburse. Everything he verified moved through the steps easily. If he had questions, the process slowed and sometimes ground to a halt.

During the 1970's and 1980's, external factors helped the bank grow. Chicago's re-birth in the gentrification of its neighborhoods meant a continual series of applications for home loans, remodeling and repair loans, construction company and supplier loans, and other loans related to a booming real estate market. Deposits soared.

Smart and aggressive developers were buying older apartment buildings in the ethnic neighborhoods near Lake Michigan. They converted these old, lovely, and large apartments into condominiums for the city's more affluent younger citizens who were beginning to move back in from the suburbs. The State Bank of the Community had a central location to many such neighborhoods and was the perfect lender for this army of rehab entrepreneurs. Lee Ryan was the perfect man to lead the charge.

Fran organized an efficient loan-processing department that was precisely what the bank needed. Ryan had been right in choosing her for the job. When a real estate loan application looked marginal, Fran would have a detailed write-up for the loan committee explaining why the loan should be rejected. On the other hand, when a loan passed the underwriting department, she submitted a detailed report to the loan committee explaining its acceptance. Ryan chaired the loan committee with two bank board members, along with his lending officers and bank senior staff. Eberstark attended each meeting, but he allowed Ryan do his job and never interfered with his decisions.

By attending the weekly loan committee meetings, Fran was presenting and displaying her skills in lending and underwriting to the people who mattered most: the officers, board members, and decision-makers at the bank. She enjoyed the weekly stage to showcase her talents. But what really added to the thrill of these meetings was the catered lunch. The meetings began at 11:00 a.m. on Wednesdays in the boardroom. This was a large room with floor-to-ceiling glass windows overlooking the parking lot of the bank on the south side of the building. The room received the southern sun so it was full of tall green plants that the maintenance staff pruned and watered carefully. Eberstark loved his plants. Because of the sun glaring in the boardroom, shades were lowered to keep the room from overheating.

The focus of the room was a long glass conference table that sat sixteen. In three areas at the center of the table were pitchers of water and glasses, ashtrays, and coasters. Each place setting was set before the meetings by a capable and conscientious bank employee, Mrs. Lazar. At each place setting she set a coffee mug, water glass, three-ring notebook with the loan committee's report for the week, a yellow legal pad, and a State Bank of the Community pencil.

The meetings were opened by Ryan, who reviewed the loans outstanding, the loans that were expected to be paid off in the next month, and the gross deposits in the bank current as of the close of business the last Friday before the meeting. He would then turn the meeting over to Fran just as Mrs. Lazar was escorting the local deli delivery into the boardroom.

The menu was the same: corned beef, roast beef, German rye bread with and without seeds, Swiss cheese, Munster cheese, mustards in many flavors, spices, and horseradish, and good vinegar potato salad and coleslaw. Fran's mouth always watered as the trays arrived and she was always distracted as the committee members lined up to fill their plates just as she was beginning to read her report and review each loan with this committee. She was at one end of the table and all that wonderful food was at the other end.

One might think that Fran, as a presenter to the board, would be unhappy with the people getting out of their chairs, standing up, moving around, sitting down, and munching away on food. No, that was not why she was upset. What really got to her was the fact that she did not have the first choice of these luscious, pink lunchmeats. Although her family life had always been secure, she had eaten her share of leftovers. She didn't care to repeat the experience in her adult life. As a child she had prided herself on getting to the kitchen before her brothers and making herself the tallest mile-high sandwich anyone had ever seen. Then after eating it she excused herself to the bathroom.

After the committee fed itself, there was still plenty of food remaining for Fran to make her sandwich, but she resented not being able to be first in line. Her ever-growing paranoia made her wonder if the men scheduled the meetings just to deny her first choice of the choice cuts. And the torture of waiting made her perspire.

On more than one occasion, Fran would be describing a real estate loan for a customer named Ben Kornblatt and she would slip and say, "I want to begin to review the Ben Corn Beef loan." There might be a chuckle from the committee members, but Fran would laugh at herself in that defensive way that she would when she was embarrassed. She would correct herself and go on, her eyes darting back and forth between her papers and the delicious spread on the table. There was something else Fran resented about these lunches. There was no mayonnaise for the sandwiches and Fran loved her mayonnaise.

The committee meetings always ran smoothly, a tribute to Lee Ryan and Fran Kontopolus. The bank was growing and becoming more profitable. Not being on the bank's board of directors, Fran never attended the bank board meetings with the chairman of the bank board, Mr. Hogan. When the meetings ended and the board dispersed, Hogan would walk to Fran's desk, stop, and tap his index finger on her desk three times. When she looked up he would say, "Job well done, Ms. Kontopolus." To Fran, or anyone, such a compliment was as if Zeus himself reached down from Mount Olympus to offer a blessing.

As the growth of real estate lending continued, Fran got to know the customers well. She saw the carpenters and plumbers who bought a Chicago two-flat, fixed it up, and sold it. She got to know the pools of immigrants who took whatever money they had to buy an apartment building, placed themselves and their families and friends into the apartments, then repaired and maintained their first real home in America. Although she was an integral component in making the American dream come true for many people, she really didn't give a rat's ass. She had dreams of her own.

Fran convinced Ryan that she could and would be more effective in his department if she actually had an opportunity to go see the properties and construction projects for which the bank was making the real estate loans. The bank had a small pool of cars for employees to make field calls, and each week Fran reserved a car and drove to see if what was supposed to be built was being built. She met developers onsite and began to get a handle on what was going on in the neighborhoods.

She made it part of her day to stop for breakfast near construction projects that the bank was financing. At the local coffee shop, she would ask the wait staff about the building being renovated across the street. She knew the workers frequented the local restaurants for coffee and meals. Fran would ask the staff if they saw construction activity or if they heard any construction-related gossip. The waitresses always knew the local angles and were the best source of information. Fran hated to do it, but she always tipped heavily.

Fran found a bonus in lunching with these real estate developers. The practice was to meet, eat, and talk business. These men wanted to be generous to Fran because she made the decision about how generous, and how quickly, the bank would be generous with them. In the day when martinis were not unusual during lunch, Fran would have her two martinis at one of the many neighborhood steakhouses. She was taken to Louie's on Ashland, Bassett's on Irving Park, Cello's on Clark, or Willie Joes' on Chicago Avenue. Fran became a restaurant maven. When she called a customer she would like to meet to see a project on a certain day, the savvy customer would make a lunch suggestion.

It was not unusual for Fran to say, "No, I've eaten there lately, I prefer the Blackhawk or the Italian Village," or one of the more expensive places near downtown Chicago. She was as obvious as hell, but the developers didn't mind. The outlay was a pittance compared to what Fran could steer their way. After lunch she would excuse herself to the ladies room. Customers and restaurant staff alike wondered how she could eat so much without "porking out" more than she did.

Borrowers knew that this was the way to do business and they fed her heartily. They found it unusual but did not really care when Fran completed her meal, steak, salad, pasta, potatoes, dessert, and two drinks, and began to eat from their plates too. She would direct the wait staff not to throw any food away, but to place it in doggy bags, even the bread and rolls, and she would take it all with her. After telling the waiter to do this she would turn to the borrowers and ask, "Do you mind if I take this home for my dog?" The borrowers, of course, never objected and no one knew Fran had no dog.

She liked the new position and likely would have stayed as support for Ryan forever. She actually began to like him. He was someone she could not push over as she bullied her way around the bank. She liked the intimidation and she liked being part of his team. Her paranoia was always with her, but she felt more secure because she had created a position that would be difficult for anyone else to fill.

Five years passed and Fran worked at her job well. The bank continued to expand. Eberstark suggested at a meeting of the bank board of directors that a new position be created, an executive vice president who would report directly to him. Under the executive vice president would be the vice president, real estate loans commercial business lending, the trust department, private banking, personnel, the teller line, and maintenance.

Eberstark had serious banking business to conduct locally, regionally, and nationally and needed to have an officer at a level just below him to handle the daily management grind. This person would have to be a trusted, long-term bank employee who knew where State Bank of the Community had come from and would want to help lead it into the future. Lee Ryan was the obvious choice. He was loyal, trustworthy, and had a long, proven track record of success. There was simply no question as to who should fill the new position.

Hogan and Eberstark took Ryan to lunch. He knew what was going on and understood and looked forward to the new arrangement. The meeting was cordial, as most of the meetings with State Bank of the Community executive officers were. Each man ordered a scotch on the rocks before lunch. The meeting was relaxed and matter-of-fact. Ryan was asked whom he would suggest to fill in his shoes as vice president of real estate loans and without hesitation he named Fran Kontopolus. This is what Hogan and Eberstark had anticipated and they heartily agreed. They knew her Dragon Lady reputation, but they also knew that she would most likely be a lifer at the bank. Fran was not someone likely to meet a man, get married, and leave pregnant one day. They all knew that she was married to her work. They all agreed that their steps should be implemented by the beginning of the next month. They had three weeks to put their plan into action.

CHAPTER FOURTEEN

F ran was happier than she ever had been. She had moved up further than she had dreamed by becoming the first female vice president in the history of State Bank of the Community. This promotion made big headlines in the business press. Fran's mother insisted that she attend church the following Sunday to give thanks, true enough, but also so Ma could show off her daughter to the community. Bragging rights. "We always knew Fran would go far. I hear your daughter is now a waitress. How wonderful."

When a new lender was showcased in the press, new borrowers showed up like long-forgotten relatives just after a distant cousin has won the lottery. Some were credit worthy, many not, but they all talked a good game. Regardless of their status or gift of gab, the only way to borrow money from State Bank of the Community was through Fran Kontopolus. Connections with Ryan or even Eberstark or Hogan were useless. "Sorry, Bob, but you'll have to see Fran about that." Fran was right up there at the bank. She had money and power, a company car, bonuses on loan production, an expense account, and now she controlled the loan meetings.

But better than all of that, Fran controlled the menu for lunch. She knew that there was more to a good meal than just a German deli platter. This awesome responsibility required considerable thought and she began to consider all the options for catering lunch.

She needed an assistant for another type of catering, someone to handle her business and personnel needs. An assistant was also a visible symbol of her new power. Others in upper management had their secretaries run out for cigarettes, buy a gift for a wife or child, or any other number of non-business-related tasks. Fran needed one of these "gofers," but one that would not undermine her, someone who would not feel competitive and who she could trust. She needed an assistant who could help with the loan report preparation documents, binders, and statistics of development trends, and most important, someone to order a small refrigerator for the boardroom where she could store her goodies, which included chocolate candies, original Coca-Cola, and a large bottle of mayonnaise.

Choosing a person from food services to work in her department was unusual to say the least, but Fran, who may have spent more time in the cafeteria than any other bank employee, chose Ms. Navarro, a recent immigrant from the Philippines. The woman was perfect. She was a hard worker, insecure, and easily intimidated. Fran liked Navarro because she was always friendly and did not withhold the extra plop of whip cream on the pudding dessert in the cafeteria line.

Fran knew she could train the woman just the way she wanted. Navarro would have no bad habits to unlearn. During loan committee meetings, which no longer included Eberstark or Ryan, Fran was in charge. The board members who attended were older men who had helped organize State Bank of the Community with Hogan in 1947.

For attending the loan committee meetings each week, these men, these founding fathers, received a free lunch, a small payment for attending, and an afternoon away from their wives. Often one or two would doze off. They were non-confrontational and agreed with everything Fran presented. They were happy to come to the meetings, happy to pretend to be accomplishing something, and happy to go home feeling important. As far as having any real impact on banking operations, they were nothing more than dead weight.

A real perk for Fran was having Navarro stand first in the food line on her behalf. Fran was always boasting that her staff was trained better than any other staff at the bank. One Saturday afternoon Fran took Navarro to the local German deli and showed her just how to order the meats, breads, and cheeses that Fran liked best. She spent that afternoon showing her assistant how the mustard, butter, and mayonnaise should be spread to get the desired texture and combined flavor. After all, Navarro had worked in the cafeteria. She was used to food preparation, and after some practice, Fran had what she wanted, a person who could make her food the way she liked it and assist in her every need.

The loan committee didn't really care who lined up first anyway. The older board members never even noticed. Some were amazed at how wide Fran could open her mouth when eating that mile-high sandwich. They would stare at her with bent necks, attempting to see if she displaced her jaw like a snake eating a fat, juicy rat. Attending this part of the meeting was not unlike going to a freak show in a traveling carnival. A few of the older and more traditional members were "put off their feed" at her performance and left without eating so much as a potato chip.

Navarro made her boss the mile-high sandwich from the meats and cheeses Fran most loved. One afternoon she forgot to spread the mayonnaise. She was used to being treated poorly by her alcoholic father and her alcoholic husband, so Fran's yelling and screaming, which were routine, did not seem to faze her. Abuse was just part of the job, but the day she forgot the mayonnaise created another chapter in the book of "The Dragon Lady Rages." Fran noticed the slip-up upon inspecting the sandwich when it was placed in front of her. She took a deep and angry breath, stood up, and exploded. She picked up the plate and threw it across the room. The plate crashed against the wall, leaving meat and cheese dripping and slithering toward the carpeting. She demanded that Navarro make another sandwich and this time get it right. Fran's face was as red as a bare butt after sitting on a marble bench in a steam room.

The outburst woke two of the older board members who were just beginning to doze off. Navarro never missed a beat. A plate shattered against the wall was far better than a belt across the back from her father or a rabbit punch to the stomach from her husband. She bent down and picked up the meats and cheeses and cleaned up as best she could. Fran stormed her way to the food station. The meats and cheeses, lettuce and tomatoes began flying across the table and onto the floor as she made the sandwich herself, piling the ingredients higher than ever. The food was spilling off the plate. Then Fran opened the small refrigerator in the boardroom and grabbed the mayonnaise jar. Fortunately, there was enough remaining to make a proper sandwich.

Fran emptied the jar with the knife clinking and clanging against the glass bottom. The noise permeated the room. In anger, Fran thrust the empty jar into the trash basket with a crash and yelled to Navarro, "Never let this happen again. You better get two jars, pronto!"

Fran's screeching was heard throughout the bank and Navarro, with tears in her eyes, ran from the room. Abuse could be tolerated, but it should not be public, she thought. She bounded down the stairs, through the revolving doors, and was seen running to the local market to buy more mayonnaise.

Fortunately, Eberstark and Ryan were out of the bank when this disturbing incident occurred. The bank employees knew better than to say anything to anyone. The managers at her level either figured it was none of their business or were just waiting for Fran to let out enough rope to hang herself. Either way, no one ever brought it to the attention of senior management.

The tale of the "Mayonnaise Fit" was told over and over again until one day something happened to complement the story. Apparently a substantial amount of a tasteless and fast-acting laxative was mysteriously and carefully blended into Fran's mayonnaise. On this particular meeting day, Navarro spread more than an adequate amount of the dressing on Fran's mile-high sandwich, even layering it gingerly between the slices of meat. Fran took her sandwich in hand and chomped away quickly and eagerly, as often was the case.

Shortly, like a scene from a cartoon, Fran got red in the face, her eyes began to tear, and she grunted and grabbed at her stomach. Fran jumped out of her chair and made a mad dash out the door, bee-lining it right to the semi-private ladies room. The door slammed shut and the loud noise of the bolt locking the door echoed down the hall. After thirty minutes of waiting, one of the older board members decided that the day's meeting should be adjourned.

As the boardroom emptied the maintenance man, Bill, entered the boardroom to begin cleaning. As he passed his cousin Ms. Navarro, he gave her a wink. They brushed elbows and she returned to her desk.

CHAPTER FIFTEEN

The primary job of the vice president of real estate loans was to develop new customers and hold on to those customers through professional relationships. Relationship building was not one of Fran's strong points, but magically, with the new promotion and new title, she found that relationship building was really quite easy when you controlled the purse strings. No matter how rich or successful or connected the applicant was, she always sat in the power seat.

Once borrowers were informed that Fran was the vice president of real estate loans, gifts began arriving in droves. Greeting cards with well wishes, candy, lunch and dinner invitations, and more were offered as supplicant after supplicant came to the mountain. This was the protocol, and Fran ate it up. Suddenly she had friends! Invitations to the ballet, the opera, major league sports, and other events arrived by phone, letter, e-mail, and in person. Fran was taken to some of Chicago's most exclusive private dining clubs for dinners. She never had it so good. As a person starved for attention and who had never had friends in her life, she was a grateful recipient of these favors. Although she lacked social graces and often embarrassed her suitors, the invitations continued to arrive. "Yeah, the old girl splattered béarnaise sauce on the mayor's daughter. What the hell. She just approved a quarter million-dollar loan. 'Hizzoner' never did that for me."

The senders of these gifts, all men in the business of developing real estate, were playing the game of "seduce the banker." They were pros at it and Fran fell right into their hands. Although she never lowered the bank's lending standards, she did approve certain borrowers' loans more rapidly than others.

By the time she was promoted to the loan department, Sonny Vulich had multiple loans financing a number of projects with the bank. When he discovered that this repulsive woman was someone he would have to work with he was sick to his stomach. Image meant a lot to Sonny and to have to shake hands with someone like Fran, to have to sit in a meeting with her, made him angry. He was cunning. He knew that people like her required a little kindness, attention, and a liberal dose of flattery. Acquiring the money she controlled would require a certain amount of seduction. He knew that when one sleeps with dogs, one wakes with fleas, unless one uses de-lousing powder before going to bed. He mentally prepared himself for the challenge ahead.

Sonny was the first borrower smart enough to send her a bouquet of flowers, and although he wasn't the first to send chocolates when she was promoted, he was the first to send her the finest Swiss chocolate in Chicago. In fact, Sonny was the first with everything that he could send Fran to get on her good side. He sent her gifts for the holidays and gifts from his travels when he took a vacation or business trip. He noted her birthday so she would receive a card every year. On the anniversary of her promotion, he sent a copy of the same bouquet and an identical box of chocolates he had sent to her years earlier. Each year the box of Swiss delights got bigger.

Sonny got all the money he needed, was looked upon as a friend, and became a confidant of Fran Kontopolus. He admitted to himself that he was a pretty sharp operator at that. Sonny knew that it was good business to have other banking relationships, and he did borrow from other banks. But Fran just made it so easy that there was no reason for Sonny not to choose State Bank of the Community as his primary lender.

Borrowers with smaller loan requests and certainly those who did not come bearing gifts were placed at the bottom of the food chain. When a long-term customer asked why he had to wait longer for a loan approval than he was accustomed to, he was informed that other customers had better seats at Chicago Bulls games. She was that bold. Fran, excited to have "friends," could not see that many of her customers only acted as if they cared for her. For the borrower, faster approval equaled more deals and more profit. What was a couple of $300 meals compared to a $3 million low-interest loan on the fast track?

These new friends provided the social experience she had been dreaming of all her life. Fran had never been so busy after work and on weekends. A few borrowers invited her into their homes for dinner and to meet their families. She was invited to christenings and weddings as if she were a member of the family. She knew they were all buttering her up and she loved it. Who deserved more attention and perks than she?

One borrower, a manipulative man who had a questionable reputation, began to date Fran. He took her to dinner and movies. After a couple of dates, her little heart was missing beats. Never having had boyfriends, she had never learned how to communicate intimately one-on-one. She was awkward, she was sloppy, and she was often embarrassing. But this customer had a motive. He needed money to purchase and renovate a flophouse he wanted to turn into a small hotel. He knew how to lead Fran on. After a few dates, he called her at her office one day and requested a $6 million non-recourse loan. Non-recourse meant that if the deal fell apart he would not have to guarantee the loan personally. His money would be safe from any creditors.

Fran got the loan approved as he wanted. After the closing of the loan and the funding of the project, the customer never called Fran again. He did renovate the property and was a success. According to his partners and friends, he entered six months of intense psychoanalysis after the loan closing. To this day he walks with a tremor. He got his loan, but he had climbed to the top of what was to become Fran's enemy list.

Fran's enemy list increased and included some of Chicago's most popular and well-respected real estate developers. Once on the list a loan request might be buried forever. One of her targets might be requested to produce sixteen years of tax returns for a loan approval. Another might be required to produce a credit report for a pet. She had grown men and women, professionals all, jumping through hoops like trained lions in a circus. Her techniques for vengeance became legendary.

A minor infraction or ill-conceived perception of a customer might land someone on the ever-growing list. Like the emperors of ancient Rome, supplicants had to come bearing gifts. If not, "off with their heads!" Figuratively, of course.

When Fran became the vice president of real estate, she changed the rules. Ryan would review the loan and make a decision on the credit-worthiness of the borrower and the project. Assessments were made on the merits of the deal. Old customers had built a rapport with the bank and had established a more casual way of presenting their proposal to Ryan. He would reject or accept on an informal basis, subject to review by the loan committee. Established customers soon learned that those days were over.

Fran Kontopolus had a big appetite, a big appetite first for food, and then for power and money, money, money. Her appetite could never be satisfied. Her massive ego shouted, "This is not enough. I want more, more, more!" The next gift or perk had to be better than the customer's last.

Some people have an extra body part, a bit of the human anatomy never found in a medical textbook, never found in an x-ray, never found on an ultra-sound or any physical examination. This was the driving force behind Fran. That part of a human being is called "the greed gland." Fran was a big woman with an oversized greed gland.

Borrowers talked among themselves. Many were friendly competitors who belonged to builders and real estate clubs. They shared strategies, techniques, and horror stories about the demon in the bank. At one meeting, Fran became the topic of discussion. One member let down, then another, and still another, until Fran Kontopolus stories were the evening's topic of laughter and ridicule. These men needed the loans she controlled so they could never be honest about her repulsiveness to her face. But behind closed doors they could not stand her. The golden rule states he who has the gold makes the rule and Fran had the gold.

One member told a story about Fran insisting he escort her to a trade show and take her out for dinner afterward. One member stated that he was requested to have his cousin, a jeweler on Wabash Avenue, sell Fran jewelry at cost. Another told a story in which Fran demanded he purchase the brick for a small house he was building from Fran's cousin Andreas. Of course, anyone planning a banquet had to order their fish from DK Fish Company.

The drinking and the stories continued throughout the evening and way past midnight. By the end, the members came to the conclusion that Fran simply could not get enough for herself. One jovial developer who had remained silent through most of the night stood up. He took his glass in hand and said, "Ya know, I propose a new club with Fran Kontopolus as the president, vice president, treasurer, secretary, and entire membership. Let's name it the 'I Can't Get Enough Club.'" Everyone laughed and toasted to the president of the new club. "May she rot in hell."

CHAPTER SIXTEEN

For a good number of years Fran prospered as vice president of real estate loans. The borrowers became used to dancing with the ogre. Fran, on the other hand, felt she finally had the true friends she had always wanted. When the ruling tyrant received gifts from her servants it would reinforce her tyrannical behavior. The subjects providing the gifts would mask their feelings, acting as enablers reinforcing the heavy hand of the tyrant. Thus, Fran's basic behavior did not change because she was receiving continual reinforcement for her rude, crude, and slovenly ways. She never wavered from the bank's goal of investing deposits into real estate loans. And the longer she maintained her position and State Bank of the Community grew, Fran was successful and regarded as a valuable member of the team.

Many tales have been written and stories retold of people who sold their souls for money and power. This was certainly the case with Fran's customers, but it didn't apply across the board. Word got around and the real estate professionals of higher character refused to deal with Fran Kontopolus. Certain potential customers avoided her at all costs. There were other friendly banks in Chicago and money was always available for a good deal.

"There's no way I'll work with State Bank of the Community. Every time I come out of that woman's office I feel like I need to wash my hands." The statement was far from an exaggeration. Even in the most important meetings, she would be snacking on powdered donuts, a greasy sandwich, or some melted chocolate something or other. Fran found it most frustrating to have some of Chicago's best-known and well-respected real estate borrowers and developers choose not to work with her. As successful as she was, she wanted every big developer as a customer. She felt she deserved it. Fran wanted to show off and brag about her long list of clients. Yet she could not capture the entire market place.

Then national politics hammered the economy. Markets have always changed and fluctuated. During the late seventies' presidential administration of Jimmy Carter, inflation hit the United States hard. Paul Volker was the Federal Reserve chairman. He felt that to control inflation, interest rates should be increased. So he began to increase rates to slow the economy. Interest rates rose and rose and rose until they exceeded twenty percent. Double-digit lending rates halted borrowing of any sort. Large multi-national companies declared bankruptcy. Volker's actions succeeded. The economy slowed so much that the national economy began to shut down.

When businesses pay more for borrowing money, the first cut they make to increase or maintain profitability is to lay off employees. It's not vicious. It's not evil. It's not personal. It's math. A minus B equals C. Expenses minus employee salaries and benefits equal profitability or at least temporary stability. For many young people just starting careers it was, "Welcome to the real world, kid."

Millions of workers were laid off as unemployment increased and the United States floundered in a deep recession. The impact on the real estate market presented itself in a few ways, none of them pleasant or profitable. For builders who borrowed on adjustable rates tied to the prime lending rate, their developments were no longer profitable. The increased cost of interest ate away at the profit. Buyers could not buy homes or condominiums and the residential real estate market practically disappeared. Not being able to sell their property forced builders to go into foreclosure and give property back to the banks. Builders of office buildings, shopping centers, apartment complexes, or any type of property, for that matter, tried to stay in business, but rates were stripping away their profits. Banks that paid interest to depositors found that they were increasing the interest rates due to depositors but not getting a return on money they had lent out to builders, businesses, and real estate borrowers. Those banks that paid out more than they received began operating in the red and running at a negative cash flow. The dilemma that State Bank of the Community had was basic—stay alive.

Fran saw this crisis on the horizon as the Fed raised rates slowly and steadily and with no end in sight. Her customers were having problems and that meant that the bank was going to have problems. Fran was bright enough to contemplate this challenge over and over in her mind. Board members and executives were expecting the worst, but Fran devised a plan. She saw the blood on the streets not simply from her customers but from those borrowers who always evaded her.

Fran appealed to Eberstark for a special meeting to present a plan. He agreed and called on Ryan to join them. Fran proposed that State Bank of the Community create its own balance system of deposits versus the interest rates they would charge customers. Typically a bank would lend money at a rate higher than they would pay depositors. Fran suggested that if the base of borrowers she developed would move their savings accounts, money market accounts, and other interest-bearing accounts to accounts that were referred to as "demand deposits," accounts that are non-interest bearing, the bank would no longer have the obligation to pay interest on many millions of dollars they were now obligated to pay. On the flip side, the bank could lower the strangle-hold rates that were putting their customers out of business.

This was an aggressive idea. Ryan and Eberstark listened carefully and liked what they heard. This was a revolutionary concept that could keep the bank in business and help keep their customers in business. Banking was not creative and no other bank was this innovative. This might be a great plan if the board approved it and it was legally feasible. State Bank of the Community did not want to own a portfolio of real estate and did not want to foreclose on good customers.

Fran had another idea she kept to herself. She thought that if she could put this program in place, she could attract those borrowers who had avoided her to deposit their money at State Bank of the Community and move their loans to the bank. That's how she could seduce them to work with her. Business was the only seduction Fran could offer.

The idea brought her respect and attention from Eberstark and Ryan. Eberstark told her he would review her suggestion with the banks attorneys and the board of directors. Now don't think that every borrower in Chicago ran to Fran Kontopolus for their money. People who are true to themselves don't give up their character and moral standards. But this was a tough time for the economy. Standards had to be modified. Those at risk of losing everything were drawn to State Bank of the Community and Fran Kontopolus. Once the word was on the street that there was a way to possibly preserve assets, business people of higher character lowered their moral standard and became Fran's customers.

Fran's brilliance helped the bank and brought her a following that became obligated to be loyal to her. Depositors took less on their deposits as long as they could hold onto their real estate. The fishmonger's daughter's power was growing exponentially.

CHAPTER SEVENTEEN

The years became decades and Hogan and Eberstark were getting older. Their small investment in 1947 had grown into many hundreds of millions of dollars. It was time to look at retirement and the future of the bank. The principal shareholders and the senior board members with them from the beginning decided it was time to sell.

Selling the bank had been a background discussion in general terms for many years. Nothing lasts forever. Timing is everything and Hogan and Eberstark wanted to set a smooth transition in place. They wanted no shocks that would damage or perhaps even destroy their "baby." After the recession ended and business was back to normal, large banks, looking to expand into the neighborhoods of Chicago, had an appetite to acquire community banks. In preparation for the sale, and to make the offering a little more desirable, State Bank of the Community opened four small branches in the city, increasing their presence and franchise value from one location to five. With careful planning, the owners knew it would be a valuable acquisition candidate. The process involved hiring a firm to prepare the appropriate documents to qualified suitors. A confidential placement offering was prepared, showing the financial history of the bank and its projected long-term growth. The board of directors ordered the offering to be submitted first to the largest national and downtown banks. The matter was to be conducted confidentially. If a sale became public, depositors might withdraw their money and employees might start searching for new jobs. Panic followed by a significant drop in value might follow.

Obviously, the employees were not informed of the intent to sell the bank. Only after the papers were signed and the due diligence period of the acquirer was complete would there be an announcement. The offering was not on the street long when a unanimous decision was made to sell to another prominent financial institution, the First National Bank of Chicago.

Once informed of the pending sale of the bank, the employees of course were nervous. They wondered if they would lose their jobs. There was curiosity as to what the new management would be like. An uncertain future produced anxiety and there was a nervous tension throughout the bank each day. For the first time in years, Fran was scared. As the new purchaser investigated and inspected all aspects of bank operations prior to closing the deal, a key component of the merger was knowing what personnel they should keep, offer contracts to, and who should be let go. Fran had a good lending record and wanted to stay with the new administration. This was, after all, her power base. The new management decided that her intimate knowledge of the loan portfolio made it a necessity to keep her. She was offered a one-year contract.

Suddenly more confident in her position, she used this opportunity to hold out for more money and she easily got what she asked for. The new owners needed people who knew the new acquisition intimately. After the transition they could be kept on or let go. Additionally, Fran's department was one of the most profitable. For the time being at least she was an asset. The bank was sold, the shareholders made a fortune, and leadership was transferred with a minimum of shock.

Fran thought she could run her department as usual. But with the closing of the sale came a new boss to oversee the real estate loan department, an experienced banker with a different operating philosophy.

The mission of the new leader was to teach the First National Bank of Chicago's culture to Fran. She was expected to master it, pass it along to everyone in her department, and monitor a successful implementation of their policies, procedures, and expectations. Fran did not like the way the big bank conducted business. From the start, she knew she would collect her salary and at the end of her contract, after she collected every red cent due, she planned on heading right out the door to find a new seat of power.

CHAPTER EIGHTEEN

Fran had no loyalty to the new bank and could not get over her resentment of the way the sale of Sate Bank of the Community took place. Although she had no ownership, she had dedicated her life to build the business and contributed to its growth and prosperity. She had plotted, executed, whined, cried, bullied, threatened, and ruined careers to get where she was. She was due! Fran was angry. Hogan, Eberstark, and Ryan owed her. Precisely what they owed her was more than she could verbalize, something somewhat intangible yet immensely rewarding. Fran was jealous, angry, and upset that events were so out of her control. She had to compromise to get along with the new management team. Her frustration and anger increased her nervous eating. She soon gained fifteen pounds.

During the countdown to the end of her contract, Fran let it be known in selected and trusted areas of the banking community that she was looking for a new home. She became a commodity to be bid on, and headhunters, those who find jobs for experienced banking professionals, were looking to earn a large commission or hiring fee for placing Fran Kontopolus at a different bank.

Fran did not like the large corporate setting of the First National Bank of Chicago. She wanted a more controllable community bank environment. About this time, a brilliant banker and entrepreneur began expanding his family's suburban bank within the city neighborhoods, Roosevelt National Bank.

Tom Steiner was a Harvard University graduate. His father began a community bank in a western suburb of Chicago years earlier. Tom learned well the business of banking after he graduated from Harvard. With Tom's initiative, his father's community bank was on a path to growth. He was an extremely refined man who surrounded himself with other intelligent young men who actually resembled Tom in height, appearance, and dress. This group of yes-men looked like a group of clones. They wore round tortoise shell glasses, white shirts, bow ties, and always had their cuffs rolled up. Steiner was quietly brilliant and in a matter of five years under his control had acquired a significant group of banks geographically close to the old State Bank of the Community. Steiner's bank expanded rapidly and they now needed an experienced lender to run their real estate loan department. Fran's name was submitted by one of the head hunting firms.

Steiner had never met Fran Kontopolus, but knew she was an established and successful real estate lender. Those who knew better warned him, but Steiner thought Fran might be the figurehead he needed at one of his locations. He was particularly concerned with the lending department at a branch in the Lincoln Park neighborhood of Chicago's north side. Lincoln Park become popular as an area of renovation and gentrification during the late 1960s when hippies came to Chicago for the notorious democratic convention and found its Victorian apartments and lofts inexpensive and a likable lifestyle. Located near the lake front, Lincoln Park was one of the hottest and trendiest neighborhoods in Chicago. The hippies became yuppies as they grew older and spent millions if not billions changing the face of the neighborhood into a modern suburb.

The Lincoln Park branch of Roosevelt National Bank was a great depository, but it was underperforming in the real estate lending arena and Tom thought it could use a boost. The bank management staff consisted of his clones and not one of them was up to the task. He needed a strong lender to lead loan origination. Fran was approached to meeting with the personnel department and was offered the job as head of their Lincoln Park branch.

The members of the board and management were traditional banker types, men with white shirts and ties. When Fran attended her first loan committee and met the staff, they realized she was not exactly a fit. She was loud, unrestrained, and her obnoxious behavior did not fit their image of a professional banker. The clones weren't very good at innovative management, but they were experts at maintaining the proper image.

To be successful as a lender someone in Fran's position needed credit authority, which is a lender's ability to make loans at certain levels without having to receive a loan committee's approval. The lender's credit authority was a mainstay and important part of the lender's ability to conduct business. The lender needed a certain amount of independent decision-making ability for customers who needed answers on the spot. At State Bank of the Community Fran's credit authority was $2.5 million, a very large amount in its time. This provided her with an ability to accept or deny a real estate loan based on her individual experience with a customer and his or her level of bribery. Every loan was required to be officially acknowledged by the loan committee, but if the lender could tell a customer that his or her loan was unofficially approved, then the borrower knew he could make his deal. The paperwork certainly needed to be prepared, but at that point the borrower knew he could proceed with confidence. This was an accepted practice in lending to provide better customer service.

Fran had earned her credit authority by making good decisions throughout her career. Those decisions often included caveats requiring borrowers to deposit funds in the bank and to provide verification of work progress. Borrowers were held to the highest standard, which helped make State Bank of the Community profitable and a mainstay of the real estate development community.

At Roosevelt National Bank Fran was provided with credit authority not to exceed $1 million. She was shocked. The $1 million limit was an embarrassing and emotionally damaging slap in the face.

Fran's customers exceeded this borrowing limit in every real estate loan. By lowering her credit authority, she was placed in a position forcing her to present most if not every loan proposal to the loan committee for approval and criticism. She did not like this at all. Fran felt she was too important to explain herself to her new employer.

The requirement to assign a $1 million credit authority was purposeful on the part of the real estate lending group. Although she had a remarkable track record, the new employer did not really know her. The bank had a "you must prove yourself to us first" attitude. From the start, Steiner and his group felt a need to keep tabs on the new hire. A number of things about her just did not fit. The executive committee did not like Fran's behavior, presentation, or the image she projected to their customer base. They did not like many of the customers she invited into the bank and the baggage that came with them.

Fran had only been at work a week when the gifts began arriving. Steiner felt this was inappropriate and that gifts were obvious bribes that meant granting favors in the future. This was against bank policy, and he required her to return all the gifts and not to accept any more. The new "law" only added to her resentment toward bank management in general and Steiner in particular. Many people Fran had seduced to move to State Bank of the Community for her liberal lending practices were ready to come to Roosevelt National Bank all right, but Roosevelt was not ready for them. Management's plan was to bring her into the bank's culture and channel her considerable skills into more ethical behavior. But first they had to make sure she had only limited power and control until she proved herself worthy of greater trust and responsibility.

Steiner was a quiet man to those on the way out and he was quiet to Fran from the moment he met her. No matter how she tried, she could not get her customers in to bank at the Roosevelt Bank. The real estate business was again experiencing a good market and most borrowers established a lending relationship with banks that made borrowing easy. This was not Roosevelt National Bank. Moving deposits and a banking relationship was a business burden and one that most people did not look forward to. Fran was fighting an impossible battle to show the executives that she could bring in profitable accounts. "They courted me, brought me in, and now they won't let me do my job," she complained.

Fran had been successful in lending to customers and making money for State Bank of the Community, now the First National Bank of Chicago. But if the choice was for customers to remain there and borrow money easily enough or choose to leave and contend with starting over, many customers made the decision to stay at the First National Bank of Chicago. For some their decision was partly based on the relief of not having to deal with Fran Kontopolus any longer. Fran had worked hard to earn the disgust of customers and she was a burden to have a business relationship with. One of the major reasons they had stuck with her for so long was her willingness to be bribed. Other borrowers could enjoy a more refined business experience now that she had left. Money was money and when the choice was to go back to Fran or elsewhere, elsewhere offered a more pleasant experience.

Fran faced another crossroad in her life. Her salary was good, as was her benefit package. But she was the laughing stock of the bank, she had no real power, and she was frustrated by just coming to work. She was angry and unhappy—a deadly combination in someone like Fran Kontopolus.

Then during this challenging time, the worst in her career, her father died. Dimitri Kontopolus had a heart attack and collapsed face down in a pile of fresh fish at his store in the middle of a busy Friday afternoon. He fell forward after making a large sale to the local Baptist Church group, who had just purchased twenty-five pounds of catfish for their Sunday fish fry. The impact of his fall caused drivers traveling east and west on Seventy-ninth Street to claim that they actually saw fish flying in the air. When Dimitri Kontopolus was pulled from the fish bin, his cigar was still in his jaws. The undertaker had one hell of a time extracting it from his mouth.

When Fran received a call from her brother Ray on her cell phone, she dashed out of the bank and into the white Mercedes 190 the bank was leasing for her. She picked up Ma and drove as fast as she could to the store.

As the Kontopolus family was preparing for the wake of their patriarch, Fran was drowning her sorrow in a huge slice of blueberry pie. The mind has the ability to create surprisingly real images from the strangest things, clouds in the sky, sand on the beach, patterns in a rug, and even in berries and gel. Fran saw an image of her father. She shook her head and when she looked up from her plate, she stared at the sky and saw another image. She saw a fish entering a bank vault. This was an inspiring image. She knew in her heart it was a message from the Almighty. She was charged with opening a bank, *her* bank. The Bank of Kontopolus would be a memorial to her father.

She would do it while working for Tom Steiner. *Why should I waste my time trying to make Steiner rich? I'm not bringing in any of my old customers. I'm going to quietly and covertly set up my own bank,* she thought. Fran was a champion at burning bridges and she promised herself that she would have her plans made no later than thirty days after the burial of her father. The will of Dimitri Kontopolus provided that he be buried in his beloved Delta 88 Oldsmobile. The family wanted to comply with Papa's request, but in the best judgment of the funeral director and their priest, the car was donated to the church to be used as a fund raiser. Fran's mind was already on other matters. She would show Dimitri that she could take care of the family.

And with the new bank she would satisfy her addiction to money and power. She would finally have enough. As with all addicts, she was lying to herself.

CHAPTER NINETEEN

F ran had no savings to invest in her own bank. She was a spender. Customers frequently commented how unusual it was for a person whose life was real estate lending not to own a home, condominium, or town home. Despite her significant salary and benefits package, she lived paycheck to paycheck and never missed an opportunity to buy new clothes or a new pair of shoes. From the time years earlier that she diverted money into her own savings account, she never saved a dime. Her apartment in downtown Chicago was a rental, yet her furnishings were expensive. With six months remaining on her contract, Fran could collect a paycheck from Roosevelt National Bank while secretly working on her own project. To her mind such unethical behavior wasn't a betrayal. It was payback.

Her first step was to contact lawyers, business consultants, accountants, and others she had a working relationship with and paid fortunes to while working at State Bank of the Community. Since the sale of the bank, these people had one less client and substantially less income. Fran knew that if she fed them a little business from Roosevelt National Bank she would create a new loyalty. She was, of course, correct.

To refresh her relationships with these essential professionals, she contacted them first by phone and asked if they would be available to do some work for Roosevelt National Bank in the form of reviewing or preparing documents. Once she had money flowing into their offices she would be in a position to call in favors. Fran already knew that any opportunity an attorney had to bill more hours was an opportunity he would not pass up. So that was the way she began her task. An attorney who had worked for her at State Bank of the Community had done the legal work for three de-nouveau banks, new banks. She did not think highly of him, but needed someone who would do his work on nothing more secure than a promise. This guy was the perfect sucker. He had access to investors and he could be bought cheap.

Fred Belker worked for a medium-sized law firm. He was a pompous individual with an ego as large as his billing rate. Fran knew that his greed would drive him to do the work she needed and that his ego was the way to reel him in and bring him down. Fran laid out the temptation. Lawyers operated their businesses or practices for profit. They charged a client for phone calls, e-mails, and faxes. The billing rate for Fred Belker was $350 per hour. Fred would, as some lawyers do, inflate his billing hours. The unwritten rule in the legal profession was charge and if caught let the client dispute.

In the markets of old, merchants would set a price and a buyer would bargain until the two reached a compromise. Clients rarely argued with their attorney. Lost in a world of confusing rules, regulations, and "legalese," they were vulnerable. They thought that their attorney always represented their best interests. In corporate America, whether the business was manufacturing, service, or banking, if employees were not spending their own money, they didn't care how outrageous an attorney's bill could be.

Fran was free with her own wasteful spending and she was extremely free with the money of Roosevelt National Bank. A famous old story began with a forty-year-old lawyer walking down a busy street in downtown Chicago when suddenly he found himself in heaven. He looked around and in an instant of disbelief asked St. Peter, "Where am I and what happened?" St. Peter replied that he had died of natural causes and was now at the moment of final judgment. The young lawyer responded that he had never been sick a day in his life and was in perfect physical health. St. Peter then asked him if his name was Richard Richardson. The lawyer responded, "Yes, that certainly is my name." St. Peter replied, "According to the hours you have billed your clients, you are ninety-seven years old and have lived a long life." Fred Belker was one of these lawyers.

CHAPTER TWENTY

Fran called Belker and started her chitchat. He was excited to hear from her and anxious to take on any jobs she had available. While listening, his mind wandered to his firm's partners meeting conducted every Friday morning. The following Friday, just two days away, he could report that he was bringing in a new client and a big one at that, Roosevelt National Bank. The rule was the more billing, the more bonuses partners received and Belker loved money as much as Fran.

He had a forty-five minute conversation with her that was primarily social in nature. He asked how she enjoyed working for her new employer. She told him business was great and that she was excited about her wonderful new opportunity. She lied. He asked about her family and told her how sad he was to learn of her father's passing. He asked about the city's newest restaurants and insisted that he take her to one or more of them in the near future. She readily agreed, not lying. At the end of the conversation, two things happened. First, he was hired to review a set of loan documents. The other was that Fred Belker wrote in his billing log that he had spent two hours on the phone with Fran Kontopolus from Roosevelt National Bank.

Fran sent Belker a set of documents, which for all practical purposes needed no review. He quickly read them and sent a redlined version back the following day. This was a test. She had sent him a copy of documents he had prepared for a loan from State Bank of the Community some time ago. It was his work. When the documents were returned, as she expected, he had marked up the papers as if he had never read them before. Standard covenants and paragraphs had been eliminated and

87

re-written. Fran knew he would likely do this rather than pay attention to the actual work and call her to discuss the possibility of her having sent him his old work by mistake.

Belker, of course, never read the documents. He gave them to a young associate who the firm billed at $150 per hour. The associate spent three hours going over the work. Then Belker added another three hours to the bill for a total billing time of $500 per hour for three hours work, or $1,500. Fran knew she could have Belker in her pocket when the bill from his firm arrived at the end of the month. His firm's charge was two hours for their phone call and six hours for document review for a total of $ 2,200. Fran walked the bill into the accounts payable department with a box of chocolates for the clerk and had the bill paid and mailed that same day. Instead of failing her test, he had passed with flying colors. Her plan was in the works and the first member of her secret team was in place.

Over the next few weeks, Fran reviewed Belker's website to familiarize herself with the banks he had organized during the previous three years. These banks seemed to make money and do well. The State of Illinois website, which disclosed the public information about banks, rated them as profitable. After Fran felt she could conduct a sensible meeting with her new lawyer, she invited him to dinner, on her expense account. Belker, being a savvy attorney, also billed Roosevelt National Bank for the time he spent watching her scarf down a huge meal.

During dinner Fran told him, in strict confidence of course, that she wanted to start her own bank and promised that if he assisted her in the organizational phase of putting the whole thing together, he and his firm would be the bank's counsel. She would also provide him with an opportunity to buy stock in the bank at the initial offering price. "Work with me and keep your mouth shut and we'll both get wealthy," she said. Belker's greed gland began throbbing. He actually licked his lips.

She told him that he would be paid well for his work, but since she had no money now he should bill extra hours to Roosevelt National Bank in monthly statements. She would personally walk his charges through the accounting department. Later he could catch up with billing when her bank had received its state charter and was open for business.

Belker was comfortable with this deceptive practice, as he had been doing this to other clients for quite some time. He agreed to look into the matter (on his free time, of course) and help his old pal, poor little Fran, get out on her own.

Fran closed the meeting by asking him when she could expect an outline to direct her on organizing her bank. He knew that he really had very little work to do because of his previous work setting up other new banks. But Belker, who felt he was leading the charge, suggested that he meet with her weekly for the next two months to get the details together. More meetings meant more billing. Fran didn't give a damn as long as she got the information and direction she needed and that Roosevelt National Bank covered the tab.

After dinner, as Belker waited for his car to be brought around from the valet parking attendant, he thought that it would not be unreasonable to bill Roosevelt National Bank for four hours for that evening's work. When Fran's car arrived she told the valet to hold it for a few moments as she had forgotten something in the restaurant. Her stomach felt as if it was going to burst and she headed for the ladies room as fast as she could.

Belker and Fran dined at the best restaurants in Chicago, choosing a different one each week to avoid being seen too much at any one place. "Let's just keep moving around town. We don't want to establish a pattern," she said. At their first meeting, Belker brought a large satchel of offering memorandums from the banks he had worked on. He gave them to her to read and review before the next meeting. She asked him how much capital was needed to begin a bank in Illinois. He chuckled as he stuffed a jumbo shrimp into his mouth, chewed on it while appearing lost in thought for a moment, and swallowed. "Look, Fran, the state requires a minimum five million dollars, but don't worry. You'll find a sucker line of people looking to make money and invest in this bank. You need to be adequately capitalized up front so you won't have to raise more money right after starting. Set your goal for fifteen million dollars. Maybe you'll get nine million, maybe twelve million, but you'll get more than the five million you must have."

Fran began thinking as Belker sipped from his glass of scotch and soda. He asked her, "Who do you know who will invest with you and buy stock in the bank?"

Fran had not really given this much thought. On some level she thought that Belker would produce a list of people who would throw money her way. "Who do you know?" asked Fran.

"Well, I may know a few people, but investors are investing with and in you, Fran. You'll need to show them you're investing your own money in the bank and then you'll have to tell them a good story. They will never read the offering memorandum. People never read these formal documents with all the boilerplate, disclosures, and all those 'thereforz' and 'whereasiz.' Sure, maybe one or two will, but it's you who will have to go into to the marketplace. It's all you, Fran. First, I would ask your family and friends."

As she sucked down her garlic mashed potatoes, Fran became worried. Belker was right. She would have to show that she could invest money in the bank. But she had no money. Her family didn't have any real capital. Everything was tied up in the fish store. And she had no real friends to tap. *Damn,* she thought. Every real estate deal she financed had multiple investors but the principal investor always used some of his own capital to show his confidence in the project. There was just no way in hell she could do that.

"For a fifteen million dollar raise how much should I invest?" said Fran.

"More than fifty thousand dollars. One hundred thousand is a better number. One hundred thousand is respectable. No one can argue with one hundred thousand dollars. That will prove your personal commitment." He could see the discouragement in her eyes. She scraped up a mouthful of potatoes so she wouldn't have to speak.

Belker continued. "Look Fran, here's how these other guys get rich. None of them have real money. They all borrow from family and friends for their share in the investment. Your dad must have left your mom some money. Have her lend it or give it to you. You need an employment contract with the new bank. Remember these investors aren't putting their money into brick and mortar. They're investing in you, right? The holding company board of directors has to hire you or they have nothing. So I write you a big fat contract that the investors will accept as the protocol. You should have a compensation package, a damn fine one. We begin with a salary of two hundred thousand per year plus the following: in addition to an expense account, leased car, club memberships for dining and so on, you will receive stock and stock options each year. That, my friend, is how you get rich."

Fran swallowed, took a drink, and looked up, a tiny glimmer of hope in her eyes. He continued, "Initially the stock has no value. In fact, the stock of any privately held corporation has no value until the company is sold or goes public, when the stock becomes liquid. So investors won't blink when you receive ten or twenty thousand options or shares of stock at the end of each year. At that time it's basically worthless. That's good for you. Over five years you'll have hundreds of thousands of shares and options. We offer you a ten-year contract and we include a clause that says you'll receive an additional seven percent of all outstanding stock when you either leave or the bank is sold. So you can't lose. Over the years you can increase your salary, you'll receive retirement money, deferred compensation in one form or another, and I'll think of more items to include in your contract. You can't go wrong with me, Fran. I know what we can slip into the contract on your behalf."

Fran was elated after hearing this speech and ordered a double dessert to satisfy her excitement. Belker ordered another scotch and began to mentally add several hours to his billing time.

CHAPTER
TWENTY-ONE

Fran, now unhappier than ever with her new job, wanted to test the market for investors interested in her clandestine plans for a new bank. With the right financial support she might even quit her job at Roosevelt early and just work on opening the new bank. Fran admired Sonny Vulich. After all his courting, she also thought of him as a close and dependable friend. She asked him to lunch. She made sure they were seated in a corner away from other diners. Even so, she spoke in a near whisper. "Sonny, I'm thinking of starting my own bank." Sonny almost choked while sipping his water. "I need money and want to know if you'll invest five hundred thousand dollars?"

Sonny sat silently. The gall of this woman was amazing. His brain worked fast. Fran was smart, ruthless, and driven. He knew her scheme might lead him to an opportunity to make a lot of money. Like Fran, money was thirst that he could never quench. If he said yes that would commit him to investing $500,000. If he said no, it would ruin his relationship with Fran, a connection that had provided him a lot of loan money throughout the years. He thought carefully and was quiet for a few moments.

Fran was accustomed to his quiet and thoughtful nature when responding to a serious question. This was his style. He was a thoughtful man about important matters and wanted to be perceived that way.

He cleared his throat and lifted his napkin off his lap, smoothing it out as he began to answer. "How much money do you need to start your bank?"

"Well, the state regulators require a minimum of five million dollars, but I want to raise ten million."

Sonny thought a bit longer. He knew that the ultimate objective of small banks was to be acquired by a larger bank. That was when the shareholders received their big payday. But more important, Sonny knew that Fran could then become an even more powerful and generous lender. Sonny's career path had taken him into large projects such as old industrial sites in which he could build subdivisions with homes, mid- and high-rise buildings, shopping centers, and other highly profitable projects. Sonny knew that if Fran had a bank, it could become his bank, his primary lender, and that borrowing would be easy. Sonny wanted to encourage Fran.

"Fran, five hundred thousand dollars is a lot for one person, but I know many people and am sure I could help raise that amount for you. Go for it, Fran, you deserve it. In your father's name, do it." Sonny's emotional support was what she needed to go forward in forming the bank.

When State Bank of the Community had been sold and Fran departed, Sonny was in a financial quandary. He wanted to continue to borrow from Fran, but the restrictions placed on her by Roosevelt National Bank made borrowing a challenge Sonny did not want to endure. For old times' sake he did re-finance some safe, small investment properties with Roosevelt through her, but more for lowering the rates than for the relationship with Fran herself. The lower rates simply came at a good time. One thing that Sonny did maintain was the giving of the bouquets, chocolates, and more, but he was savvy enough to send them to her home. Fran was equally savvy and never mentioned these gifts. He knew that although he could not do business with Fran at the Roosevelt Bank, she would somehow change her situation and turn things toward his favor in the future. Clearly, that time was coming quickly. Fran and Sonny were beginning their dance of deception.

CHAPTER
TWENTY-TWO

Fran was determined to avoid repeating the personal and financial fiasco that happened to her at the sale of State Bank of the Community. She wanted a bank and wanted all the money, power, and control that came with ownership. One problem blocked her path. Fran had never saved money. Sonny would roll his eyes whenever her name came up in discussions during parties or at a get-together with friends. He would laugh or chuckle in the way people did when a distasteful topic surfaced. That was Fran, a topic, not a person. Sonny repeated the same comment over and over for years, "Here you have a real estate lender, a 'really big' real estate lender. A woman who has lent millions, maybe billions of dollars to real estate developers, and she has never even bought a one-bedroom condo."

Sonny was an accomplished liar and knew Fran would never believe anyone who repeated his words because in the real estate community he was too "big" to be doubted. He had invested years getting her loyalty and devotion by deceiving her with his friendship. She looked up to Sonny and made quite a tidy sum on fees from his loans. He would kid her, "You are wearing the Sonny Vulich line of designer fashions. You are dripping in the Sonny Vulich line of jewelry designs. You look good in those new pumps and high heels from the Sonny Vulich line of Italian imports. You look classy in that car from the Sonny Vulich showroom." She wasn't under his thumb; she was under his spell.

Fran knew that when she had to, she could be financially seductive and she knew that a seduction was necessary to get investors. One of the key elements of seduction was to promise positions on her board of directors. It was common for community banks to be formed by a group of investors who became the board members who controlled every aspect of the bank's operations. The typical makeup was a family or a group of successful businessmen who wanted a little diversity. Directors had a ground floor opportunity to capitalize on their investment. They received fees and stock options as compensation during the time the bank was in business. Their eventual goal was to go public and capitalize on their liquidity or sell to another bank within five to ten years. Long-term thinking was never part of the process. Greed for short-term profits drove the enterprise.

After much thought, Fran developed a plan. She would offer directorships only to those who invested as initial organizers, those who provided seed money. Her plan was to assemble a board of fractionalized people. Sonny, of course, would have a seat on the board, but she needed people who she could count on not hanging around for very long. People who were older, who had diversified backgrounds, people who could help get the charter from the state, but who would depart quickly because they were old and tired.

She wanted yes-men. She wanted directors who would, like the old board members at State Bank of the Community, come for the free lunch, a small check, and fall asleep at board meetings. She wanted people with vulnerabilities who she could easily purge by innuendo, accusation, or, if necessary, blackmail. Her plan in the first five years was to replace the initial board, the group who put up the money and who would work hard to organize the bank. She wanted to fill in the seats with her family members and friends, again a group she could control. Fran knew if Ma and her brothers from the fish store were on the board they would always defer to her. Unfortunately, they did not have the money to invest. She would have to look elsewhere.

CHAPTER TWENTY-THREE

Fran began a list of potential investors as Belker suggested. She had the confidential financial statements of many borrowers, a potential gold mine of opportunity. This information had been accumulated from confidential loan files secretly stolen from State Bank of the Community. She kept them at her apartment where she studied and plotted. She knew certain customers would be more willing to invest than others. But who? Who should she approach first? Who would bring others with them?

Knowing the behavior and characteristics of her customers, people she had worked with over the years, made it easy to eliminate those who would not invest. *Why waste time with a bunch of short-sighted losers?* she thought. Members of the prime investor list were customers who owed her for favors she had extended to them over the years, people she knew would invest because it was payback time. These were people who she extended dates for loan payoffs, reduced loan fees, or otherwise went out on a limb for. And many were the people she knew she could tempt with promises of continued favorable treatment.

She added to the list a list of second-class potential investors, names of people she owed favors to. Belker was a typical example. He could easily see filling his pockets with the promise of new banking business. He would jump at the opportunity. They would all invest in her bank. Her list consisted of architects she could use to help design and build her bank, lawyers she could feed work to, business people who needed loans, and people who owned supply and service firms from whom she could purchase office supplies, coffee, and furniture for her bank.

She thought about her plan every day, all day and all night. She was obsessed. As Belker told her, if she could promise a board seat to an elderly relative or friend, then family and friends of that person would certainly invest their money in her bank. Of course, retired bankers—she thought of them as a bunch of saps—were going to be her first choice to purge from her board. She needed retired bankers to prove instant credibility for the new bank, but she wanted this bank for herself and her family. If she needed to make pawns of investors and board members, well, she knew how to make pawns of people. That was how Fran had spelled success throughout her career.

She had Sonny's support, and that was good enough for her to know she was headed in the right direction. Hadn't he already committed to $500,000? Of course he had, and Sonny's commitment was what Fran needed to launch her bank. Thank God for Sonny.

Fran also needed a leader, a figurehead for her board. She needed a clean, upstanding person, someone like Steiner, but entrepreneurial, known in the community, and someone who would draw investors. But who? Fran decided to attend a lunch program hosted by a local builders club. The president, Adam Berg, was conducting the program that day. Berg was a bright forty-five-year-old developer who was well respected throughout Chicago real estate circles. He was generous of money and spirit. Berg was exactly the man for the job, someone who would help disguise her plot. But she did not know the man beyond his reputation. She had to find a way to meet him and persuade him to get involved in this new venture. Adam Berg would be a feather in her hat.

When she returned to Roosevelt Bank, she discovered that Berg was not a customer. *That's it! I'll approach him to borrow from the bank. I can justify a meeting with him and invite him to lunch. That makes sense.* By asking around, she found out that Berg had a small rehab project in the planning stages. Fran had her secretary call Berg's office to set up a lunch meeting. Fran received a call back from his office confirming the meeting. She was thrilled.

She could not sleep the night before the meeting. She had to look her best and feel rested and alert. The sleeping pills her doctor suggested had helped her through the long and frustrating days at Roosevelt National Bank. They would get her through this night. She considered how she would behave at the lunch meeting. She knew she would have to mask her poor manners, avoid her usual stream of profanities, eat daintily, and keep her knife, spoon, and fork on her own plate. Berg certainly knew of her, but how much did he know? How much did that knowledge matter when it came to money and opportunity? He had never banked at State Bank of the Community. What had he heard from the banking and real estate communities? She wondered these things as she dozed off with the city lights of Chicago twinkling below.

CHAPTER TWENTY-FOUR

She suggested a local pub near Berg's office for the meeting. It was empty during the day, the burgers were great, and it would be quiet. Berg didn't care where he ate lunch. In fact, many days he ate in his office as he was not one to go out to lunch for sport and waste the afternoon that way. "If we're going to do business, let's do business and forget about the three martinis," he always said. Not that he was a workaholic, but lunch meetings were not his thing. He really did not know Fran, but he knew of her. He liked meeting new people, and despite the rumors of her behavior, he was the type who liked to make up his own mind from direct personal experience. Now that Fran was at Roosevelt Nation Bank, he thought meeting her was just good business.

After sitting down and ordering iced tea, Berg listened as Fran began discussing Chicago real estate development and gentrification. She outlined her history at State Bank of the Community and of the neighborhood projects she financed. She told him of the many successful developers she had helped start in business. And she told him of how she enjoyed being part of the Roosevelt National Bank team.

Berg listened and could tell she knew her profession. He had never met some of the players she described, but certainly he had heard of all of their names and reputations. The conversation continued and she asked him about his career. He told her how he started as a real estate broker and slowly started climbing the developer's ladder. He spoke about taking on small, manageable projects in various neighborhoods and eventually moving on to bigger and bigger projects. He was very confident of the city's real estate future and his own.

He told her of a twelve-unit condominium conversion he was planning in the Ravenswood neighborhood and she jumped at the chance of financing it. The amount of the loan was within her credit authority and would be a slam-dunk. She told Berg she would go out of her way to make the transaction seamless. "I'm not the 'last of the great guys,' Adam. I just want you to know how much I want your business and how well the bank and I will serve your financial needs."

By the end of lunch, Berg agreed to let Fran originate the loan. As the weeks followed, Fran personally supervised every aspect of the process, and Berg closed his loan and was underway on construction. Two months into the project Fran called him and asked to visit the site and walk the project. She wanted to use this as a guise for her real agenda, soliciting Berg to invest and join her group of organizers.

After exploring the real estate project, Fran changed the conversation to her bank. She explained that she was offering an opportunity to a select few to get involved as organizers. She wanted the organizers to contribute $25,000 each to fund the organization. The money would go for legal expenses, meetings, and supplies. If the bank was organized and received its charter, then the organizers would have their $25,000 issued as stock.

Fran asked if he would be a board member with the expectation of raising money. He listened, asked questions, and told her he would think about her proposal over the weekend. On Monday he called her cell phone. "Fran," he started, "this is Adam Berg. I like your idea. I am definitely interested in becoming one of your organizers."

She could not believe her good fortune, Adam Berg in her court. What a break. Now she could use his name and reputation to reel in other investors. "Adam, I'm so flattered you'd like to invest with me. This is going to be a great bank. I promise. We'll make a splash in the real estate community, you'll see. Thank you, Adam. I will never betray your trust."

"Fran, please have two placement memorandums sent to me. I want to share one with my attorney, Earl Lasman, if you don't mind."

"I will, Adam, I will. They will be coming from my attorney, Fred Belker. I'll call him right away. Call me or Belker if you have any questions."

"Okay, Fran, thanks for the opportunity. I'll have a check ready for you in two days. Shall I send it to your office at Roosevelt National Bank? They must be very proud of you."

"No, no, Adam, I'll pick it up myself. Thanks again." Fran snapped her phone shut. She was so excited she drove around the city that morning looking for sites for the bank. She was fantasizing where she would locate the heart of her empire. Fran was as happy as she had been in a long time.

Berg hung up the phone and stared at the blue sky. Something inside him told him that this woman was trouble, but he did not listen to his inner voice. Even people who have a good moral character become enticed with success and Adam Berg was not immune.

A bank board member, he thought. *This is promising. How could this go wrong? In ten years the bank will sell and I'll add to my retirement portfolio.* Adam knew of many successful men in the Chicago real estate and banking community who made fortunes investing in banks. He wanted to join their ranks, and this was getting in on the ground floor.

CHAPTER TWENTY-FIVE

After meeting with Berg, Fran searched her mental Rolodex looking for customers who did not have the time to serve but who had a retired relative or parent with enough credentials to sit on the board. The effort did not require much time. Her group of organizers had to be diverse (according to her definition) and, most important, malleable. Fran was bright enough to mask her intentions so that the poor saps actually believed they were being selected because of their merit. She created a story that she even began to believe after repeating it so many times.

"I want a diverse board. A board made of people with experience in all areas of business, not just banking. I want a place where I can glean information from people who have 'been there' before. I want and need people who know what business needs and wants in Chicago—lawyers, accountants, businessmen, retired bankers, stock brokers, and real estate developers. And I want women and minorities on my board. This bank will represent everyone in our community. Everyone."

But that's not exactly what she wanted. She wanted yes-men as in yes *men*. Fran hated women in business and most women in general. The taunting and laughter behind her back during her school years had never left her. Neither had the memories of the cute, feminine, and bitchy women of her early working years. She would never include another woman on her board. Never. Fran was vain, very vain, like the wicked queen in Snow White. "Mirror, mirror on the wall, who's the best damn businesswoman of all?"

Her diversity speech was far from the truth. But it was a great story and investors had no reason not to believe it as they were subject to getting rich and this woman was going to lead them to those riches. They heard that Adam Berg, his attorney Earl Lasman, and even Sonny Vulich were investing and they wanted to get in on a good thing too. As long as Fran was the only female banker in Chicago, she could be at the top of her field. No competition, no fear. But she needed organizers to invest money in the bank. She had three, but she needed a lot more seed money to get started.

Fran found the likely prospects within her files. She met with each man individually and gave her stump speech and promise of wealth to those who joined as an organizer. She called and solicited real estate developers and attorneys who could raise money. Ten men, carefully selected and seduced, would become the holding company and bank directors and receive options as their compensation, rather than cash until the bank was profitable. Fran wanted organizers who were a cross section of people who brought different resumes to the table. The other members of her organizers were attorneys and real estate developers. These men, she knew, were young and greedy. She could promise them legal work and favorable loans. The attorneys who sat on bank boards were frequently fed work for the bank in the form of document preparation for loans, collections, and trusts. Real estate developers always needed to borrow money. Fran picked these men because of their sphere of influence and relations with clients and partners who had money to invest.

She was convinced that she could tempt them with money, money, money, and in fact, she was right. The perception that Fran strove for was no different than what Mark Twain wrote about one hundred years earlier. She used the same technique Tom Sawyer used to persuade his friends to beg him to let them paint Aunt Polly's fence. Fran had men lining up to meet with her to invest in the new bank. After months of looking for organizers, she finally had a core group committed to helping launch her bank. In return they would be rewarded with seats on her board of directors. These men were Adam Berg; Earl Lasman; Stephen Drury, a fifty-year-old entrepreneur and attorney; Sonny Vulich Jr.; Max Rudman, an ailing seventy-seven-year-old retired CPA who lived with a colostomy bag; Mr. Balt, the father of a home inspector and a retired eighty-year-old corporative executive who was quickly entering senility; a seventy-year-old retired banker, Mr. Friendly, who had a slight Parkinson's disorder; a sixty-five-year-old retired banker with a severe case of psoriasis, Mr. Harris, who needed to stay in Florida most of the year; and Michael Pischer, a thirty-five-year-old stockbroker who had excessive debt from a business failure and four children to support. He needed the money. He only made the final cut because of the recommendation of another organizer, and Fran could see how easy it would be to put him under her thumb. The final member was an awkward builder, an Irish immigrant named Maloney who had a slight stutter and was always red in the face. He spoke so fast it appeared as if he were going to run out of air and collapse. He was a very excitable chap.

Her initial work was completed. She had her $250,000 to organize the bank. Fran decided to have lunch with each organizer and during these meetings obtain a financial commitment for their respective stock purchase and a commitment for what they felt they could raise by selling stock to their family and friends. She tallied more than $10 million in commitments. Now the job was to get the checks. With ten men of influence, a mere $1 million per person was not a stretch. Fran knew her group well, well enough at least to exploit their capabilities.

The younger, still active members were greedy and would go along with anything she proposed for no other reason than padding their bank accounts. They would be with her all the way. The older and ailing members were among the elder statesmen of Chicago's business and banking community and were like the members of the board of State Bank of the Community. She could count on them for attending meetings because of the incentive of the free lunch, a small check for participating, and the prestige of being on a board. They would never be against her because they wouldn't really know or care what was really going on. This group would be her loan committee. Fran knew that she could count on them as the yes-men she needed to step out of her way for loan approvals.

The organizers were a supportive group. They donated office space to Fran to set up shop. They gave their names and reputations, time and loyalty, anticipating that it would take one year to organize the bank.

CHAPTER
TWENTY-SIX

F
ran had never run a bank before. Persuading investors that she
could organize, operate, and make a bank profitable was a major
challenge. Sure, she had a reputation as a successful real estate
lender, but running an institution was a significantly larger challenge.
With greed in their eyes, people see and hear what they want, and they
wanted to see dollar signs. They gave her a free hand. With time running
out on her Roosevelt National Bank contract, Fran's plan began with
entertaining potential investors on Steiner's nickel.

Under the pretense of business origination, she spent every afternoon away from the bank over long and expensive lunches that were
charged to Roosevelt Bank. She knew what she was doing and the customers never thought about who was paying for their meals and drinks
because it was simply protocol that the banker paid. She was carefully
following a recent banking trend. A few groups similar to hers started
what is referred to as de-nouveaus (new banks) during the late 1990s.
The catalyst to open new community banks was in part due to the disap-
pearance of well-known and established community banks that were being gobbled up in mergers and acquisitions by larger banks. The reality
was that mergers made way for new community banks.

Customers missed the ease of the neighborhood bank versus the
mega-institutions. Fran's pitch made good financial sense. She cleaned
up her language and spoke simply and logically. "Look, there are fewer

banks where the bank employees know the customers and have sensitivity to the entrepreneurial challenges that present themselves in business. I want to start a de-nouveau that can reach out to my old customers and at the same time appeal to new customers. I want to make doing business with my bank easy." She presented a detailed argument based on the State Bank of the Community model, a bank with a level of service that was vanishing. Fran went on to say she had the formula to get banking back on track. This simple presentation was one that was difficult to disagree with. Most people had had similar experiences when their banks were absorbed by a larger institution. They lost their identity. A new culture entered the scene and they frequently moved their business to another bank.

Once when Sonny met with her during the process, he gave her a warning. "Fran, you have to hire experienced people. You need other bankers on your board of directors and you need people at every level who understand banking. You have no experience running a bank, and if you want to succeed, you must surround yourself with people who know what they're doing. I insist on it." Sonny was the only person in Chicago who could use the word "insist" on Fran and get away with it.

She knew Sonny was right, but she did not want to be overshadowed by competence. She had to be the president and one day chairman of the board of directors. She went on a clandestine search for potential employees, being careful that no word leaked out and found its way back to Roosevelt. She had her organizers, bankers, real estate developers, and attorneys help with the search. The overriding question was basic. Could she control the new hires?

Fran and her newly formed board went to the state to convince them that they would be trustworthy enough to be granted a charter. The appeal worked. The state loved them as they were not a typical group and seemed to have great prospects for serving their community. They received the permit to organize.

Now came the hard part. The group had to raise $10 million in hard dollars, not promises, to open their door.

CHAPTER TWENTY-SEVEN

The next six months were busy, fast, furious, and very stressful. During those months, Fran steadily gained weight, but she hit the streets like the middle-aged money whore she was. No prostitute ever worked the streets of Chicago with more energy or greed. She was selling a dream and took herself seriously enough to get serious attention. The middle-aged whore appeals to a lot of middle-aged men, especially the whore who makes the pimp the most money. Perhaps it's the experience factor. Fran didn't really know beans about running a bank, but she was an expert at sleaze. "Hey, Joe, you wanna party?" Her pitch was a little more sophisticated, but the meaning was the same. She would wake every morning in her high-rise rental apartment as the sun above Lake Michigan drove painful spikes into her eyes. The muffled sounds from the surrounding apartments were like the beating of a bass drum. She would lie in bed unable to move due to the hangover from the sleeping pills washed down with vodka that was a fixture of her evening ritual. Her paranoia was so deep that she could not turn off her brain in the evenings to relax and go to sleep. Drugs were the only solution.

Fran would stagger to the bathroom, turn on the lights, and look at herself in the mirror wondering, "How on earth will I pull this off?"

Her motivation: ego, money, and power. The possibility of failure added to the motivation. And her paranoia. Fran was a paranoid person, all right, and paranoia drives the bully. From the time she woke up to the time she took her evening elixir to get to sleep, she wondered who was out to get her. In her heart she knew the answer, everybody.

Fran was taking a risk trying to start a bank on the sly. That risk wouldn't diminish even after the new bank was open for business. All eyes would be on her, not the bank. She needed to show the real power brokers in Chicago's business and banking community that she could not only start a bank but also run it. The difference between "run" and "ruin" is the letter "I."

Fran had worked hard to build a reputation as a difficult person and for the first time realized the down side to that image. She was afraid of being unemployable if she failed. She had no real friends in the banking profession, only acquaintances. None would want the Dragon Lady as an employee. She needed money to live, as she had no savings. She needed the paycheck from this new venture bank to survive.

If Fran could pull this off, she would have power. She could not be removed and would have to be accepted. She could not organize and start a bank alone. She needed others and she hated sharing the limelight. Fran also hated and despised all the men who were helping organize her bank, but she had to use them. Fran wanted it all for herself. She resented the influence and enthusiasm that these men had for her endeavor. They were committed to the project, essential to it, yet she couldn't stand the sight of any one of them. Once the bank was organized and open they would be purged from her board of directors. She needed them now for their influence, but that would be only for a short time. She had built them up and she would most certainly tear them down.

But by the end of the first month of fund raising, Fran had commitments of less than $250,000. This was a far distance from the $10 million she needed. Fran played up every commitment she received even if the dollars had not immediately followed. She pushed, bullied, cajoled, promised, and lied until the synergy started. Money began to accumulate. Her organizers were coming through. She was so relentless that successful business people invested $25,000, the minimum investment, just to make her go away. But the money began to add up, and once the momentum started one investor told another and another told two more and they told two more. Within six months $10 million was in the escrow account.

CHAPTER TWENTY-EIGHT

Investors were invited to a final "Rush to Raise," a cocktail party held high above the city at the exclusive Metropolitan Club. The purpose was to increase the money raised to open the bank and introduce shareholders to one another. This was an opulent affair.

The sky was a dimming blue and the city gleamed as the sun set. Servers passed through the crowd with platters of large shrimp, delicious hors d'oeuvres, and glasses of expensive champagne. The bars were pouring generous drinks and the investors were enjoying themselves as only those who aren't paying a dime can. No one considered that the party was costing more than $50,000 of their investment money. They didn't care. Fran Kontopolus was entertaining and for once she had organized something with class.

The organizers attended the event with their investors. And like a telethon for a charity, the front of the room was dominated by a chart in the form of a thermometer showing dates and dollar amounts raised so the participants could see how the money came in.

After an hour of socializing, Fran was introduced by the soon to be chairman of the board, Max Rudman. He had been retired for some time. Actually he was forcefully retired from his accounting firm for malpractice. Max was a glad hander. He bragged about being both an accountant and lawyer who never practiced law. Fran's bank was his opportunity at redemption, probably his one last chance. Max's downfall was being lazy and sloppy. He presented himself as a "senior senator" type. He fit Fran's plans perfectly.

When first approached to join the group of organizers, Fran believed Max would purchase a large portion of stock. He committed to $250,000 and she duly recorded the promise in her records. He wrote her a check for the initial $25,000 and then denied making any larger commitment. Interestingly, Fran liked this. Max lied the way she did, so she knew exactly how to read him and to control him. He was the oldest member of the group of organizers and he was the rubber stamp Fran needed. She assured Max a three-year board term. She had him in her pocket for the first 1,095 days.

Max's job that evening was to introduce Fran's speech to the group of 150 or so attending the party. His way was genteel and patronizing and he had a practiced way of repeating himself. He used this method for emphasis, thinking it made him sound authoritative.

"Friends, friends, we don't often have the privilege to meet and get to know on a personal level someone with the outstanding character and characteristics of Fran Kontopolus. This woman who has become a legend, a legend in banking in Chicago, will set forth a new dedicated system of community banking. This, at a time when community banking has been lost to the big banks that gobble, gobble up the small banks we used to know, trust, and do business with. Does anyone know your name when you call your bank? Remember when they did? Boy, I remember when I was just out of the Army and I needed to open a checking account. My community banker knew my name, the name of my family, my friends, and my friends' friends. Boy, they could help me along the way with anything I needed. Friends, as the sun goes down outside, we are present for a sunrise in here, a sunrise for Chicago banking. You have provided the life blood, the capital for the new Sunrise Bank in Chicago. Yes, under the leadership of Fran Kontopolus, Sunrise Bank will deliver the quality personal service that went out of style years ago. A style we miss, don't we?"

The room exploded with a cheer. Some of it was even legitimate.

"It is my privilege and honor to introduce to you the president of Sunrise Bank, a woman with knowledge and insight into the business of banking, a woman of courage and a woman of conviction, the woman who, well, without whom we would not be here right now, would we? Ladies and gentlemen, I give you Ms. Fran Kontopolus."

Every greedy investor stood and applauded.

Fran was having her day all right. She had some cocktail sauce on her face from the jumbo shrimp platter. She caught her mother's eye as she walked across the room. Ma was giving her the familiar direction that she had given so many times before, pointing to Fran's cheek and making a motion to wipe off some food.

Fran stuck her finger in her mouth, wet it, and then wiped it across her face, catching the sauce on her finger. Her finger popped right back in her mouth and she licked it clean and wiped the saliva onto her dress as she approached the podium. In the tight black knit dress that had become Fran's uniform she looked like 250 pounds of ground beef stuffed into a 220-pound sack.

Just as she approached the podium, she miss-stepped and twisted her foot. Suddenly Fran's heel broke. She fell on her right knee, tearing her hose. Blood began flowing from the knee.

She fell at the feet of the new chairman. Rudman, who could no longer bend down to tie a shoe due to the weight he had accumulated around his belly, quickly pointed to two busboys who were retrieving empty plates and glasses from the cocktail tables. "Uh, boys, boys, can you help the lady please?" The two Mexican busboys, who spoke "Spanglish," got the idea and immediately bent over to help Fran get up from the floor. The men helped her roll over then grabbed an arm. As they pulled, they were brought down on top of Fran.

Mouths dropped open as the two busboys bumped their heads into one another. One investor commented that this scene reminded him of a Three Stooges film. This drama, with Fran taking the role of the victim, added to the event. Two more busboys helped the first two to their feet. Now four men were pulling the woman of the hour off the floor.

Once on her feet, with torn hose and a small cut bleeding down her leg, Fran took the mike at the podium. Her mascara was running from the tears of embarrassment.

"Friends" she started, as her voice was choked up, "I wanted to show my papa, up in heaven, that I could open a bank in his name and in his honor. With your help, I am doing that now. I had more to say to you wonderful folks, but I must sit and mend my wound. Does anyone have a band-aid? Ow! I appreciate your confidence in me and in Sunrise Bank. Now enjoy the food and refreshments. Thank you."

Fran's brothers and Ma approached the front of the room. Her mother, wearing the cheap dime-store wig, came running. "My Franny, my Franny," she screamed. The audience rose and applauded awkwardly this time. Fran turned from the podium with a limp just pronounced enough to get sympathy. To her right was a station where waiters placed plates and glasses they retrieved from guests before taking the items to be washed in the kitchen. Fran saw three meatballs and a slice of German cocktail rye bread. Without missing a beat, she grabbed the plate from the tray and began wolfing down the food. The taste of the sauce made her feel grand.

CHAPTER
TWENTY-NINE

In late November the charter to open arrived from the State of Illinois. Now the bank was ready to go. The months following "Rush to Raise" were a time of planning and hiring. Just to the west of the site where a building was to be constructed for Sunrise Bank, two trailers were installed as temporary offices. The construction time was projected at less than one year and it was not usual for a new bank to begin in a trailer or temporary facility.

Interviews were conducted to hire the staff, including tellers, lenders, private bankers, security personnel, managers, secretaries, assistants, and others. Stationery, deposit slips, envelopes, and connection to banking systems all needed to be ordered and put in place. Marketing, advertising, and public relations plans had to be developed. Despite the enormous workload and responsibility, Fran knew what to do and set forth the process in an organized and well thought out way. The organizers were transformed and became the board of directors.

Fran's goal had been reached and she had her bank. She knew that she had to start manipulating, shaping, and bending the board to her will immediately. She once again began meeting with members individually. She made appointments to the most important committees with the weaker and older members. She repeatedly used the same approach. As retired men, they could attend, without distraction from their various interests, the many meetings that these committees would require. The bank and the community needed their direct involvement, she said.

Fran would have preferred no board members and no board meetings. The bank had been designed from the beginning as a monarchy. She often daydreamed about herself as Queen Fran and even had a queen's crown she had purchased in a garage sale as a kid. She kept the crown in a drawer in her home wrapped in red velvet and would, in stolen moments, place it on her head and stare at herself in the mirror on the wall. What she never considered was that her kingdom had to be more stable than that of the Dr. Seuss character Yertle the Turtle.

Yertle the Turtle thought of himself as king of all he could see. But from his little rock he could not see much beyond his small pond. He commanded that all the turtles in the pond climb on each other's backs so he could climb up and see farther. The stack got higher and higher and the backs of the turtles began to hurt. Then after a turtle on the bottom of the pile belched, the tower of turtles collapsed and Yertle fell into the mud. Fran never considered that she might fall. Instead of a skinned knee, she might suffer a greater loss—a bruised ego.

CHAPTER THIRTY

Banking rules mandate a board of directors, and Fran was obligated to conduct monthly meetings regardless of her feelings or desires. The board raised the initial capital with friends, relatives, and business associates. Expectations ran high for the new bank. They expected Fran to come through on her promises for rewards, which included stock grants, options, cash for meeting attendance and chairing committees, and any other little perks that came their way were what everyone was waiting for.

But Fran was determined to divide the loyalties of her board so she could ensure that it would remain *her* board. Before a meeting, she would select a member as a pre-ordained committee chair. Rather than have decisions made by the board, which required votes and discussion, her handpicked yes-man would automatically slide into the chairmanship. The presentation of that board committee chairman would be announced under new business on the agenda. In reality, it was a matter of old, settled, and "let's move on right now" business. Naturally, the board member was pleased with the appointment and the other members were not going to oppose their friend's new position, so no discussion ensued. Fran got what she wanted each and every time.

Fran had her self-esteem on the line with the business and banking community at large. She had to make things work. Her board didn't really concern itself with real bank management. That was Fran's problem. They were carried away by their own inflated egos. They shared with the people within their sphere of influence that they were members of a bank's board of directors. That they were all going to be rich through this new business venture didn't hurt either.

When asked why there were no women on the board, Fran quite logically stated the obvious. Because there were so few women in high positions in Chicago banking, her search for the right candidate with the right credentials would take some time. She wasn't about to appoint an unqualified person to the board just to meet an arbitrary quota. The organizers took Fran at her word and the matter never came up again. There was no way in hell Fran would put a woman on the bank board. She did not want the competition. What whore wants to share her street corner?

A group of investors were partners in a powerful, yet understated, law firm in Chicago. The senior partner of the firm, Bernard Farin, was an elder statesman in his late seventies. He was a well-connected king maker, a man behind the scene in Chicago politics and influential in many business circles. He told his partners to invest in the bank and the group brought over $2 million to capitalize the bank. Farin was a friend of the family of Adam Berg.

Farin called Fran to appear at his office, and when Bernard Farin called, people jumped to his command. Chicago works as a city because its business community, like politics, is a matter of favors. I do for you now you do for me later. As Fran arrived in the lobby of his downtown law firm's offices, Farin was napping in his fifty-ninth floor corner office. At this point of his career, he had nothing to do other than have lunch and listen to people who needed his advice. Bernard Farin was a political and business Godfather now. He still wielded great power, but his life was far different than that of his younger days.

After World War II, as a young man, he was acquainted with the Shah of Iran and traded in oil tankers and brokered oil deals internationally. His family's connections with the inner workings of the City of Chicago went back three generations. He was a powerbroker in the local, state, and national Democratic Party and friendly with the Kennedy family.

There was always room in Irish politics for a smart Jewish family. Bernard Farin's uncles were judges and businessmen and his father was treasurer for the county. Legend had it that his father had assembled the land that was sold to the county to build the Cook County hospital in the early 1920s. Bernard's confidential net worth was estimated at well over a billion dollars. Farin's political and business value was priceless.

As the door to his office opened, he was jarred awake from his pre-lunch nap. "Fran Kontopolus is here, Mr. Farin," said his secretary.

"Sit down, Fran." Farin never spoke, he barked. Fran, who was accustomed to a father with a bark, reacted as she did as a child. She sat down and remained quiet, not to speak until spoken to.

Farin was not one for small talk with anyone and never asked for opinions. He told people what he expected and they did it. "Fran, the money from my partners pushed you over the top. We got you twenty percent of the dough you needed. Put one of my guys on the bank board." Fran was not expecting so blunt an order, but she listened as she knew Farin's power and influence.

"Ever hear of Everett Miller?" Fran shook her head no. "Didn't think so," said Farin. "Everett Miller is a black man influential in government lobbying in Illinois. I know his family well. I want him on your board. He will open doors for the bank." He sat back and waited for her response. He knew what it would be, what it had to be, but he wanted to see how this woman handled herself.

Fran was speechless. Although she often spoke of diversity, Fran was a racist and having a black man on her board was unthinkable. Worse, she knew that Miller would report her every move back to Farin. But she also knew that with a phone call Farin could put a hold on a building permit, instigate a regulatory investigation, or have her bank charter questioned due to a minor detail. His influence could be reflected in many ways.

As the seconds ticked away a thousand thoughts crossed her mind. She wanted out of that office. She wanted to call Sonny Vulich. She wanted to stand up and throw a hissy fit and tell Bernard Farin where to shove his damn millions. The checks were cashed and the money was hers now. Who did he think he was telling her, Fran Kontopolus, what to do? As Fran looked at the many photographs of Farin and world leaders that covered his office, she suppressed a smile as a bead of sweat trickled down her forehead.

Fran looked at the old man who could call presidents or world leaders and have direct access. She accepted the undeniable and just nodded her head and told him to have Everett Miller call her. She knew when she was cornered.

"And he needs to have a long term on the board that is automatically renewed. You will see his value as time goes on," said Farin. She was dismissed.

As Farin looked away, Fran stood up and meekly walked out of the room. She didn't want an eleventh board member, not at all. Fran usually knew how to get out of obligations and promises she had made to people. But this was one that she would have to live with. She could not get out of this one, at least not for the time being. She was a master of spin and some angle would sooner or later present itself. It had to, she thought.

During board meetings, when Fran was reminded of promises regarding stock options, board committees, board compensation, commitments, and more, she would defend her neglect of attention to those matters by stating that after consulting with the bank's counsel, Fred Belker, she could not deliver on those items at the moment. Whatever it was could not be done, according to Fran, because Belker told her so and that was it. "Gentlemen, the well-being of Sunrise Bank must come first. Rest assured each of you will get what you have so richly deserved." Belker never knew his most important role, Fran Kontopolus' fall guy, because he was never present when she made these representations.

Belker was part of Fran's bigger plan for control and had been promised large rewards for his work in organizing the bank. He held the party line even when asked about an issue by a board member. Fred was a yes-man. He agreed with whatever he was supposed to have said.

When he did attend a meeting, Fran would give him a glance from across the table and as she addressed her descent from a promise, Belker sat poker faced and nodded like a bobble-head doll.

CHAPTER
THIRTY-ONE

Inherent to Fran's way of thinking was a premeditated plan for the corporate demise of people she viewed as in her way. This feeling had been established upon hearing her father telling his friends that the way to success in business was to "kill the competition." She took that message to heart far more seriously than her papa ever meant. After careful thinking and planning, Fran decided that she should separate her board into two groups. The first would be the bank board of directors, which would have the responsibilities for the day-to-day operations of the bank. The members of this board were the older retirees and executive officers of the bank. The board would meet monthly.

The second group would be the members of the holding company board. The holding company was the entity that actually owned the bank. This group would meet quarterly and would hear about the business of the bank after, way after, it happened. This schedule gave Fran a lot of maneuvering time if needed. Although the bank board of directors reported to the holding company, the company directors had no input in the running the bank. She decided that she could include the bank board members on the holding company board too. That would save time. Yes, that's what she would do. If she included the members of the organizers on the holding company, her plan would not be as obvious. And if she could get these men to go along with her direction without controversy she would know that she had the power to control them and the destiny of her bank.

As she had observed at State Bank of the Community, the elderly were less confrontational; they wanted their lunch, payment for attending meetings, and to be left alone if they fell asleep. They had no desire for principal or fight. She chuckled to herself as she visualized her elderly board of directors at meetings wiping their noses with washed-out gray handkerchiefs, dripping food on their clothes, dozing at meetings, and farting while dozing. She knew she could get away with anything with this pathetic group. They were the perfect board. She did not announce this separation to her board until two weeks before the opening of the bank.

As she had done in the past in using Belker as the fall guy, she explained that they would have to be split in two as counsel had pointed out some members may have conflicts of interest. Some of the younger members were involved in developing and investing in real estate. By being on the bank's board, she explained, they would be exposed to confidential deal-making information that would allow them unfair competition with the bank's borrowers. Fran felt it would be morally wrong and she could not expose the bank's customers to board members who might "steal a deal" or compete with a customer.

The lack of experience of this "devoted" group of men let this go as they had before. They wanted to believe her. They wanted their perks. They wanted to avoid responsibility. The bank was chartered and in organization and this was her first real test. Fran could divide and separate these men with amazing ease. This set the precedent. From then on, they would continue to follow her like sheep to the slaughter. Fran's set rules became the standard at the bank with no discussion and no opposition.

Her suggestion was not industry standard, but these men knew no better so they believed her. There was a code of ethics that bank board members were supposed to uphold and it was not unusual to find bank board members who were in the same businesses that banks loan to. In fact, members who behaved the way Fran described could have, and would have, been terminated for cause or an ethics violation. But no one questioned Fran. They simply did not know better and didn't see her bigger plan in the works.

The group on the holding company board would be the power brokers, the aggressive, opinionated men from the group of organizers.

At the quarterly meetings these men would respond to larger issues if any came up, but could not respond to the day-to-day decisions Fran wanted to control. The set-up was perfect. She could add more yes-men to the bank board should she want to. She could just as easily create a situation to remove anyone she wanted.

The holding company board was just as perfect for the surprising new star in Chicago's staid banking circles. Fran announced the division to the two groups in the last meeting of the organizers. Rudman led a toast, "Boys, and Fran, of course, boys, some claim success is due to the grace of God. Others claim success the result of hard work. Well, I've been around for some time in the business world of Chicagoland and I must say we have experienced both the grace of God for bringing Fran Kontopolus to us and the hard work that this knowledgeable woman provided this last year. Without Fran we would not have become friends and without Fran we would never have gotten true community banking back in business. Drink up, everyone."

Glasses were lifted and then brought to the mouths of the organizers. Fran drank too. She thought of her father and how she seemed to have done what she set out to do. So far, so good. Her next steps were to get rid of these bozos and take over the bank. She did not know how she would do it, but she would do it just the same. And she wouldn't waste a second getting started.

The meeting was also a dinner and Fran decided to order two desserts. As was often the case, a forkful of chocolate cake had fallen in her lap. She had one more piece of business to discuss and waited until coffee was served. Before the evening meeting was concluded she asked the organizers to approve an increase in her salary. Fran's reasoning was that she needed more money to live the lifestyle of a bank president. If the bank was to be successful, the leader should look successful. She also complained that she had been underpaid in organizing the bank and was due justifiable compensation for her sacrifice. A shocked look appeared on the faces of the organizers. They were not expecting this request. Everyone was stunned by her audacity.

Fran looked to Max Rudman, who was chairman of both the holding company and the bank board. Rudman, having sat on and been a member of other boards before, knew how to be a successful chairman. Make no waves. Do what management wants and keep your board seat at all costs. After a long silence Rudman loudly cleared his throat and spoke.

"Boys, Fran's right. Frankly I thought she was underpaid from the get-go. I was surprised that she gave so much of herself to this group. We certainly don't want to have a bank president unhappy, do we? Not our bank president. We don't want other banks looking at Fran without the respect she deserves, do we?"

Adam Berg raised his hand. He had enthusiastically endorsed Fran to many investors including Bernard Farin. Fran had approached Berg as one of her first investors and organizers and conferred with him frequently. Berg spoke up, telling the board members that he thought the timing for such an expenditure was premature for a bank that had not made a dime. Certainly a raise was appropriate a little further in the future, but the bank had not opened yet, there was no profit, of course, and the uphill battle was just beginning. He could not understand how Fran could request more than the $120,000 per year she was earning. Fran's true colors, her gluttony, were finally beginning to show. "Don't you think this request for a pay increase, considering we haven't even one dollar in deposits, is a little premature?"

Fran's eyes became red with hatred.

Berg continued, "We can visit the salary increase for Fran in six months or anytime, but on behalf of the shareholders, I just think our obligation is to do things in an organized and prudent manner. Nothing personal, Fran, but, as you've said before, the bank has to come first."

A discussion ensued with board members chatting back and forth their opinion of Fran's request. Fran's face was fire engine red and her breast was heaving up and down. At a glance one would have thought volcano Kontopolus would erupt any second and start spewing red hot venom out of its big mouth. What made things even more bitter was that Berg had so cleverly used her own words against her. Bastard!

Sensing the right moment, Rudman cleared his throat again and began to speak. "I think it's a fair request to pay our president a president's wage. So let's bring this to a vote." Rudman winked at old man Balt and Harris, a retired banker himself who knew the value of a free lunch and a board seat. Rudman turned and nodded to Michael Pischer, the youngest organizer who sold his soul to Fran for a paid position as a vice president of the bank. These four-yes men quickly raised their hands in favor of a raise. Slowly other board members' hands rose. The one hand not raised was that of Adam Berg.

"Passed and carried," said Rudman.

Fran's heaving began to settle, but she was sweating profusely and the armpits of her dress were soaked. She was still boiling mad. She looked at Berg and thought to herself, *He is the first one to go.* Fran was on a mission. Get Adam Berg.

As time passed the obsession to purge Berg from the board would become more pervasive than making the bank successful. Fran got her salary increase, of course, but in her mind the amount of money was just not enough.

Purging both food and people was becoming a regular part of the life of this woman.

CHAPTER
THIRTY-TWO

The core of banking success is a simple formula. Get deposits, make loans, and make a profit on the spread. Knowing this, Fran had been meeting with her customers during the bank's organization, not only to get them to invest but to open accounts, deposit money, and take out loans. Fran approached Sonny and his family from the start.

Sonny Jr. had a place on the holding company board, so it was a natural that he should become a major depositor and customer of the loan department. So Fran focused on the rest of the family through its patriarch. She shamelessly indulged Sonny and his family to seduce them to move their money to her bank as well. Fran took Sonny and his wife and their adult children to both the theater and the symphony. She took them to the horse race track and professional basketball games. She bought them dinner at the finest restaurants. Sonny was at a pivotal point of his career. He was on his way to becoming one of Chicago's largest residential builders. And knowing this, Sonny wanted something too.

As a young boy in Hegewisch Sonny had developed patience. It was a survival mechanism. One of the old neighborhood customs was to imbibe frequently and heavily. It was not unusual for Sonny's father, Duke, to drink till he was plastered. When this happened, gentle dad became an abusive father who would slap Sonny around. This physical abuse from an alcoholic father was motivation enough to leave and move north. Sonny hated Hegewisch and after leaving never wanted to return to the neighborhood that had a tavern on every corner. Oh, he would buy, sell, rent, and trade property in such neighborhoods all day long, but he would never, never live in that environment again.

As a child his patience was developed as he hid quietly in a small basement storage area, avoiding a drunken father who would beat him just for sport. He learned as a youngster how to hold his breath, then breathe slowly, evenly, and silently when his father would search the house for him. He learned how to control his bladder and hold his pee for hours. Sonny developed patience, all right. He knew what Fran was up to and he let her stay out on a limb for quite some time. He enjoyed having the tables turned, having real power over someone else's life, and he enjoyed Fran's generosity. He didn't care about her spending the organizers' seed money. But in the same way he would not commit to investing money in the bank when they first met, he would not commit to moving his deposits and loans. She needed him and he knew it.

As the initial deadline approached to raise money for the bank, Sonny's plan was to jump in at the last second. He waited until she had raised the $10 million. He waited until she was ready to officially close the period for investors and make her announcement at the cocktail party. Then one night at dinner, when Sonny was alone with Fran, he told her that he would seriously consider becoming a customer of the bank, likely its largest and most profitable customer, if she would make him a promise. He would come on board provided he was assured of an interest rate on his deposits of at least one percent higher than market rate and an interest rate on his loans that was one percent lower than the market rate. If she would make that promise, he would always be ahead of the float. If she agreed he would invest $100,000 to purchase stock and she would be guaranteed his son's vote on her side as well as his customer loyalty, and he would initially move $1 million into an operating account.

Fran needed the guarantee that every board member would be loyal to her. This was Sonny Vulich talking. She knew that she would not have to disclose her promise to anyone. As for the stock purchase, at this point it did not matter that Sonny wanted to make an investment. Enough money had already been raised to start the bank, but she wanted him on her customer list and she would do anything to get his accounts and loans. As a prominent customer his name alone would bring in some business. Fran immediately agreed to Sonny's terms. She wanted a guarantee that Sonny Jr. could always be counted on to be in her camp.

"As long as you make me the loans I need, we vote Fran," he said.

Fran had not been this excited about anything since the chocolate fountain at one of her brothers' weddings. She gobbled her dessert feeling more powerful than ever.

CHAPTER
THIRTY-THREE

The bank charter was in hand and the bank would open in a few weeks. Fran felt empowered, but she also felt the effects of her sustained efforts. Being the Dragon Lady, the Wicked Queen, and the financial equivalent of Typhoid Mary all rolled into one had taken its toll. She was tired and thought she was due a break. President Fran was ready to make a significant executive decision and it was to goof off at a critical moment. She would pack up and go on a vacation. She would leave Chicago and leave the opening set-up to her staff. She hopped a plane to Jamaica for two weeks. She wanted to return nice and tan for her opening. And knowing how large white women were treated so well by the native Jamaican men, she was also lookin' for some lovin.' Wielding real power had brought out Fran's horny side.

When her staff was informed that she was taking a vacation just two weeks prior to opening, when everything was coming together, when they most needed a leader, they could not believe it. She informed her board president by sending Rudman an e-mail on a Friday afternoon. Her plane left Saturday and there was no way he could contact her to discuss "some plain old common sense." She left Chicago without preparation for her weary staff, which was expected to work twenty-four hours a day preparing the temporary banking facility in the dead of winter.

Fran had purposefully refused to create a chain of command. She was the general, the admiral, the queen. There was no fall-back plan should anything happen to her, nor was anyone clearly in charge in her absence. Somebody even in temporary charge might grow to like it and she wasn't about to take that chance. To make matters worse, the staff was deathly afraid of making a mistake, which meant they were afraid to make decisions. Cell phone service on the islands of the Caribbean was not always accessible and anyway Fran left word not to be disturbed. She told her staff that she would phone them every few days. They were unprepared for the opening of Sunrise Bank. They knew they would suffer the wrath of Fran should they do anything incorrectly so they were quite cautious and did as little as possible.

One of the higher paid vice presidents who came from Bank of America and was heading commercial loans, had transferred to Sunrise Bank for an excessively large signing bonus and the large salary offered to executive employees. He had no prior experience with Fran Kontopolus and did not know her or anyone else from the community bank culture. He was a corporate employee from a national organization. For the past month Brett Pomerance had gritted his teeth each time he had to interact with Fran Kontopolus. He was seduced by the money, as were others, but his central nervous system and conscience were in chaos working in her bank. After a couple of weeks of firsthand exposure Brett saw Fran's reputation come to life.

He was in disbelief that he had sacrificed integrity for money. He knew he could never introduce her to his wife or kids. It would have been embarrassing to admit to those who had respect for him that this horrid woman was his boss. Brett had joined the bank while it was in organization. He was hired after all the money was raised and about ninety days before the official charter arrived. Fran was very demanding of her staff and Brett was instructed to leave his cell phone turned on at all times so she could reach him should she need to discuss something in the middle of the night. There were a number of occasions when his sleep was disturbed by a phone call by a less than sober Fran who ran on and on about nothing of real consequence. He had never experienced such disrespect. His wife began to wonder if this move was a good one for her husband. Brett was earning more money now than ever before and this lack of basic courtesy seemed to be part of the job.

But as time went on the foul language Fran used in the normal course of the day was becoming intolerable. He could not imagine bringing a client into the bank and introducing them to a slovenly foul mouth. And that was just a symptom of much more serious problems. His boss was a beast, an inexperienced beast who could never create, she could only destroy. His credibility was at stake. When Brett found out about Fran's absence just when the bank was opening he was stunned. On the second day of her vacation he informed Michael Pischer he was quitting the bank. He was able to get his old job back immediately at Bank of America. The night he quit, Brett slept better than he had for months.

CHAPTER
THIRTY-FOUR

When the bank officially opened its doors, Fran had everything and everyone in place. Her board of directors was positioned just as she wanted them on the holding company and the bank board. A divided group stacked with impotent yes-men. The staff lived in fear of her intimidating and humiliating tactics. There was no second in command. Fran was the go-to guy, the slave driver and commander-in-chief. People of the backwoods South had the most appropriate designation. Fran was the "she bear" of Sunrise Bank.

In addition to a golden brown Jamaican tan, Fran returned to Chicago with other things. Specifically, she had new ideas to benefit her and her family. Fran knew that the power of money was strong enough to buckle morals and ethics. She planned to solicit her board members who were in the real estate business.

Sure, the federal government had "Regulation O" prohibiting preferential treatment of bank board members as borrowers. So what? She had placed her real estate people on the holding company board not the bank board. Thus they were removed from the day-to-day operations of the bank. To the Fed, they were now invisible. This would stretch the rules of borrowing money. From Fran's perspective, however, this was in effect her money and she could do with it as she damn well pleased.

The holding company board members would jump at this opportunity. They would be easy prey and rush to borrow at her gracious lending rates. When a bank placed a loan on the books income immediately showed up on the ledger. She would look good and not have to work hard for these quick loans.

For some board members there might be some resistance, she knew that, but in Sonny's case, his son, not him, was on the board. So she could funnel Sonny as much money as he needed indirectly and without a direct paper trail. Sonny would like that, she thought. Fran figured that other members' loyalty was for sale and she had the right price in those favorable loans. She would go out of her way to spread money around to enlist them into her camp.

Fran was told of Brett Pomerance's departure while she was still in Jamaica. She did not care much for Pomerance anyway and was happy to see him out the door and gone. He hadn't sucked up to her the way she had expected, and anyway he had all the makings of a self-righteous pain in the ass. The loss of his considerable signing bonus could easily be written off as the cost of business. If questioned, she could always refuse to comment, adding a little hint that perhaps someone had discovered a bit of scandal in his background. She still needed someone available 24/7, a man who would attend evening dinner meetings with her and escort her to real estate, banking, and charity events. Pomerance's marriage and family life would have interfered with her agenda. The replacement for this position would have to be an experienced commercial lender, but she would have to make sure he was single and a stud. She could not be seen with just anyone. Fran knew that she could contact a headhunter, a company that received a commission to place employees. They would have a file of young studs eager to break into a well-paying job regardless of the strings attached.

While in Jamaica, Fran phoned her brother Ray. She instructed him to set up a dummy corporation in Chicago. He was about to become one of those headhunters. She would direct him on how to advertise for bank employees, how to interview and evaluate people, how to keep proper records, and how to spot those special people whose loyalty would be for sale. She had him order a business phone number with voice mail under the name of REWRES Headhunting. Phone bills went to the address at the fish store. This way she could funnel the commission for hiring bank employees to her family and no one would be the wiser. It was a perfect plan. She could make this work.

A headhunter earns 20-30 percent of the first year's salary of an employee. During the first year of operations for the bank, employees continued to be hired, and with each one, a commission was paid to RE-WRES Head Hunting. During a slump she even fired someone just so she could pump some capital into Ray's company. Within the first year of the bank, during which hiring was essential for new positions and new responsibilities, Fran paid her brother almost $300,000 in commissions. Members of the staff were encouraged to use the services of REWRES, and to make sure her loans remained favorable, they did. She was living up to her father's motto of always taking care of the family first.

Fran recruited staff from competing banks. She knew that offering a generous signing bonus would entice a move from senior level management. Considering the level of banking expertise in the city, she had a nice gene pool to choose from. She had worked her entire career building a reputation as a difficult and unforgiving woman, a true bitch of a boss. If not for the signing bonuses and salaries extremely above market level, and certainly above the budget for the bank, few would have knocked on her door. The money was great, but the price tag was costly. No one liked the ogre and more than a few learned to hate the very sight of her.

Fran was calculating in every respect. She knew the challenges she would face in finding senior staff. She also knew that new businesses were expected to operate in the red for the first few years. She counted on that and had worked it well into her plans. That early red ink would hide a lot of wheeling and dealing. She also knew that at the end of the first year the budget would have to be increased to cover those high salaries. The bonuses and salaries were necessary, but there was also another motive. With senior staff receiving such high compensation, the president's salary would have to be adjusted upward, way upward. She would simply explain to the bank board that to be competitive she had to offer money, big money, to experienced people. They would believe her and the money would flow, much of it directly into her own account.

The salaries of her staff exceeded the bank's budget, but that would not be reported until the end of the first quarter of the second fiscal year, so the holding company could not react on a timely basis. Thus Fran created a loyal staff by overpaying each person. Her ultimate motive was to increase her salary exponentially relative to the employees' salaries. Employees could not earn as much as she did, now could they?

CHAPTER
THIRTY-FIVE

S unrise Bank opened and Fran continued to spend money like the proverbial drunken sailor, not a bad analogy considering her increasing intake of expensive vodka. She had $10 million to play with and play she did. For the first time in her life, Fran could pretend she had a life. As the new structure grew, she planned to decorate the bank as if she was decorating a palace. The private bathroom within her office would be opulent with mirrors, a dressing area, and cabinets for all of her toiletries and personal items. She even put in for a small refrigerator and microwave. The furniture for her office would be top of the line. Jackie Kennedy and Nancy Reagan took less time decorating the White House than Fran took decorating one office in one bank. Chicago's finest decorator was brought in to handle the public areas. Fran did her own designing for her office, which meant the colors were garish and the materials miss-matched. Fran made the common mistake of thinking expensive automatically meant "class."

With the bank open for business in temporary trailers, the directors and employees looked forward to Fran generating the business and getting the loans she had guaranteed, but often she was nowhere to be found. She spent the first months of operation at Chicago's Merchandise Mart with her interior designer, already looking for ways to upgrade the bank's image. She met with countless advertising agencies, most of whom had prepared speculative campaigns. She toured the offices and even a few factories of bank suppliers to make sure they were ship-shape. It was all make-work.

On days when she came to work, she established that she could be expected to arrive no earlier than 11:00 a.m. Then she would depart for lunch promptly at noon. Her regular lunch place was the Huron Café on the Chicago River. The staff knew Ms. Fran, as she was called, and promptly delivered her regular lunch of pork chops and double baked potato with cheese and chives.

The shareholders and board members were active in sending their friends, clients, and business associates to the bank for loans. But the loan applications by borrowers sat awaiting approval because Fran made it clear that she was the only person in the bank who could ap-prove loans. Sure, she had hired an expensive staff to underwrite loans and gather data, but Fran insisted that each step in the loan process had to go through her. She had to read each application, approve the choice of the appraiser, read and approve each financial statement, read the pro-forma and prospectus, review the biography of the borrower, review the borrower's tax return, and more.

Her inaction created a bottleneck in the loan approval process. Banks usually approved loans in periods that ranged from one month to six weeks. To remove any possibility of success by employees Fran did not allow her staff to make final decisions. This pace created criticism at board meetings when loan review was on the agenda. Members of both boards received complaints from their referrals that they could not get loans approved in a timely fashion. It was embarrassing. "I thought you had some real juice with the loan committee. What's going on over there?" The question was usually followed by a board member stam-mering, stuttering, and promising, "I'll, uh, look into it, okay?"

The loans that sailed through like a fast sloop racing on the wind were the loans that Sonny, his sons, or partners needed. If a borrower had an affiliation with Sonny, loans were pushed to the head of the line and turned around quickly. Approval usually took less than one month.

During her search for a commercial loan officer, Fran interviewed and hired Ron Kevin. Kevin was a vice president at Exchange National Bank and had twenty years of experience to his credit. When offered the job, Kevin, who had worked hard at a downtown bank, realized what the real job was. He was to become a banking gigolo. He accepted $50,000 as his signing bonus and a salary of $125,000. He made sure he had a great severance package. Kevin had been divorced for seven years and had time on his hands. A playboy who did not want to work hard, he was out to take advantage of anyone at this point of his life. Fran provided him a great opportunity. Kevin's first assignment: escort her to every design showroom in the Merchandise Mart in Chicago and roll play husband and wife shopping for furniture.

Ron Kevin was six feet tall and handsome. He seldom wore a tie, had a well-trimmed mustache, and always wore a handkerchief in the breast pocket of his jacket. He made a striking appearance. Fran interviewed much better qualified men for the position, but none was single and none had his looks or physique. He had even been offered a few modeling jobs by local photographers and had accepted. The money was okay, but the exposure in Chicago magazines and newspaper ads got him laid, a more important form of compensation for the young banker.

Kevin wanted to slack off on work for a while. "So what?" was his attitude if he needed to go to events with Fran. He didn't care if he spent his days shopping at the mart rather than calling on customers. He liked this pseudo-gigolo position where he was paid well, had an unlimited expense account, and did not have to work hard. As long as this chubby little slob did not make sexual demands he was fine. Ron was a "taker" like Fran and Fran did not care what he took financially so long as he performed as she wanted him to.

As an extra perk, Kevin had a leased car, not a Mercedes 500SL, as Fran now drove, but a Lincoln Town Car. Fran leased this style of car for Kevin because she wanted to be driven around as if he was her chauffeur. She would insist on riding in the rear seat of the Lincoln on the way to meetings, claiming that her legs were stiff from walking on the treadmill at the health club in her building. He knew what she was up to. Fran had it good, just as she planned.

CHAPTER THIRTY-SIX

The eighteen months in the trailer passed quickly for some and much longer for most others. Time dragged out in ever-increasing painful degrees. Nearby, the permanent structure rose from the ground like a tree in the forest. Each day workers and customers saw encouraging progress as brick was added to brick, concrete was mixed, and windows and doors were installed. The construction workers frequently visited the bankers inside the trailer to get out of the cold and drink the hot coffee and eat the cookies that the bank provided. Fran boiled at this modest down time. Luckily, before she said anything, Sonny explained how construction went faster and there were fewer problems when the owners treated the workers as if they were human. "Piss off the right guy, Fran, and you'd be amazed at how fast half your crew comes down with the flu."

Most people working at the bank thought these men and women were part of the team and fit in like family. It was sad for some to think that one day these people who were friends would be leaving.

That day finally arrived and construction ended. The new building was complete. The furniture arrived and shortly bank operations moved from the trailer into the expensive structure. In comparison to similar community banks, Fran's office was twice the size of what one might expect. With a salary higher than that of presidents of larger banks, she thought she deserved the square footage as well because, to Fran, size mattered.

Her projection that her board of directors would always be steps behind her with information about the bank's finances worked perfectly. The loss in operations was anticipated so why disappoint anyone?

At board meetings discussion ensued when reviewing the bank's expenses, especially when line items for entertainment and non-essential expenditures came up. If Fran showed a tear or threw a tantrum and showed emotions, the men would cower. Max Rudman would instantly come to her aid and share examples from his years as a CPA of successful companies that started in the red. It was essential, he emphasized the word, essential that Sunrise Bank's president look successful to the community. He always came to Fran's rescue.

But even Rudman knew that her spending was excessive compared to other banks and businesses. He was concerned with the bank's performance. He had received multiple calls from borrowers who could not get loans approved. These were good stable investors and shareholders. Other directors called him to share their concerns when their investors and clients were treated poorly by Fran and her staff. The men were embarrassed and humiliated. They had gone out on a limb for Fran in proclaiming her capabilities and objective for success, but she did not have the common courtesy or basic good business sense to treat them and their people with efficiency.

These customers or future customers were the lifeblood of the new bank. These were the bank's future, but Fran had a motive, of course. That was to piss off the directors so that they would resign the board so she could replace them with people she controlled. She had no care or respect for the work they did putting her in business. She wanted it all for herself.

CHAPTER THIRTY-SEVEN

The relationship she established with Ron Kevin was what Fran wanted. She would call him all hours of the night and on weekends just to talk. He was always available. He would take her calls and use the mute button on the phone while doing other things like entertaining women in his lakefront condominium. Fran talked on and on and on about nothing, completely unaware of his indifference. There were times when Kevin dozed off or grabbed a fast shower while she droned on. They were like a married couple in a bad television skit.

"Yes, dear…uh-huh…okay…that so…uh-huh."

"Are you listening to me!"

"Yes, dear…uh-huh…okay…that so…uh-huh."

"Again with the talking," he would say to himself. "Why did God create a telephone mute button if not for moments like this?" Kevin was going to goose this job for as much as he could get. What were a few annoying calls in the long run?

The problem with Kevin was his public ridicule of Fran. This was his Achilles heel. He would make snide and condescending remarks about her in front of staff, board members, customers, and sometimes right to her face in public. Since Fran never had a respectful relationship with a man, she did not expect much, so she never seemed to react to his comments. Board members were surprised at his behavior and lack of respect. They were shocked that she let him get away with it. Granted he was not wrong about what he said, but he now appeared as the bully and she as the victim.

Even Max Rudman was turned off by his behavior. Board members began to question Fran why she kept the young man on staff. Kevin did not generate business, was paid extremely well as a kept man, and then humiliated her publicly. This was not good for business.

"Fran, you have to do something about Kevin."

"Oh, he doesn't mean anything."

"He's ridiculing you on the street, for Chrissakes."

"That's just his style. He's harmless."

"Get rid of him before you get hurt."

Eventually Fran realized Rudman was right. He had become disgusted with Kevin's behavior and it broke her heart that she had to fire him. She needed him. In her mind she had created a fantasy romance. But once she began to see, really see how poorly he treated her, she knew what she had to do.

Fran had consulted with Berg from the beginning of the organization process. She trusted his opinion. On the day the bank opened, Adam was the first of Fran's loyal following to transfer multiple checking accounts to the bank. It was a snowy day in January and the bank operated in the shabby trailers. But Berg arrived with his bookkeeper and opened fifteen accounts at Sunrise Bank.

As the personal and professional crisis with Kevin was peaking, Berg came to the bank to make a deposit. Fran asked him into her office to discuss firing the ungrateful son of a bitch. "Adam , I know I have to let him go, but I don't know what to do." Alone and with someone she trusted, Fran allowed tears to roll down her face.

Berg, who had supported Fran from the start, was most vocal about Kevin's behavior. He told Fran that it was in her best interest to remove him from her staff as quickly as possible. He paused a second before speaking, looking for the right way to illustrate his point. "I recall a maintenance man at one of my buildings telling me a story of an old wood chopper in the backwoods of Georgia. As he reached down, a huge diamondback rattlesnake popped him in the left hand. The old man knew his heart wouldn't stand the poison and the shock. Without hesitation he chopped off his hand before the venom had time to spread. It was a simple matter of lose the hand or lose the life. Do you understand my meaning?"

She nodded in the affirmative as he continued. An employee who humiliated her publicly was poisoning her position in the banking community, he warned. "Fran, he's not trustworthy and he has to go. You must have someone with you at the termination meeting. A witness is important. I suggest that another vice president or even two people from management be present to witness the firing. I'm afraid of this guy. Don't fire Kevin without someone else present at the meeting."

Fran promised she would have someone witness the meeting. Berg soon departed the bank. She was awake all night knowing and dreading what had to be done. This was the first night she did not call Kevin at home. She would look at the phone, pick up the receiver, dial six digits, and hang up. Sleep required a few pills and a couple of shots of vodka.

The next day Fran sent for Kevin to come to her office. This was not an unusual request, but today was different. When he arrived she asked that he close the door. They were alone, no witness was present. She had ignored Berg's advice because she knew things would get emotional. It was inevitable that she would break down and cry at some point. No bank employee would ever be allowed to see her show a sign of weakness.

Fran began to cry hysterically as Kevin sat coolly on the sofa in her office. He lit a cigarette. "Ron, my Ron," she sobbed, "you have embarrassed me too many times. I can't take it anymore. I loved, I mean, liked you very much for the work you did and I don't understand why you treat me so poorly. I have no choice other than to fire you." She blew her nose so loudly the little trailer shook.

Kevin had known that this day would eventually come and he really didn't give a damn. He had a severance package and he knew what to do next. He asked Fran for a check for his six months' severance pay. He wanted it now. Fran wanted the painful, embarrassing meeting over as soon as possible. She placed a call to accounting and the check was delivered.

Kevin immediately departed with his check in hand and opened an account at another bank that same day. The check cleared within two days, and within seven days of being axed, he filed a sexual harassment lawsuit against Fran and Sunrise Bank. The lawsuit was part of Kevin's long-planned exit strategy. He had maintained a record of the phone calls at all hours of the night. He kept a record of all the weekend meetings Fran demanded and the after-hours "dinners" he was forced to endure. All the time Fran had been playing Kevin, she had been playing right into his hands.

Kevin knew that sexual harassment lawsuits were rarely played out in court and his records certainly could substantiate harassment. Fran was floored when the court papers were served on her. Her ego bruises were huge. She could not believe how cunning this man was. She had treated him so well.

On the advice of Fred Belker a settlement check was prepared for $50,000 to Ron Kevin, along with a settlement agreement. The agreement committed Kevin to withdraw the lawsuit and keep the matter quiet forever. Fran cost the bank an additional $50,000 before the bank earned their first dollar, but it was not her money and she soon forgot about the incident.

CHAPTER
THIRTY-EIGHT

S unrise Bank began to develop a rhythm and a life of its own. Employees were required to be at their desks and ready to go at 7:45 a.m. Fran entered the building no earlier than 11:00 a.m. Her entry was as predictable as her daily attire. A tight black knit Chanel-like dress, black high heels, and garish jewelry was her uniform. Her dark hair was over-sprayed. At fifty-four years old she claimed to never have had a gray hair, but everyone knew better. Fran was now tipping the scales at more than 250 pounds.

As she exited her car in the bank's parking lot, she would clumsily stumble in her heels all the way across the parking lot. Her frequent hangovers didn't help her mobility. Employees watched her from the security televisions in the bank. Using the various cameras positioned around the lot they could zoom in and watch as she put on lipstick, pulled her bra strap, or picked her teeth.

At first it was the security staff that laughed at the tyrant as she "adjusted herself." Their laughter became so noticeable that employees of the bank told one another and like children in school looking for their teacher to return to the classroom, created a lottery to determine who would have the opportunity each day to enter the small security room and watch the ritual. They called it "Franny's Follies" or "The Mornings With Fran Show" and there were always critics in the audience.

"Well, she certainly got the fattest role."

"A staggering performance."

"Chewing up the scenery again."

Even after the pulling, combing, stuffing, and re-stuffing performances were completed Fran rarely entered the bank without toilet paper on her shoe or Danish on her face. She walked on her toes due to the height of her heels. Often she had the maintenance man run (literally) to the local shoe repair store when she shattered a heel.

Jan Everest, a private banker and wannabe cartoonist, drew a series of cartoons he titled *Comical Tales from the Shoe Rack of Ms. Kontopolus*. This comic book series circulated weekly and told the story of Fran's shoes and their desperate lives. Each pair had a face on each toe. Looking at the shoes lined up on multiple shelves in her closet, the reader could view the multiple faces expressing themselves to one another. Each had exaggerated and usually sad or painful facial characteristics. They complained of their plight to one another and hoped not to be chosen to be worn. As the alarm clock rang at 8:00 a.m. and Ms. Kontopolus woke with a grunt and even the occasional wall-shattering fart, her shoes would attempt to avoid the inevitable curse of supporting her weight and being stretched beyond their limits from within.

Fran spent an extraordinary amount of money on shoes. She was the Imelda Marcos of the banking business. She may not have had a fetish for shoes, but she did have an obsession for them. She collected and treasured them.

Each week "Mount Everest Publications" related the latest tortuous adventures of these "poor soles." The tales would describe plots of how the shoes would try to avoid being worn, stories of the old shoes telling the new purchases of their soon-to-be sordid existence, and stories of "wears and tears." Some comics described the plight of looking up at the world and what they saw from their perspective. One series told the tale of shoes wriggling free and escaping never to be seen again. One week featured a pair of gay loafers trying to come out of the closet. Another issue featured a pair of heels with a toilet paper "beard."

The stories were always narrated by the oldest shoe in the closet. He started each comic by saying, "Oh, hi, folks, welcome back to the closet. I'm Old Shoe, the oldest surviving shoe of Fran Kontopolus. My mate, rest his soul, is long gone. Today I'm going to share with you the tale of…" The story changed week to week, but the theme was always the same. It ain't easy carrying the weight of Fran Kontopolus. The comics were actually quite funny and the bank employees looked forward to the new stories.

Jan Everest was a good cartoonist and writer of the comic script. This was his creative release on the weekends. That was until Fran found copies of the strips in the desk of one of the personal bankers. After the employees left for the day, Fran stayed at the bank. She had nowhere else to go. She required security guards remain in the bank in the lobby until she departed the building.

Being paranoid, she would wait until the bank was empty and then rummage through the desks of her staff. No one was exempt from her suspicions. Fran would open picture frames to see what was stored behind photographs of loved ones. She would look inside open bags of snacks people kept in their desks. Nibbling as she looked, she tried on shoes kept under desks, inspect files, and searched through each and every drawer. She never found anything worthwhile that would support a mutiny, but she remained paranoid just the same.

Then one day in the desk of a new hire she found six editions of *Comical Tales from the Shoe Rack of Ms. Kontopolus*. She read each one getting angrier and angrier. A clock in the shape of a gyroscope sat on the employee's desk. She set the comics down, grabbed the clock, and threw it across the office. It hit an oak door leading to the office of Michael Pischer, leaving a dent in the wood. The clock crashed to the floor and broke on the granite tile. She was furious.

That night, she rummaged through the desks of all of the staff, one by one, drawer by drawer. The security guards who were used to extended hours worked very late that night. They rolled their weary eyes at each other and tried to ignore Fran's raging.

"Bastards! You're all bastards! All of you!"

Everest was good at his job, liked by his fellow workers, and was a harmless, grandfatherly type with a few years left to retirement. The next morning when he arrived at the bank he was called into Fran's office. Before he could offer a greeting she threw the comic books in his face. Before firing him she dressed him down and publicly humiliated him as an example to anyone who might think to expose "The Emperor Has No Clothes."

After this, on a typical day, Fran would enter the bank like a stampede of buffalo. The energy that followed her was like the tail wind of a jet plane. Papers would fly. Fran would stop, point to an employee at his or her desk from across the lobby, and scream some accusation or criticism. "Where is the coaster that should be under your coffee cup?" "Why are there loose papers on your desk?" "I don't like sleeveless blouses worn by private bankers."

Anyone could be a victim and, at some point, everyone was. If an employee was not at his desk, Fran would sit in his chair and wait unit he returned from a bathroom break. Then she would question him with unnecessary intensity, wanting to know where he had been and for how long. After these outbursts she would enter the elevator and go to her office. Her assistant was required to have a fresh pitcher of ice water and a plate of cookies on her desk, fresh flowers in place on the coffee table, and a box of Fannie Mae chocolates placed beside them. Each day required a new box of chocolates, new cookies, new flowers. And God forbid they should not be there.

One day Diane, Fran's assistant, offered her a suggestion to replace the Fannie Mae candies with a bowl of fruit. Upon hearing this Fran got angry, pushed her nose into Diane's face like a baseball manager in a home plate dispute with an umpire, and yelled, "I don't eat fruit!" That was a lesson to Diane to always do what she was told. Dietary innovation was not welcome at Sunrise Bank.

Once in her office the door would slam shut and Fran would call her mother. A line of loan officers who needed to see her about loan approvals would form outside her office. Occasionally one or two might get in to see her before she left to eat lunch. The staff was becoming more and more frustrated as they could not complete their work. A few minutes before noon, like little soldiers waiting for inspection, her commercial lenders or other officers waited in the lobby of the bank to join Fran for lunch. Each day she would tell her assistant who was to join her, regardless of their workload, appointments, or conflicts. The selected individual would have to arrange his or her day, at the last moment, of course, to appease the boss. Hungry or not, ready or not, overworked or not, it was lunchtime with Fran and there were no options other than harassment or even unemployment. And often Fran did not have business to discuss; she just wanted someone to socialize with.

Her assistant would call ahead to the restaurant of the day to prompt the host to make sure Fran had her favorite table and her standard fare. Fran did not like to wait to order in a restaurant. She wanted her food and wanted it now. She returned from her daily lunch at 2:00 p.m., and once back at the office the work would begin. She would meet with her assistant and review the business of the day. After this, Fran would meet with the lending officers to review the loans. By then it was already after 4:00 p.m. and Fran kept her staff around well into the early evening as she reviewed the details of their loan write-ups. "Bankers hours" had an entirely different meaning for the officers and staff at Sunrise Bank.

Nothing went easily in getting loans done. Often Fran would be critical of information and demand more details, adding new requirements that the loan officer knew nothing about prior to the meeting. Then the same thing would start all over again. Where it might only take an application, a write-up, a review, and an approval for a loan to get approved at another bank, Fran's process was torturous to both her staff and customers.

Staff would frequently go home frustrated at the end of a long day. They would have liked to have completed their tasks. They knew that the next business day they would receive a call from their customers wanting to know when their loan would be approved. Knowing that they could not tell the truth about the process, they created excuse after excuse as best they could until in some cases the customer gave up and applied for their loan at another bank. Fran, who was so paranoid about screwing up, was making every management mistake in the book.

CHAPTER
THIRTY-NINE

As time went on, business at the bank established certain patterns. Fran developed a preferred list of customers who received priority on all services as well as, of course, an enemies list. There were people she disliked who found it frustrating to attempt to conduct any serious business with the bank. People with good reputations and business practices had difficulty getting even a checking account opened correctly. Some became so put off with service that to think of attempting to borrow money from Sunrise Bank was out of the question. The bank's budget was never up to date and spending for goods, services, and salaries was excessive. Fran, who was cocky and overbearing at her best, was becoming worse.

Rudman was getting nervous. He had assumed the role as chairman of the board so he could have another feather in his cap before his life was over. He collected feathers like Fran collected shoes. They were essential to his dwindling sense of self-worth. But Rudman could not continue to be the absent-minded defender of Fran's increasingly unprofessional behavior any longer. Board members called him sharing their concern about the bank not being profitable, about dissatisfied customers, about Fran.

To raise $10 million to capitalize the venture, 250 people had invested money and they expected returns well beyond a bump in the interest rate on their deposits. This large group of people was composed of the family and friends of directors, people they met frequently and often daily. They were experiencing difficulty doing business at the bank. Rudman was receiving call after call. At first he could talk his way out of things, but the number and intensity of calls was accelerating. The pressure was mounting on board members, especially the chairman, as more and more people used them as sounding boards for their frustrations.

Calls were coming in to board members at home in the evenings and on weekends. Rudman's conscience, his wife, was at home when the phone would ring. Blanche was not comfortable with her husband defending Fran any longer and she did not hide her opinion from him. Worse, she did not hide her opinion *of* her husband over the matter. "When they haul her off to prison or the loony bin, are you going with her or will you stay with me?" She was a bit more than half-serious.

He said, "New businesses have to grow into their overhead" so often Blanche was repeating the phrase in her sleep. In fact, the overhead was growing horrendously, but the profits were not. Fran began discussing adding branches and that meant more money out the door. The bank had no capital. It was operating in the red. Rudman, an old school glad hander with his nose up many people's asses his entire life, knew what to do. He was not confrontational and was not going to get on Fran's enemies list. He wanted his title and the money he received for conducting and attending board and committee meetings.

One Saturday afternoon Max called Berg at home. Berg, whose family had invested a substantial portion of the initial capital in the bank, was the perfect person to set up as the spokesperson for Rudman and the board. In a conversation that lasted more than two hours he described what was needed to confront Fran about the concerns of board members and investors. Berg, he said, was the only board member to do this job because Fran actually listened to him.

Berg listened and took notes. At the end of the conversation he said he would set an appointment with Fran to discuss the economic concerns of the board and the shareholders privately. He was also concerned and had been for some time.

Berg had a gentle way about him. He was often the voice of reason and was frequently brought into negotiations and transactions to help get parties to agree on points and move the deal forward. He was the perfect person to shield Rudman from Fran's inevitable wrath. The chairman did not want to be ex-communicated from the board. If anything were to be seen as mutinous, let the guillotine fall on someone else's head, even if that meant a good man like Adam Berg had to go. At this point all he wanted was to complete his term as board chairman, receive his gold watch, and move on to retirement. All he had to do was to survive for another eighteen months when his term would expire. A simple year and a half never seemed so long.

On Monday Berg called Fran's office to request a meeting for later that week. The appointment was confirmed for Wednesday afternoon. He arrived on time for the meeting and sat in her office on the couch as she sat in a chair at the end of the room. He started. "Fran, I've come here by request of the board of directors. Fran, we've been friends now for many years and I know I can be honest with you about concerns that board members and shareholders have about the bank. You need to show a plan to the board, a plan showing the steps to profitability. These guys just don't see the future. Yes, we need to spend money to earn money, that's basic, but we need to see the roadmap, so to speak. The board lacks confidence and they can only get it back from you. Fran, they need you as the commander of this vessel to tell them the direction you have in mind. They need your leadership." Berg wasn't sweating, shaking, or showing the slightest sign of stress. Why should he? He had just calmly presented a logical business request.

Fran's immediate reaction was anger. As he spoke she saw his lips move, but after a moment did not hear a word he said. Blood rage filled her ears. *How dare he come into my office and tell me how to run my bank*, she thought. Another betrayal. Another bastard.

As genteel as Berg's approach was and regardless of the guidelines he was suggesting, his was a lost cause. It was doomed from the first sentence. She thought he was insulting her and being mutinous. *At the request of the board*, she thought. Screw them. Screw all traitors. She viewed this visit as a declaration of his wanting to take over the bank. That was it. She knew it. He wanted to take over her bank. Fran's paranoid pathology took over. He had to go. The volcano was ready to erupt. Her ego was bruised by the perceived challenge. She held herself back from jumping from her chair and strangling Adam Berg on the spot.

Adam was reasonable and sincere, maybe naïve, but he wanted to help Fran get over a hump and get out of a bad place. He thought his approach might allow her to listen and become sensitive to his suggestions and understand that good business is good politics. Appeasement was the topic of the day. Make the board happy so they could convey confidence to their shareholders. Cut back on lavish catered luncheons, lease a less expensive car when the lease on the current car was up, lay off an employee or two who were ancillary to the operation of the bank. Show something to the board to prove she was stepping in the right direction. Put off the expansion idea for twelve months or so.

Fran saw only a traitor spewing out false advice so she would stumble and fall. He, the conquering hero, would then pick up the pieces and save the bank. Berg had no concept as to the depth of her paranoia or that he was signing his "death warrant" with Sunrise Bank and Fran Kontopolus. He was now an enemy, a person in her way. Sicilian mobsters had a phrase, *levarse na petra de la scarpa*, which means remove this stone from my shoe. Or, less poetically, kill that sumbitch before he testifies. Adam Berg had become just such a stone. He had no clue as to the plot that Fran was about to launch against him as he departed her office. He felt good about his honesty and willingness to help Fran through a difficult period.

Driving back to his office he called Rudman to report on the meeting with Fran. He described the points he had brought forth in the conversation and how he was hoping Fran would respond positively at the board meeting the following week with a plan to convey confidence to the board.

At the same time, Fran was in her office seething. She had stopped smoking two years earlier and for the first time in years she felt like puffing away a pack or two.

Berg was now in first place on the Fran Kontopolus enemies list, a list that was getting longer every day. The way her devious mind worked, Fran knew exactly what to do and how to do it within an amazingly short period of time.

Berg had brought his lawyer, Earl Lasman, in to Sunrise Bank as a board member and organizer. Lasman had been with Berg for ten years or so and had been brought in to Sunrise Bank because Berg had a generous heart and wanted his friends and close acquaintances to succeed. He shared opportunity and he felt that Lasman would be a good fit on the board. The lawyer handled real estate transactions and had a small law firm with attorneys in multi-transactional work. He had a good knowledge base and occasionally helped to raise money for investments. Berg did not know that Earl Lasman was loyal only to Earl Lasman.

Fran called Lasman to test him based on her knowledge of that loyalty. She had given business to him and knew that money talked louder than any other voice. She demanded he visit her at her office that evening after the bank closed. He eagerly agreed.

When he arrived, he found Fran with a chocolate cream pie on her desk. She had a tablespoon and was slowly eating the entire pie spoonful by spoonful. She looked as if she was planning something as she slowly devoured the pie. There was no joy in her face. Fran was eating her sorrow and feeding her anger.

"Earl, I had a visit from your client Adam Berg today and he was quite insulting." Lasman, who was a younger version of Max Rudman, was surprised. He waited to hear more so he could figure a profitable angle for himself in the situation. Fran went on, "He burst in here today and told me that if I did not do what he wanted he would take over the bank. He wants to be chairman of the board, Earl, I just know it, and he frightens me." With this statement Fran broke into the tears she was so famous for.

Lasman listened then asked, "What do you want me to do, Fran?"

"I demand an apology from Berg and a public one at that. Who does he think he is? I work here every night into the wee hours. I bust my butt every day to make Sunrise Bank successful and he wants to take it over. I want an apology." Fran knew that if he agreed to see Berg he was loyal to her. If not, he was to be cut off and added to the enemies list.

"Okay, Fran, I'll talk to Berg. Soon." He didn't say Adam on purpose. He was already distancing himself from his benefactor.

"No, go see him, face to face, and get him to apologize. Call him tonight!"

"I will, Fran, but I'll do it from my car. I need a few minutes to pull my words together."

"Thank you, Earl. Oh, by the way, the way we're growing we'll soon need additional attorneys with your firm's experience."

He felt the pendulum of loyalty swinging toward Fran and away from his friend. "Now that I think about it, that really is something Berg would say." The words never even got caught in his throat. They came out smooth and slick like shit through a goose.

"He said that and worse."

"The son of a bitch."

Fran got up to give Lasman a hug. As she approached him he felt repulsed, but he was as big a whore as anyone whose loyalty was to the almighty dollar. He had gotten many clients to invest in real estate deals over the years and many of his investments had gone south. Clients and friends lost money while he rode high and always came out ahead. Whether his clients won or lost, he earned money on the transactions. Lasman had stopped caring about people years earlier.

Lasman knew that Berg brought him to this party, but the fees he would earn from Sunrise Bank would exceed whatever a former friend could generate. He made it clear to friends that he liked the power of being a bank board member. That and the money-making opportunities were things he was unwilling to let go. He dreamed of becoming the chairman of the board some day and then the money would really start rolling in.

As she approached him, one of her heels did their thing and she almost fell on him. He caught her and tried to hug Fran in return, but his arms could not reach all the way around her.

Once in this BMW 700 he called Berg at home. "Adam, I need to see you tomorrow morning at your office. Can you meet me there at seven tomorrow? It's an emergency."

Berg asked, "What is it, Earl? Can we discuss this tonight? What's the emergency?"

Lasman responded that it was a matter involving the bank and that it was better to talk in person. With that, Berg agreed to meet him the next morning. Back in her office, Fran finished off the pie. For the first time since her meeting with Berg, she smiled.

CHAPTER FORTY

Lasman was not stupid. He knew that he had an opportunity to show his loyalty to Fran. By being her knave he could hope to prosper with the bank's money. What he did not know was the truth, nor did he care. *Let Kontopolus play her games,* he thought, *and I'll just let the money come my way.*

He arrived at Berg's real estate office promptly at 7:00 a.m. Berg wondered what was up as Lasman was rather private about the nature of the meeting. The lawyer sat down and Berg offered him some freshly brewed coffee. Lasman had a way about him that made one feel he was ready to exit as soon as he arrived. He refused the coffee. "Adam, I heard you visited Fran yesterday."

"That's right. Why do you ask?"

"Well, Fran was upset with your aggressive nature and the demands you made. She wants you to apologize to her publicly at the board meeting next week."

"What are you talking about?" Berg was more than a little confused. Lasman was speaking in the tone of a lawyer, not a friend.

"Look, Adam, I wasn't there, but Fran called me after you left. She was quite upset. She told me you were aggressive and made comments about wanting to control the bank. Whatever you said upset her and she wants you to apologize. You can't treat the president of a Chicago bank that way."

"Earl, Max Rudman called me last Saturday and told me of his concerns about the financial and strategic plan for the bank or, rather, the lack of one. We spoke for a couple of hours. I took notes. He asked that I, on behalf of him as chairman of the board and for the shareholders alike, speak to her about the turn-around time for loans and the excessive spending and growth plans for the bank. I simply addressed shareholder and board member concerns. I really don't know what you're talking about 'my taking over the bank.' You know me better than that."

"Look, Adam, Fran works her tail off at the bank. She was quite upset with what you said," Lasman repeated himself. "She wants you to apologize to her. Publicly."

"Apologize about what?" Berg was duly confused.

"Apologize about what you said."

"Earl, I said nothing that requires an apology, believe me. Nothing at all. I told her what Rudman wanted me to tell her about the financial concerns of the board. You know what I'm talking about; you've been to every meeting. You've expressed your concerns too."

"That's a separate matter, Adam. You need to realize what you've done and make amends."

All of a sudden it hit him. In his attempt to appear neutral, Lasman was showing his hand. Whatever Fran's game might be he was a part of it. Berg realized that he should have had someone with him as a witness. He should have never entered her office alone. He had been set up by Rudman to be his fall guy. There was more at work here than met the eye. He felt foolish and betrayed. He had a bad feeling in the pit of his stomach.

"Look, Earl, you've known me for quite some time, does this sound like something I would say to Fran?"

"Adam, just apologize to her and settle this matter."

"Earl, I don't even know what I'd be apologizing about since none of what you're saying is true. Should I say I'm sorry for being honest with her about the thoughts and concerns of the board?"

Lasman did not care. He wanted to be somewhere else anyway. Often in the mornings before he arrived at his office, he was at the health club on the stair-step machine flirting with some young female attorney, accountant, or real estate professional. Although his skin was gray, his breasts sagging, and his baldness unbecoming, he thought he was a hunk.

"Okay, whatever you do is up to you," Lasman said as he pushed his chair back and headed toward the door. Moments later he called Fran on her cell phone as he drove to the health club.

Fran, asleep in her bed, had her cell phone on her nightstand. The phone rang a few times. This brought her to consciousness from her Ambien-induced sleep. As she began to say hello, some mucus got caught in her throat. Her throat clearing was deafening. "Ma, is that you?"

"No, Fran, this is Earl, Earl Lasman."

"Did you see that son of a bitch?"

"Yes, Fran, I just left his office."

"When is he going to apologize? I want him to crawl."

"Well, he's being difficult and I don't see an apology forthcoming. In fact, I'm concerned." Lasman liked to use the word "concerned" when he needed to get someone to jump to. And he knew that he could fire up Fran with it. "Seriously, Fran, I'm concerned."

"What? That's it. He is off the board," screamed Fran.

"Fran, you can't take a board member off the board like that. There are procedures."

"He's off," said Fran. "He's off-my-damn-board." She slammed her phone closed.

CHAPTER
FORTY-ONE

One Saturday morning Fran called Sonny to get together. He suggested a café she had not visited before. In fact, it was not a place she would have considered at all. She was not a small, quaint café type person. Café De Marco was a Wicker Park street front coffee house with a light menu. Fran would have preferred the café at the Four Seasons, not a colorful, artistic place filled with families with little kids ordering pancakes with chocolate sprinkles. She arrived before Sonny and seated herself in the back of the café as he had directed.

She was sitting next to a family of four, a young yuppie couple with a six-year-old girl and four-year-old boy. The parents were wearing loose sweats and sweaters. They chatted on and on about little league, the church youth choir, what to do on the weekend, and other inane topics. The little boy was eating bits of fruit with his fingers. The noise of the coffee grinder making a loud noise as it ground the blend of the day beans annoyed her as much as the brats.

At another table nearby a family was speaking just as loudly. Fran looked around and waited. She felt out of place. She was made up in her traditional black knit Chanel Lane Bryant variety of dress. The families were thin and wearing casual and workout clothing. She glanced at the table next to her once again. She could tell by the accent that the father was German. For a moment she thought back to her days at State Bank of the Community. The Ravenswood neighborhood in the 1960s had many families from Germany. This was the first time in many years that she had seen a young German man with an American wife and two kids *"sprechen sie Deutsch."*

This struck her. She was getting annoyed again as she overheard German being spoken. It reminded her of Eberstark. In fact, everything in this café was distracting and annoying. She looked around with disgust. The high ceiling, concrete floors, the artwork by talentless local artisans, the families and their chatter, the casual clothing and no makeup look of the women made her want to rush to the nearest upscale restaurant. But this is where Sonny wanted to meet and Sonny knew what he was doing.

As she watched the little girl share an order of pancakes with her mother, who was likely a size six, Fran's mouth watered. The waiter approached. He was a six-foot-tall, slim, twenty-something with a day's growth of beard and a long nose. He was wearing all black. When he stopped at her table, he shook his head to fling his long, greasy hair away from his face. "Can I take your drink order," he asked in a low, passive tone. Fran ordered a decaf cappuccino with extra whipped cream.

When he delivered the cappuccino he asked if she would like to order breakfast. Fran could hardly contain herself. "A double order of those pancakes with extra butter." She pointed to the nearest table. The waiter took one look at this overly made-up woman, who was squeezed into her dress as tightly as she was wedged into the corner booth and decided not to question this unusual request. As he walked away to place the order with the kitchen, Fran noticed Sonny entering the shop.

He walked toward her, a smile of satisfaction on his face. He said hello to the cashier and nodded to a waiter with a motion that was clear he would order his "regular." The weather had turned cool earlier that week as Halloween was just a few days away. Sonny wore an expensive sweater with a mustard-colored cashmere scarf around his neck. He unwrapped his scarf as he approached.

Sonny chuckled to himself as he thought about how out of place Fran looked in this environment. To contain his giggling he tried to mask it with a cough. He looked at her grotesque makeup and thought that a better fit for her this Saturday morning would have been a fright fest. She was certainly a freak in this bohemian café, where most of the women were thin, naturally gray, and dining on fruit and oatmeal. As he sat down, the single woman at the next table ordered jasmine tea.

"Hello, Fran. I love this place, reminds me of when I was younger." She looked around with a frown. She still didn't get it. This was no place for power players.

"What's so urgent that you needed to see me on a Saturday?" Sonny asked.

As he finished his question, Fran's order of pancakes was placed in front of her. When the waiter turned to walk away, Fran shouted, "Where is my syrup?" A silence hung over the restaurant for an instant. The customers were in shock. The waiter took two steps and reached to a station with syrup, honey, and cinnamon on small trays. He picked up a tray and brought it to Fran.

"I'm sorry, ma'am, but I usually deliver the tray of condiments after the breakfast dish." He gently placed the tray down on the table. Fran was silent as he walked away. She picked up the small traditional syrup pitcher and emptied all of it on her pancakes. "Prick." She purposely spoke loud enough for nearby tables to hear her. The noise level in the restaurant returned to normal. Fran cut into the double stack of pancakes and stuffed a dripping forkful into her mouth.

Sonny repeated, "What's so urgent that you needed to see me on a Saturday?"

Fran swallowed and told him her version of the meeting with Berg and his desire to take over the bank. Sonny just listened as she droned on and on. Sonny liked this. He liked it a lot. This was not the first time in his life when a party he was in business with complained about another partner in the deal. Sonny looked on her distress as a gift. He knew that when a management partner came to him for advice it gave him an excellent chance to increase his interest in the entity. Sonny had always been good at feigning empathy and Fran had handed him just such an opportunity on a golden platter. When Fran ran out of steam and it appeared as if she was finished with her story, Sonny sipped his coffee while looking around the café. He allowed for some silence before speaking.

"Fran, dear. I've known you for many years and I know how hard you worked on starting this bank. This is a tribute to your late father and you don't want anything to stand in your way or threaten your position." Sonny knew exactly what to mirror back to Fran to get her attention. She ate it up. "You have to wait until Berg's board term is over before you displace him. He's quite popular with the other members."

She rapped her fork against the plate. Butter and syrup spilled onto the table. "Adam Berg will never voluntarily step down." She used the fork to scoop up the goo on the table and dollop it back onto her pancakes. Sonny wanted to gag.

"No, he won't," said Sonny. "But I have a suggestion that I've used in other situations like this."

Sonny explained his plan to Fran under the noisy din of the restaurant. A smile came over her face as he told her what could be done to accomplish her objective. In closing he said, "Now, Fran, you must remember two important things. First, you must never share this conversation or even that we had it with anyone. Because if this leaks out it will undermine our objective. Second, be patient. Berg's term doesn't expire for a while. So just wait it out. His time will come."

"I knew I could count on you. Sonny, thank you, thank you!" She sighed with relief. He leaned forward and spoke softly. "Now, Fran, I need to talk to you about a loan for a friend. He's acquiring some land in Erie, Illinois, to build town homes and he's a nice guy. I need you to relieve him of a collateral obligation and loan him one hundred percent of the acquisition price and construction costs."

"No problem. Have him call me Monday morning and I'll get it done quickly."

Sonny just smiled to himself as he knew his plan was beginning to unfold better than he could have directed it himself.

CHAPTER FORTY-TWO

The bank was concluding its second year and preparation for the annual shareholder meeting was underway. The fiscal year concluded at year-end. The by-laws of the bank required the annual shareholder meeting take place no later than the second quarter of the following year. Thus the meeting should have been concluded no later than June 30. Fran did all she could to delay that meeting. What should have taken place in June was scheduled for December. Fran delayed everything she could knowing that Rudman and the board would not put any pressure on her to adhere to the by-laws.

Knowing that the expenses for the preceding year exceeded the budget approved by the board, Fran was in no hurry to expose anything to the shareholders. They continually voiced concern with the progress of the bank's profitability and Fran's ability to build and maintain a stable institution. Her history as a real estate lender was solid, but her delays and lack of attention to customers was common talk in real estate circles. She knew she would face confrontation and dissent at the shareholder meeting. She did not want a large attendance.

By creating and maintaining a delay, she could push the annual shareholder meeting back to year-end and count on two things in December. First, shareholders would be caught up in holiday planning and travel and, second, the board's compensation committee would have to approve raises and bonuses before the 31st of December. As she was "an employee" they would have no choice other than to approve her bonus and raise as part of regular year-end business. There was no time for thoughtful review performance by members of the board.

Low attendance and a tight deadline practically guaranteed her goal. Also, two directors were retiring and leaving the board, Max Rudman and Benny Balt. Though Rudman originally had a three-year term as chairman, Fran's pressure persuaded him to leave one year early. She started in on him six months after the bank opened. She would nudge him when she had him alone, telling him he was too old to be knowledgeable about current banking trends and informed him that at the end of his term he would not be re-elected so he should plan on leaving.

Max didn't need this intimidation. His wife, Blanche, wanted him out of the bank too. The calls at home, the pressure, and most of all Fran's boorish behavior were too much for a sick man. "Take the gold watch, Max, and forget about it," Blanche said. "Who needs this woman? This shtick?"

He knew the true colors of Fran Kontopolus and knew his wife was right. Max was not getting younger and his health was suffering. He had served two years as chairman of the board and could add this item to his final resume. But he had to be alive to enjoy those perks.

Fran was now in a position to replace two of the organizers. Approval of their replacements would take place at the shareholder meeting. A transition had to be seamless. Fran thought this might be her chance to become the chairman of the board. Becoming chairman and CEO of the bank was her goal. But when she discussed this with Sonny and Belker, in separate conversations, of course, she was advised by both that she would lose her challenge and thus lose power and creditability.

"Be patient, Fran," Sonny said. "Be patient. You have your entire life ahead of you. Stabilize the bank and get through the next year. Take it one step at a time. You will be chairman soon enough."

At eighty, Benny Balt was the oldest member of the board. The father of a shareholder, he had lived an active corporate life in his younger days. Balt had worked for multi-national corporations. He had spent his life traveling the world. He was asked to join the bank board in organization not simply for his credentials and resume. He was asked to join the board as an honor to his son, who in turn would see this as a compliment, invest in the bank, and bring other investors with him.

Balt was a perfect fit for Fran. He was silent or sleeping at board meetings, taking a passive seat on committees in which he did not actively participate. He was a frictionless board member who never opposed Fran, always voted with her, and received his lunch and monthly board stipend. His showing signs of senility worked in Fran's favor.

In planning for the annual shareholder meeting, Fran was looking forward to having a new chairman. When the board of directors had their monthly meeting in October, Max and Benny made their retirement announcements. This gave the board two months to fill their positions. The board put in the form of a motion that special recognition be made at the shareholder meeting thanking them both for their leadership and dedication.

Fran suggested that the board replace the two vacant seats with four new board members. The suggestion of adding more board members started an animated discussion that upset Fran. She wanted a larger majority in her favor with more rubber stamps. She recommended friends and family, but the board voted to substitute only those seats vacating. They insisted that she suggest potential board members who had a background in banking. They all agreed that more banking experience was needed in the leadership of Sunrise Bank. Before the seats could be filled, the current board of directors had to ratify the nominees who would then be voted on at the shareholder meeting. Fran was furious when the meeting was concluded and her recommendation was defeated. She considered the action an insult and a betrayal.

In her office that evening she got on the phone with Sonny. He suggested she contact a friend of his, a retired banker, someone Sonny knew would fall into his camp.

Mit Deerfield was the perfect candidate. The board could not help but approve his nomination. A tall, refined, handsome sixty-year-old man, Deerfield had a thirty-five-year career in banking. He was knowledgeable, experienced, and had a solid reputation. His background was in commercial lending, which is what the bank lacked. He was a young sixty and would have likely still have been working but the bank he was with his entire career had been sold, so he took early retirement.

Sonny's wife had a gay cousin who had worked in banking his entire career as well. He suggested Fran call Jerry Hunting. He would be a loyal board member too. Sonny called both to inform them that Fran would be calling. When she spoke to them, they were happy to be considered as board members. Fran had her replacements.

The next morning a limousine picked up both men and brought them to the bank to meet Fran. A lunch was ordered and brought into the boardroom for a meeting.

Both dressed as bankers dress, dark suits, starched white shirts, and red ties. Both had folded white kerchiefs inserted into their breast pockets. At the meeting Fran discussed the men's backgrounds and experience. She had had her secretary Google both men so she had some material to refer to. Fran did not hold back her expectation of them as board members. She clearly stated her goals. Convinced that they were on *her* team she thanked them for coming and the limousine took them home. When they departed, Fran called Rudman to report her suggestion for his and Balt's replacement. Max had no fight remaining and really couldn't care less, so he agreed to give Fran his vote. She knew she had Balt's vote. These two nominees would elevate the level of bank experience and would easily be added to the board.

Within an hour Fran had called all members of her boards to support the two replacement board members. An e-mail went out to all members that a conference call would be conducted the following day at noon to discuss the replacement of the vacated board seats. Fran addressed the bank's weakness in commercial lending in a surprisingly humble way. She then told the story of finding two experienced retired bankers with this area of expertise.

At the November board meeting the new potential members were introduced, questions were asked of them, and resumes were distributed. After the brief questioning, like clockwork, Sonny Jr. made a motion to nominate both men. Pischer made a second to the motion and a vote took place. The ayes had it and the decision was rallied through. Fran was happy. Two more votes at her direction.

In December, the shareholder meeting went as planned. Fran enjoyed a low attendance, absentee proxies in her possession and in her favor, and no controversy about the bank operating in the red. Immediately after the shareholders' meeting a board meeting took place as it was the final meeting of the year. Lunch was served. Fran ordered roast turkey with all the trimmings for this festive holiday/year end meeting. Compensation was the key issue and Fran wanted a super-sized bonus and raise.

The first order of business was to elect a new bank board and holding company chairman. Nominations came forth. Fran still wanted this position for herself and took the floor of the meeting to express to everyone that she would be the best person for the job. The board would not hear of it. She had taken too big a step. Her new members were not going to do much more than sit quietly and watch as this discussion unfolded. Stephen Drury was recognized as the most qualified and respected board member. Berg spoke on his behalf. Drury was nominated and elected.

Drury, an organizer of the bank, was an attorney and businessman. He was always well-prepared and addressed issues thoroughly and thoughtfully. After the vote, it was time for compensation to be addressed. The two new members were lacking experience to oppose Fran's suggestions; the new chairman was basking in his glory and could only be a swing vote in case of a tie. Fran presented a generous compensation package, which included a large raise for her and a bonus equal to 25 percent of her salary. Although discussion ensued, the motion to accept Fran's compensation package was passed.

Fran was leaving for her annual winter vacation; her business was completed for the year. Leaving the bank that evening her ego was as swollen as her ankles after a cocktail fundraiser. She felt satiated.

CHAPTER FORTY-THREE

Sonny received a call from Fran shortly after the board meeting. His plan was in the works. Two more members on the board loyal to him had just been appointed and they would help keep that plan on the fast track. It was Thursday and Sonny had a Thursday afternoon ritual. He hung up with Fran and opened his phone to make another call. The number was nine on his speed dial. The phone rang twice and a woman answered.

"Yes, of course, Sonny. She is at the usual place," responded the familiar voice with the Asian accent. Sonny had made this call hundreds of times over the years. This part of his life was private and kept from even his most trusted confidants. This was the avenue where he sought and found solitude and pleasure. He could be anonymous, and by being anonymous, he could be himself. The private get-togethers in a Gold Coast apartment were like going to a therapist. Like so many men, he wanted to unload with a beautiful, young, seductive woman who would physically nurture him for an hour or two each week. A rubdown with a happy ending always topped off the experience.

He parked his car four blocks away, across from a church, and walked to the multi-unit apartment building. He owned the building in one of his many partnerships. There was no doorman, just a buzzer system. He knew the code on the entry system and entered the sequence of numbers. He never thought of the thousands of dollars he spent for this service, but it was less than he paid his lawyers who still fucked him but never kissed or nurtured him.

He rode the elevator to the studio apartment. There was a lake view from the window. He could now gloat over how his master plan was unfolding so well and so quickly. He felt good, very good about himself. He saw the path ahead clearly, as though it was a winding roadway through a dense forest. He knew where the road would inevitably end, but he did not quite know the twists and turns to be negotiated getting to the end. Being patient always got Sonny what he wanted and he wasn't about to rush things at this stage.

When he entered the apartment, an Asian girl answered. He had seen her before. They embraced and he pulled two crisp one hundred dollar bills from his pocket. He then placed them on the entry table.

The shower was running and she took his sport coat, shirt, and slacks. Sonny liked a hot shower before being bedded down and serviced for the afternoon. He neatly folded his socks and underwear and placed them near a space heater to keep them crispy and warm. He gave the Asian a kiss on the cheek and she returned the affection with a soft pat on his ass.

He stepped into the shower and the warm water felt good running through his hair, on his face and back. He cleansed himself before the act. The girl was younger than his daughter-in-law, pretty, and well shaven. His relationship with his wife of thirty-eight years had diminished to going places together and dining out, but intimacy had vanished. Intimacy with affection anyway.

So Sonny looked forward to his Gold Coast haven as his reward for deceit and corruption. That day's visit was to celebrate installing his people onto the board of Sunrise Bank. Both men owed him favors, many favors, and they would continue to owe him. Sonny chuckled out loud as he thought about how clever he was. "Are you ready, Hon?" asked the voice of the young angel who would bring him to heaven within the next hour.

"I'm on my way out now. Can you make some tea and bring out your best massage oils?"

Sonny dried himself and slid into her bed. He liked the satin sheets. He didn't know if his hard on was for the excitement of the deal or the excitement he was anticipating with Angel.

CHAPTER FORTY-FOUR

Throughout the next twelve months, Fran maintained a free rein. The bank operated on a few levels. The first included Fran's disclosing to the board the business at hand before or while it was taking place. The second was telling them after the fact. She knew that new board members sat quietly for at least six months getting the hang of what was going on before they became vocal.

The third level was arrogance. Fran played favorites with customers that Sonny or Sonny and company sent to the bank. She did not always do what was healthy for the bank and good customers suffered. Sonny had many friends who wanted to emulate his success. His agenda was not so much to get these people the money to be successful, but to the contrary, his eyes were always on his success. He knew what they did not know. Simply getting the money for a deal was not an automatic road to success. He wanted to see their projects explode in the Chicago minefield of real estate development. After an explosion, somebody had to pick up the pieces, at bargain prices, and turn failure into financial success.

A failed investor sitting on the sidelines was not a competitor. A building developer who borrowed money at interest rates that were too high, or who over-leveraged the development and the equity in his home, was not a competitor. A builder with no experience in how to get permits out of city hall was heading toward doomsday. The more people

Sonny assisted in failing, the more deals would come his way. So it was important to false mentor these wannabe builders and wait until they were unable to repay their loans. He never cared how this would impact Sunrise Bank.

Fran made the loans quickly and with seamless approval because Sonny wanted them funded. And she could justify a request for a higher bonus due to her increased loan volume. The conventional system of appraisals and verifications was compromised for expediency for this select group of customers.

"Ms. Kontopolus, this loan package looks shaky."

"Sonny Vulich never made a shaky deal in his life. If he says this deal is sound, it's sound. Pass it along. Now!"

If an appraisal came through on the low side after the loan was made, Fran directed bank personnel to back date the appraisal and inflate the numbers. When a loan committee meeting prior to a board of directors meeting was conducted, Fran would explain that there was urgency and these loans had to be approved quickly so the borrower would not lose the deal and the bank suffer the loss of a loan and perhaps a valued customer.

She would shortcut the approval presentation for the board. And the board, seeing that the loan was approved and funded, had no ability to take it back. The common thinking was that Fran was a good lender and that she knew what she was doing. Sonny's name was the referral source, but his influence on making the loan was never disclosed to the board. Not much changed as conventional borrowers waited and waited for their loans to be approved.

Throughout the year, more and more letters of complaint from customers and potential customers found their way to all members of the holding company and bank board. Board members had directed clients and friends to the bank to get loans and many were simply left waiting in the wings after filling out a loan application and advancing money for application fees. A real estate loan should have taken no longer than sixty days, and when a property was under contract to close, customers expected that the sixty-day time frame, as industry standard, would be complied with.

This was not the case for those coming through the "front door" of the bank. Conventionally, banks turn around loans in sixty days. The process became bottlenecked at Sunrise Bank. It wasn't because the bank was so busy with a volume of loans, but because Fran required reading and reviewing each and every detail of each and every loan herself.

Sonny's loans and those he recommended were quickly approved, but loans for others took forever. Many took their loan application and appraisals and moved on to other banks. These people pulled their deposits with them. Within the first few years of the bank, the makeup changed. The customer base was no longer representative of the diversity of the community. It was now Sonny and his friends who made up the largest percentage of borrowers and depositors.

Board members viewed this as extremely risky. If Sonny pulled out of the bank, tens of millions of deposits would leave too. The profitability would diminish. If any of his projects or the projects of his disciples developed problems with repayment of the loans, a severe domino effect would be devastating. Sonny knew that when you owe the bank $100, the bank owns you. When you owe the bank $100 million you own the bank. The same lip service Fran gave to discussions of adding a female banker to her board was how she addressed the concentration of loans. "I'm working on it. Everything is okay. Don't worry." Seasoned board members knew "it" was never going to happen and they did worry.

Stephen Drury, the current board chairman, decided that it would be wise to bring a consultant in to advise on the future profitability of the bank and to help devise a strategic plan. Ron Muck was a banking consultant from New England. He owned a bank in Vermont and his business was buying and selling banks. His goal was to take banks public and to create liquidity, thus making his investors money. He was an expert in making banks profitable and increasing shareholder value.

Muck stood five feet two inches tall, wore a thick handlebar mustache, and dressed in, of all things, Western attire. When the board arrived on a Wednesday morning to spend a day with this banking expert they were first surprised by his appearance. A little man with a hearty handshake and bravado in his voice met them as they entered the bank's conference room. Somebody whispered a joke about "time to cowboy up." Nobody laughed.

Muck was organized and presented his strategy on profitability in a professional, experienced way using Power Point and the support of his material data in a notebook for each board member. By the end of the day, and after many questions, the board felt enlightened. He taught them many things that they had wanted to learn about creating value, long-term planning, and profitability. Drury was quite pleased with this initial stage of launching a strategic plan.

The day ended with the board members thinking for the first time about their obligation to the shareholders and themselves. Fran was noticeably upset.

CHAPTER
FORTY-FIVE

S onny often recalled memories of his late grandfather, his advice, and suggestions about life. The old man had spoken to him as a mentor when Sonny was young. He recalled his soft, raspy voice as he would speak in tones almost like a whisper. "Sonny, never get tempted by money. Money will destroy a man's ability to think clearly. It will sway an honest man and bring out the worst in him."

Sonny's grandfather saw many people become corrupt through the love of money. In fact, Chicago was well known for outward displays of corruption. As an immigrant in Hegewisch, old man Vulich saw a lot of people receive a few bucks from politicians before Election Day, sell their votes to the precinct captains and ward bosses, and compromise their beliefs as if they were just a whim. He saw money swapping hands inside the house of God, while good people just looked the other way. He saw people who did not need money, but who simply could not get enough of it take advantage of their workers, the needy, and even members of their own community by lining their pockets with substandard business practices. The Bible speaks of selling one's birthright. Money has led men from their moral and philosophic standards from the beginning of time. Sonny remembered his grandfather's warning.

But his grandfather's words were more than a warning to Sonny. They were advice, the best advice he ever received. Words are always subject to interpretation and what Sonny gleaned from his grandfather's words was simple and true. "Sonny, if you ever want to buy a man's loyalty, give him money." Sonny lived by this creed. He could identify a greedy man miles away. Earl Lasman was this kind of man. Lasman, of course, was a lawyer. As a young man he worked for a mid-sized firm and began to specialize in estate and tax planning. His law practice, as many law practices do, included real estate closings and real estate work. At the advice of a senior partner at his firm, Lasman went to night school to get his CPA. As both an accountant and a lawyer he could bill at a higher rate and act as an expert in tax matters.

Lasman read of an opportunity to purchase a law franchise that offered legal work to low-income people through an annual membership fee. The deal was that employers could offer employees, union members or not, legal benefits by including a membership as a benefit in their compensation package. A sales team would approach school boards, the hotel workers union, large companies such as Wal-Mart, and so on selling multiple memberships to employers to add to employee benefit packages. The purchase was made and the sales generated big fees to Lasman's firm.

Lasman hired a pool of young novice lawyers who would answer the phones, prepare wills and real estate contracts, or appear in court for traffic tickets and handle other minor, standard tasks. This created a nice cash flow. When he set up his firm, he solicited clients who had estate and tax planning needs. Having read Shakespeare as a student he knew that "a fool and his money were soon parted." And as a young attorney and investor himself, he could persuade his clients to invest in many real estate deals he syndicated. He found lots of fools.

In these deals, the syndicator would receive fees for putting the deal together, fees for his legal work, and monthly management fees. This formula would take money off the top for Lasman. As an example: when $1 million was required for a deal, $50,000 to $100,000 would disappear in the form of the fees, leaving $900,000 for actual investment. When a property did well and earned a profit, five or ten years after the initial capital contribution, the investors were happy. When a property lost money and the investors took a loss, this was used as a tax write-off against their other income. The investors' accountant, Lasman, justified the loss by saying, "Why pay more taxes? Take the loss."

Regardless of the fortunes of his investors and clients, Lasman always made money. A look in his eye revealed that he knew a deal might not have been good from the start. He was careful to make sure his clients always read the prospectus and signed the page that verified they knew that a loss of their original principal was possible.

Sonny could tell Lasman surpassed Fran when it came to greed. Lasman could never get enough money for himself. His long list of unhappy clients was no secret, but they signed off on the documents, meaning they knew or should have known what they were getting into, so he didn't care.

Sonny became the largest single depositor at Sunrise Bank. As a bank board member, Lasman read the deposit reports each month. He was green with envy as he watched Sonny's money grow and grow. As interest rates increased, Sonny rolled his millions into high yield deposits per his agreement with Fran. As interest rates rose, Fran never objected or charged Sonny a fee to break a CD prematurely to roll his money into a higher yielding vehicle.

Sonny wanted Lasman, his greed, and his easy manipulation in his camp. Slowly he began to refer real estate closings to the man's office. Like feeding a hungry animal, Sonny was creating loyalty and need. He was careful not to use Lasman for his personal business. But when Sonny built a town home complex or high-rise condominium building he would call Lasman and let him know that a percentage of the purchasers would be referred to his office as the firm recommended by the developer. This meant Lasman added many transactions to his bottom line each year.

Lasman liked Sonny, especially Sonny's money and connections, and Sonny noticed how Lasman would hop to when he called his office. *Another pawn, another sap,* Sonny would think to himself.

Then it happened. Sonny had an invitation hand-delivered to Lasman's office inviting him to a new investors meeting for a condominium development overlooking Chicago's lakefront. Sonny was looking to raise money for a new project and knew that the lawyer would jump at the opportunity to be a first-tier investor in a Sonny Vulich deal.

The first-tier investors would receive a higher return on their money and be guaranteed a preferred payback when the deal was done. Lasman wanted to be included, but he almost started salivating when he learned how the deal would get better. After the multimedia presentation, the cocktails, and hors d'oeuvres, Sonny sat down with him and offered him an even better opportunity. Lasman would not have to invest a dime.

He could give Sonny a promissory note for his investment, no cash, just the note. With that he could purchase five condominiums. He would sign five pre-sale contracts for condominiums committing to purchase five pre-constructed units, and then he could resell or flip these units once the project was built.

Lasman was thrilled at this opportunity. He figured that he could flip the units for a minimal profit of $50,000 per unit when the project was completed in twenty-four to thirty-six months. That would be a cool $250,000. Sonny told Lasman that this was a confidential transaction and that he was not to breathe a word of this to anyone. He agreed as his loyalty was to the almighty dollar and now a major source of those dollars, Sonny Vulich.

Lasman had love in his heart for Sonny. He no longer had loyalty to Adam Berg who was responsible for getting him involved with the bank. He forgot that he would have never met Sonny and would not have had this opportunity if not for Berg. The next day the note and documents were delivered to Lasman's office and he did not miss a beat. He signed everything and returned the papers to Sonny's office by personal delivery.

Lasman decided to send Fran a box of Godiva chocolates. Fran called to thank Lasman and asked him why he sent the candy. He replied, "Fran, next to my wife, you are the girl of my dreams."

Sonny had Lasman, all right. And from this interaction forward, Lasman was always at Sonny's service.

CHAPTER
FORTY-SIX

Lincoln Road in South Beach Miami was the perfect location for Adam Berg to escape his business on this, the last Friday of the year. He was vacationing with his family and he was seeking a little peace and quiet from the storms of Lake Michigan and the even more blustery storms of Fran Kontopolus. He usually was the first to wake. As a younger man, as a runner, he would jog the area in which he was staying, finding shops and restaurants to visit later that day.

Berg had not run for many years. He exercised each day, but running was simply too uncomfortable. A line from an old, old rock n' roll hit kept rotating through his mind whenever he glanced at his old jogging shoes. "You're not a kid anymore." His hotel was just a ten-minute drive from South Beach. At the corner of Lincoln Road and Jefferson he found the Van Dyke Café, a perfect place to sit, read the paper, and drink too much coffee while waiting for the call from his wife that his family was awake and ready for the day.

He parked his rented car at Michigan and Lincoln roads, deposited his credit card in a parking machine, and purchased a two-hour ticket to place on the dashboard. As he walked east on Lincoln Road he was drowned in the loud noise of the leaf blowers used by cleanup crews as cafés and shops were preparing for the day.

Blowing dust and debris and leaves from one place to another could be fun, he thought. The blower was a cool adult toy. It simply moved

187

crap from one man's property to another. He found a highboy cocktail table to sit at as he opened his newspaper and set his cell phone down. As he looked up, he could see the staff of the many cafés wiping tables and pouring coffee to the sparse number of customers at 7:30 a.m. He liked it this way. He knew that in the next hour or so hundreds more would mosey from their posh hotels, the Delano, the Sagamore, the Ritz, and the Loews, to Lincoln Road and fill the bistro marble tables. For now, the place was pretty much his own.

As he settled into his comfort zone and ordered his first cup of Java, Berg looked right to see a bicycle ridden by a fifty-something man with a rooster on the handlebars. Yes, in addition to the tourists, the locals would be out soon too. This group would likely drink the coffee at the coffee houses just off Lincoln Road where a bagel was round and meaty and coffee was not $3 a cup.

A FedEx package was part of his reading material for the morning. In the package was the holding company board book, which was sent to board members in advance so they could prepare for the January meeting the following week. Adam was concerned. He knew the economy was weakening. He was a student of economic trends and had been for years. Yes, even he had to admit to himself that he was old enough to have lived though many cycles of the economy. He could see history repeating itself. He sipped his coffee and watched the dog walkers as they marched along with their pairs of dogs, then he opened the package. The notebook was the traditional blue cover with *Board Book, Meeting January 5, 2008, Sunrise Bank* on the cover.

He skimmed the minutes of the last meeting and the agenda for the next. He wanted to read the reports that listed the loans and delinquency history for loans that were giving the bank trouble. In other words, loans that were paying late or not paying at all. The list had expanded over the past quarter. Money had gone out and money was not coming back. These were the loans Fran had pushed though the loan committee on the bank board level, of which he was not a member. They did not seem to be as good as she had represented to the holding company.

As tables filled with young couples and single older men, Berg read the list. A loan in Bridgeview, Illinois, for vacant land for commercial development made three years ago, $2 million outstanding. A vintage apartment building in East Rogers Park, thirty-two units for rehab delayed in construction and over budget, no pre-sales, and $2,215,000 outstanding. Five lots in the Lakeview neighborhood with two $2 million single-family homes constructed on two of the lots, but no sales, over budget, requesting additional time and money, $3 million outstanding. This loan had been made four years earlier with no equity other than the land.

As he read the names of the borrowers, they sounded familiar. He could replay in his mind the familiar ring of Fran's high-pitched voice at board meetings swearing up and down that these were old customers she had made loans to many times over the years. "And they are good loans, great loans for Sunrise Bank," she had said. The list included others. It was broken down to show delinquencies, their length of delinquency, and a watch list of loans that looked as if they were going south.

For some time Berg had been afraid of this. He felt in his bones that this was the downward path the bank would follow with the selective liberal lending that Fran covertly and overtly pushed through. He had never liked the way her compensation package was based on future earnings and loan origination. Now that the bank had a board chairman entering his second year, he hoped things would change. He knew all board members would be reading this package before the next meeting and was hoping the new chairman would call an independent directors meeting before the meeting to set forth his plan for the new year.

As he completed reading the package, his cell phone rang. It was his wife. *Time to get back to the hotel and have breakfast with my family,* he thought. He paid his bill and walked back to the car. Later that day an e-mail arrived. All board members received the same notice. An independent directors meeting was being called for January 4, the day before the formal board meeting. The subject line in the e-mail read URGENT! The sender was the chairman of the board, Stephen Drury.

CHAPTER
FORTY-SEVEN

S tephen Drury, chairman of the board of Sunrise Bank, was an extremely bright man. Many theorized he never slept. He was active in every endeavor he undertook. The son of Russian immigrants, he was taught to study, learn well, and apply what he learned. His father operated a small dry goods business in the Albany Park neighborhood of Chicago. He was a good provider to his family of both money and education.

"An education is something nobody can take from you," he often said. Drury respected and listened to his father and after college graduated with honors from law school. With law as a background, he became involved in many successful business ventures. When he was chosen as chairman of the board of Sunrise Bank, Drury had a long resume including real estate development and investment, health care, entertainment, manufacturing, and financial trading. He was always over prepared. Drury studied and researched every project he got involved in and this assignment was no different. From the moment of his election as chairman, he began reading and researching community banks and banking. He studied every document he could get his hands on regarding Sunrise Bank.

During his first year as chairman, Drury did more than just read everything he could about running a bank. He consulted with experts and attended classes and seminars. He had to be prepared, ready, and willing to take action. This was his nature. He discovered that successful banks conducted independent director meetings for their board without management present. That way, honest opinions of management could be discussed without fear of embarrassing someone or, more likely, facing retribution.

The first independent directors meeting of Sunrise Bank was called to order. Drury distributed the notebooks he had prepared. Inside was statistical information showing averages and information common to community banks. The information included average deposit size, number of employees, salary ranges, loan volume, loans broken out by type of loan and radius to the institution. It included norms in advertising spending, rent, cost of furniture fixtures and equipment, profit per employee, profit per depositor, profit percentage per gross deposit, volume of demand deposits vs. CD deposits and other yielding investments. Loan loss reserves were included and average compensation of executive officers and directors compensation. The board had never seen anything quite like it.

As the board members began reading through the notebooks, mild panic set it. Drury was serious. This was real business. Drury began the meeting. "Gentlemen, as you can see I have spent the last few weeks gathering information for your review. I take my election as chairman quite seriously. I know the investors I brought to Sunrise Bank and the investors you brought take their investment seriously. I want to know, as I am sure you do, how we should be performing compared to our peer group.

"You have more material in front of you than we can review and digest in one meeting, and for the sake of all of our time I am going to keep this meeting short. I just want to point out to you certain highlights that you need to know as we enter this new year and a new year of fiscal responsibility. This package of information compares our bank to banks in our geographic region, our deposit size, and our age. We are a community bank of approximately $300 million in deposits. We are not yet five years old and have fewer than five branches. This is our peer group."

He continued, "As you read though the book, you will see our bank exceeds the norm. We exceed the norm in overhead, number of employees, executive compensation, and ratio of real estate to commercial business lending. Our profit to earnings ratio is at the low end of the spectrum. Our CD deposits, those we pay interest on, far exceed our demand deposits, those we do not pay interest on. Our executive officer compensation is actually the highest for our size bank.

"I want you to know that my job as chairman is to keep you informed and help our shareholders see the value of their stock increase. We have some modifications to address to achieve the value our shareholders expect and that we owe them."

A discussion ensued with board members asking questions and stating their individual observations. Points were brought up that shareholders and customers had presented to board members. This independent directors meeting without bank employees and officers allowed a free discussion, and a few of the frustrated directors shared the complaints they were hearing from investors and customers.

"In closing," said Drury, "I want all members of this board committed to attend meetings like this, independent of management or staff, on a monthly basis. The meetings will not take much time. We will conduct them just before the regularly scheduled board meeting to create efficiency. I also need not say, but will for the record, that we must maintain confidentiality. What we decide together as an independent group is always for the shareholder interest and may not be well received by management, but that is the purpose of a board of directors. We must direct change and manage management when necessary to get back to a norm and increase profitability and share value."

The meeting was soon adjourned, and Drury was congratulated on beginning his second year as chairman of the board. Fellow board members felt this was a new beginning for Sunrise Bank.

After departing the meeting and on his way to his office, Lasman reached for his cell phone and pressed the speed dial button. Fran answered on the first ring.

CHAPTER
FORTY-EIGHT

January is dependably cold and bitter in Chicago and the first board meeting of the new year took place on a sub-zero day. The primary goal for this meeting was to set a positive tone for the coming year. Objectives and strategies, the budget, and a discussion of current and future market conditions were on the agenda. When board members arrived, there was a bustle of activity. Cars pulled into the parking lot. Board members entered the lobby, had conversations with staff, made deposits, drank coffee, then ascended in the elevator to the third level and walked to the boardroom.

But this day as they arrived, nervousness filled the air. Employees were preoccupied with something. Hellos were quick. No one had time for conversation. As the men exited the elevator, they observed employees in assembly line fashion copying, stapling, and coordinating material. At first glance it appeared as if a deadline loomed for a very big deal. And in fact there was a deadline, but it was for the board meeting. Fran had stayed at the bank all night with her assistant and a few others compiling information for the meeting. She was doing a lot more than simply preparing material. Those with any common sense at all knew something was brewing. And Fran was stirring the cauldron.

By the time the last board member arrived, they all seemed nervous. Sure, coffee was poured, conversations ensued, and post-holiday greetings and discussions were active, but something else was going on and no one knew just what. Figuratively many of the members were looking over their shoulders. Fran's assistant entered the room and told the board members she was delayed but that the meeting would start shortly. No meeting at Sunrise Bank ever started on time and the board members were accustomed to delays.

Stephen Drury looked at his wristwatch and then looked around the room. "Gentlemen, we are beginning this meeting with or without Fran at half past the hour. It is now eighteen minutes past eleven and I think we owe it to ourselves to keep to a schedule. Is everyone in agreement?" All heads nodded yes. They were used to taking orders too.

A silence hung in the room like a cloud in a rainforest. Fingers tapped on the conference room table. Board members looked at their Blackberries checking e-mail. Lasman was busy texting as Fran's assistant entered the room once again. "On Fran's behalf, gentlemen, I must say she is almost ready. She wanted me to share that with you."

"Please tell Ms. Kontopolus that we are beginning at 11:30 and not a minute later," said Drury.

"I will," said the assistant and quickly departed the room.

Quiet set in again. The only sound was the ticking of the wall clock. Faces grew red with anger. Lasman continued furiously texting as if he were the radioman tapping out Morse code on the sinking *Titanic*.

At eleven thirty Stephen Drury said, "Gentlemen, I call this, the first meeting of the year of the board of directors of Sunrise Bank, to order. Please note in the minutes that Ms. Kontopolus is not in attendance."

Just as the words left his lips, the door flew open with a smack against the wall and the room shook. Fran stormed in like a tsunami. She had a stack of booklets in her hands and was followed by her assistant who carried a staggered pile of stapled papers.

"Gentlemen, I think it is rather rude on your part to begin this first meeting of the year without me," she shouted. "It sets a bad precedent. I have important material for the board for this meeting and at least you could have waited."

She was as red as a fire truck and sweating as she paraded around the table to her reserved spot. She was wearing her traditional black knit dress, which looked wrinkled and stretched. She was unkempt; her eye makeup and pancake foundation looked as if they were layers thick.

Fran and her assistant began distributing material to the board members. The sound of notebooks and papers being slapped on the table had a certain rhythm. No one had time to think or speak. It was as if the air in the room had been sucked from everyone's lungs.

"Gentlemen, I thought we would open this first meeting with some material, some special material today," she said.

"Fran," Drury stated gently, "you are out of order. I've called this meeting to order, and according to the agenda, the first order of business is the review of the minutes of the last meeting. We have an agenda. Let's follow it, please. Is there a motion to waive the reading of the minutes of the last board meeting and accept the minutes as written?" Drury asked. A member made the motion, which was seconded by another. The minutes were approved.

"Thank you," said Drury. "Now let's move on. The next order of business is..."

"I want to make a motion to table and postpone today's agenda for a special presentation," Fran interrupted.

"Fran, what is going on here?" said Drury.

"Gentlemen, I think that for the sake of the new year I need to share some very important information," she said. Her voice was full of passion.

"Okay," said Drury, "if there is a second to the motion on the floor?"

"I second the motion," said Michael Pischer, the lackey vice president Fran had hired to interface with the employees.

"All in favor?" said Drury.

"Aye," most replied, with Lasman barking the loudest. Both Drury and Berg were noticeably silent.

"Okay," said Drury, "we will table the agenda until the next meeting. Fran, since you've made this motion and things have changed today, would you like to explain please?"

"Yes, I certainly will. Gentlemen, I have placed in front of each of you material to show how we rank in our peer group according to other banks in Chicago. I want you to see that we're right in the norm for our expenses."

Everyone looked to each other with astonishment.

"Let me go on," said Fran. "I think there's a movement to show that salaries, overhead, and profits are not what they should be.

Nothing could be farther from the truth. Look at the data in front of you and judge for yourselves."

The board opened their booklets and began looking at the spreadsheets and charts. Although it showed Sunrise Bank favorably in each category, the banks compared were not of the same size or in the same geographic location. The banks were larger or smaller and were located in different cities or even other states. In each category Sunrise Bank was shown in the median of good revenue, similar deposit gross, average salaries, and overhead. The board knew this was not "apples to apples." It was ad hoc at best.

In real estate, one of the best ways to value a property is to use "comps," short for "comparables." The prospective buyer looks at properties within the same neighborhood as the property being considered for purchase. For an accurate valuation, the comps must be for similar-sized properties, with similar amenities, similar features, and so on. If comps for dissimilar properties are used, the appraisal cannot be accurate. Fran was using dissimilar comps to make her point. She was, in other words, "cooking the books."

"Fran," said Drury, "the material you've presented us doesn't seem appropriate."

"Are you calling me a liar?" Fran barked back. Board members were in shock.

"No, Fran," Drury said calmly, "I didn't call you a liar. I said that this is not appropriate material."

"What are you talking about?" Fran crossed her arms in a huff.

"Fran, look at the salary comparison on page six," Drury said in his measured way. "You have your salary as president compared to the president of Lincoln Bank. Now Lincoln Bank is the largest bank in Chicago. It is currently owned by a Swiss holding company. Sunrise Bank is not Lincoln Bank. We are not a 210 billion dollar bank. Your comparison is invalid."

The board members knew he was right, unquestionably. Drury went on page by page, looking at the comparisons. He did not need to do more than point out the obvious. Banks in small towns in downstate Illinois were not comparable to banks in Chicago. Banks that had big losses didn't make Sunrise Bank look profitable. The discussion continued page by page. Fran looked as if she was going to erupt.

Drury was calm and collected and simply approached the material in a businesslike manner. The calmer he was the more dramatic was his effect on the board and Fran. Then the inevitable happened. The eruption came, the tears, the sobbing, the cracking of the voice. Fran began to put on the show of hurt feelings. This, of course, was done for the benefit of the board members. Her assistant handed her a box of tissues. Only Drury and Berg thought it interesting that the assistant had thought to bring tissues to a board meeting. The tears accelerated. The men did not know what to do first. This was Fran at her finest, which was to say Fran at her worst.

She accused Drury of trying to undermine her and of wanting to take over the bank. "This is a power grab, plain and simple!" She moved on with her story of how when her father died she had had a message from above that she should open a bank. Her father was looking down at her while she was on a mission for her family and friends. "His ancient heart must be breaking at this...spectacle." Just as she was waving her finger at Drury, she stopped as if she, heartbroken, could continue no more and headed for the door. The board members sat in silence looking at one another. The two newest board members, the refined, retired bankers who had sat on multiple boards their entire lives, did not know what to say.

Just as she opened the door the silence was broken by a delivery boy who said, "Is this where I deliver the lunch?"

Fran knocked him aside as she ran from the room.

Lasman was stunned—not at her performance because he had expected it. Fran had left without grabbing the sack of food.

CHAPTER FORTY-NINE

The room was hauntingly silent as the food was placed in the chafing dishes for serving. Once lunch was in place, old man Friendly, the oldest board member and one of the organizers, rose, walked to the counter, and began filling his plate. The rest of the men followed until all board members were sitting and eating quietly.

Drury spoke, "Well, gentlemen, I find it interesting that Fran would compose a presentation to contradict my confidential discussion of yesterday. I'm dismayed that one or more of us told anyone of the content of our meeting. In fact I'm quite disappointed."

Friendly stood and walked to the counter for a second helping. Friendly ate fast and always went for seconds. "I don't like this one bit," said Friendly with his back to the group. "Not one bit. I didn't tell her, boys, not me. Who is the blabbermouth? I want to know right now!"

"I don't want to address this now," said Drury. "Not now. But this is a problem, as all of you can see. It's a problem on two levels. First, we must be able to trust each other or we can get nothing accomplished. Second, this outburst and deception, well, this is not acceptable behavior. We have our work cut out for us. I'm going to go to Fran and see if I can get her back to the meeting. Excuse me."

Drury rose from his chair and left the room. The men finished their lunch. Half an hour later Drury returned. After sitting down he spoke. "Well, gentlemen, she will return in a few moments. She was quite upset and was crying in her office." He rolled his eyes. "I convinced her to return. As I said she'll be here in a few minutes."

Ten minutes passed by and Fran appeared. She was red-faced and looked tired, as if she was exhausted from crying. She took her seat and then got up quickly to fill a plate of food. "This is cold," she said loudly and grabbed for the telephone. She pressed three numbers and screamed, "Get up here right now!" Clearly, the ranting and raving and crying hadn't taken the fire out of her. No one knew whom she had called. Moments later Fran's assistant entered the room. "Fill me a plate and throw it in the microwave until it's hot." Without missing a beat her assistant piled a plate with food and left the room.

"Fran, can we go on with the meeting please?" asked Drury. Fran just nodded.

"Would someone like to make a motion to expunge what occurred earlier from the minutes so we can start over?" asked Drury.

"So moved," said Berg.

"Seconded," said Friendly.

"Okay," said Drury, "I called this meeting, the first meeting of the year of Sunrise Bank, to order. Is there a motion to dispense with the reading of the minutes of the last meeting?"

"So moved," said Berg.

"Seconded," said Friendly.

"All in favor say aye." The vote was unanimous. "All present voted in favor with dispensing of the reading of the minutes." Drury hit the table with his gavel. "Okay, let's start with new business."

Lasman looked at his wristwatch. *This meeting is taking too long*, he thought.

CHAPTER FIFTY

The first person to leave board meetings was usually Lasman. Before the agenda was over and the meeting adjourned, he would excuse himself and leave the room. Although he offered a sound reason, and he *always* had a sound reason, his behavior disturbed the other board members. He made it seem as if meetings took too long and he had more important business elsewhere. In fact, usually he headed to his health club or country club, but no one ever knew where he really went. Today was a little different. Fran asked him to stay for the entire meeting. She wouldn't put up with any of his usual excuses, so he agreed without comment other than a whispered, "Damn it."

He stayed, but the delay made him churn inside. He wanted to get out, but his greed gland ran his brain and he knew that staying friends with Fran and Sonny would line his pockets. He didn't pay much attention to the business at hand, but he did stick it out. As the meeting finally wound down, his anxiety began to diminish. He began packing the overloaded, worn leather briefcase he always carried with him. He wanted to be the first to leave. He allowed no time for small talk. He just wanted to get to his car and get to the health club. His wife was at their Florida home all winter and he enjoyed flirting with the girls at the club.

Like many men in their late fifties who are pale and bald, paunchy and have gray teeth, Lasman had no sense of how woman viewed him. He flattered himself. He had married a woman who depended on him for an allowance and had no sense of money or business so he got a lot of flattery at home. Better than that, he could deposit her in Florida to spend the winters with her girl friends chatting, drinking coffee, gossiping, taking exercise classes, and shopping. He was free to do as he pleased and that's why those long meetings made him feel shackled.

As the gavel dropped declaring the meeting closed, Lasman ran out the door. Barely saying goodbye, he was not going to wait for the elevator to arrive. He bounded down the stairs to the ground floor and out the door to his car. He pressed the button on the key chain, the lights flashed, a dual beep was lost in the splashing slush kicked up by a passing bus, and the car unlocked.

He opened the trunk, threw in his briefcase, and grabbed his gym bag. With bag in hand, he opened the driver's side door and climbed in, started the car, backed out of the parking lot, and was off. The health club was less than a mile away and he was already visualizing what machine he would use, what news program he would watch on the individual TV monitors, and how he would initiate a conversation with the nearest sweet young thing. He could have driven blindfolded he knew the route so well. Lasman parked his car in the club parking lot, grabbed his bag, and pressed the lock button on his key chain after taking six steps from the car.

While in motion he opened his wallet and took out his membership card. He entered the club and flashed the card at the entry desk. He bounded up the stairs to the men's locker room. Once there he walked to the same area he always used and grabbed one of the lockers. He placed his bag on a stool, unzipped it, took his gym cloths out, and began to undress to "dress out" in his workout clothes. These were an old wrinkled t-shirt, Adidas shorts, and old, beat-up running shoes. It was the sad uniform of a man who, in the words of an old country song, was "trying to prove he still can."

Just as Lasman was placing the padlock on his locker his cell phone rang. Figuring it was his wife, he glanced down ready to press the ignore button. But to his surprise the caller ID gave Fran's direct line at the bank. He glanced and glanced again, stunned for a moment. He let the phone ring for a few more times and then opened it and placed it at his ear. He gritted his teeth when he heard the familiar shrill voice.

"Earl, Earl, I need to see you right now, get back to the bank at once."

Lasman slapped his forehead with his other hand. "Fran, what's going on?"

"Earl, they're out to get me. I need to speak to someone I trust."

"Fran, I just got to a meeting, I won't be free for a while."

"Earl, I said now!" Fran was screaming. Other club members around Lasman heard the shrieking voice as he held the cell phone away from his ear. They nodded wisely, thinking he was being chewed out by an irate wife.

"Okay," said Lasman, "I'll be right there." Fran hung up the phone and he just stood there. A cold sweat appeared on his forehead. He was turning red with anger. He slowly undressed from his gym clothes and began to dress again in his suit. He knew this was going to be a long night. He was angry when anyone took his time and imposed their selfish needs upon his selfish needs without being billed for the time.

Even as a young father a generation earlier, he never woke when his children got up at night. He never went to school to meet the kids' teachers. He could not remember how many times he lied to his wife about meetings so he could stay at the golf course longer, get a massage, go to dinner with friends, or just have another round of scotch and soda.

His desire for money was so great that he could not risk his emotional and physical needs when Fran called. He wanted more. He knew his board seat was up for renewal at the next election and he did not want to lose his seat. Lasman walked slowly out of the locker room and down the stairs. He entered his car and drove back to the bank. He popped two Tums into his mouth as his stomach was producing a significant amount of acid. It was burning and the burn matched his burning anger and resentment.

CHAPTER
FIFTY-ONE

L asman pulled up to the bank and called Fran from his cell phone. The bank was locked and all except the security guards were gone. Fran pressed a button behind her desk and a buzz emanated from the front door of the bank. The guards were stationed in the lobby as usual. He nodded hello as he pulled the entry door to the bank and the door opened. He stepped in with the walk of a condemned man headed up the final thirteen steps. This gallows had an elevator. He pressed the button. The doors opened and he thought *the fiery mouth of the dragon* as he entered and pushed the button for the second floor.

Fran's office door was closed but he could see her fat form through the slim window at the side of the door. She was pacing. He lightly tapped the door and then entered.

"Earl, Earl, can you believe Drury? He wants to take over the bank. I know it. He and Berg want my bank. I can't have this just when things are going so well for us." She was either delusional or lying.

He listened as she droned on. If he would have thought about it, he could have predicted her attitude. In truth he could care less how this fat embarrassment of a woman felt. The more he knew her the more he hated her, but he knew being her ally would be good for Earl Lasman. Money was riding on his performance. "Fran, sit down and catch your breath. I'll get you some water. No one is going to take your bank. You know you can count on me." He walked over to the sink and filled a glass with water.

"I feel better just having you here, Earl. You are my friend, aren't you? You care about me and this bank. I know you do. I want you to stay for dinner. I ordered something special knowing you would be coming back. I need to talk to you. I need you to make me feel secure and not threatened. I knew it wouldn't be good having Drury as chairman. I should be chairman of the board."

Lasman felt as if he had swallowed a rock. His stomach felt heavy. This was going to be a long night. His plans were ruined. But he could not leave. He knew leaving would ruin his chances. To hell with her, he thought. Earl Lasman should be chairman of the board.

CHAPTER
FIFTY-TWO

Within the City of Chicago, tourists and locals alike often enjoyed a glimpse of the past by checking out the vintage housing stock, which dates back more than a hundred years. Prior to the Great Chicago Fire in 1871, the houses, streets, and sidewalks were made of wood. After Chicago's infamous fire the city was rebuilt in brick and stone. A style of building that became popular in those days was known as the center entry six-flat. It was most commonly constructed on a lot 50 feet wide by 125 feet long. The building on that lot did not take up the entire piece of land. It was set back from the street, often leaving room for a garage or a parking lot behind the building. When these buildings were constructed, they were rental apartments. Often an owner would live in one unit and collect rent from five tenants or an extended family that lived in another apartment or two and shared in the mortgage payments.

The apartments were three-bedroom or four-bedroom units with a living room, dining room, and kitchen. The basements were used for laundry and storage. Sometimes one would find a "summer kitchen" in a basement. In the days before air conditioning, it was cooler to prepare food and sleep below grade rather than in a sweltering apartment upstairs.

After World War II ended and the GIs returned, a housing shortage developed. Couples got married and wanted to start families. Apartments were in low supply as new housing had been at a standstill since the Great Depression. Owners of many multi-unit properties including center entry six-flats saw an opportunity. In the case of the six-flat, these properties could be cut up and divided into twelve units or more. In the case of the six-unit becoming a twelve-unit, there were front and rear units. Six tenants could enter through the front of the building while six could enter through the back. This created more units and more income for the owner.

Sonny had invested in a "cut up" center entry six-flat in the Lakeview neighborhood early in his real estate career. These buildings were an inexpensive way to get invested into property ownership and the growing real estate market. They were also a tried and true way of living in a unit and letting your tenants pay your mortgage. When Sonny left Hegewisch, he bought a "cut up" six-flat and lived in one of the units. He never sold that building. As the years passed, he renovated the property, de-converting the small units back to larger apartments of their original size. He installed individual heat and new kitchens and baths. He de-converted five of the units in his building on Southport Street. The remaining unit stayed as two cut-up units.

Sonny rented the five large units and one of the small units and kept the rear small unit for himself. This unit was his retreat or his sneak joint. When Sonny wanted to take a nap or watch TV and not be disturbed, he could sneak over to Southport Street and hide out. In the days before cell phones, this was the one place he would not be disturbed. Over the years the unit was renovated and made into a clubhouse with a card table, full bar, and a refrigerator fully stocked with cold beer and snacks. Every Thursday night Sonny would run a poker game for a select group of friends there.

These friends were people who did business with him. A plumbing contractor, an electrical contractor, real estate agents, bankers, aldermen and politicians, people in the stone supply business, hardwood flooring suppliers, and architects were among welcome guests. The guest roster dictated who would win and who would lose. There was never an even shot at these games. When Sonny needed favors from an alderman, he would invite his foreman and other staff from Sonny's company. He would give them money to play with and instruct them to lose to the alderman. A happy alderman was one who granted favors. And many aldermen departed the Southport property thinking they had actually won all the money stuffed in their pockets. They were happy to grant

Sonny the zoning changes and variances he needed to build more units and make more money. Sonny was one of the few real estate professionals who realized that to win big sometimes you had to lose a little along the way. Sonny was a good loser in these, and only these, situations. Actually, he was the winner!

He did a large volume of business and became very successful over the years. It was an honor and a privilege to be invited to his private hideaway. When a real estate broker or some other businessman wanted his business, it was Sonny who walked away with the pile of dough.

Occasionally Sonny would invite some old friends to shoot the shit and just play cards. One evening after the infamous board meeting his guests consisted of his two retired banker friends, Mit Deerfield and cousin Jerry Hunting, who were just completing their second year on the board of Sunrise Bank. Earl Lasman had recently joined the inner circle and was a regular hanger-on.

Kent Shem was also invited. Shem was an idiot plain and simple. Everyone knew that. He was the type of guy people would feed false information to and then laugh when he passed it on as gospel. He always thought someone else had the answer to success. Shem could not be honest if his life depended on it. There were a number of stories about his chameleon-like behavior. For Sonny, he was just another soldier in his little army of pawns.

When Sonny wanted a message delivered to or about someone, he would call Shem and tell him who to call and what to say. Shem would never use his judgment whether or not it was a good decision. If Sonny said or implied something, he would jump through flaming hoops like a trained circus animal to do it.

For example, Sonny might call and say, "Kent, don't you think it would be a good idea if 'so and so,' who is running for office, held a sponsored lunch in support of his candidacy?" Shem would of course agree. "Then Kent," Sonny would continue, "don't you think the president of the local home builders association should sponsor an event for the person and ask those in attendance to bring checks for his campaign?"

Kent, of course, would then call the president of the Home Builders Association and convey the direction by saying, "You know, Mr. President, many of our members have called and asked me to advise you that you should have a lunch for candidate 'so and so' and raise money for his candidacy. In fact, I think that if you asked around, Sonny Vulich would agree." Using this method Shem would be the spokesman and Sonny's message would be conveyed from someone else's mouth. In intelligence-gathering circles, Shem would be known as a "cut-away," someone between his superior and anyone else. It was an appropriate term. Should Shem ever make a major mistake or embarrass Sonny, he could easily be "cut away" to take the fall and no one would ever be aware of Sonny's involvement.

At the card games Shem could always be counted on to drink too much, lose money, and talk too much. If he was brought in to consult with someone on a deal, he would brag about his influence. He held no confidence entrusted to him. Sonny found he could make money by using this weakness to his advantage. A couple of drinks and Shem would tell Sonny all about his business at the card table or in a "let's just you and me have one more nightcap" session after the game.

If he listed a small retail property with Shem and brought him into a partnership he was assembling, the pawn would stay wrapped around Sonny's finger. Sonny had a plan for Shem, a big plan, but that was for later.

Shem was in the current game for a purpose. The five men started playing cards and, of course, the discussion was about business, the economy, the weather, and the bank. Sonny knew that the retired bankers had experienced their first board meeting of the year and was interested in finding out about their take on everything. He had to wait until the right moment.

A few hands of cards were played and beers were consumed. Shem liked a cigar and always brought a few to impress others. He lit his, offered them around, and dealt the cards. He liked to deal because it made him feel in control. Sonny was sipping his Diet Coke when the right moment arrived to begin his inquisition. "Kent, did you meet with Fran yesterday to discuss the refinancing for your office building?"

"Nope." The cigar in the side of his mouth bobbled slightly. He had begun to smoke cigars when a club he joined consisted of many cigar smokers. One member always kept his cigar in the left side of his mouth at all times and he tried to resemble that look. He thought it conveyed power.

"She wouldn't have been available yesterday," said Hunting.

"Why not?" asked Sonny.

"We had a bank board meeting all day yesterday. The first of the year."

"Really?"

"Oh yes," piped in Deerfield, "quite an experience."

"Unbelievable, in fact," said Hunting.

"What happened, if I may ask?" said Sonny.

Deerfield answered. "Well, let me put it this way. I was a banker at Lyons's Bank. I must have attended well over three hundred bank board meetings. This one takes the cake."

"Oh yes indeed. I didn't utter a word, not one word, the entire time. I was speechless," said Deerfield.

"How interesting," said Sonny.

"Oh my, my. It was frightening, in fact! Quite scary," said Hunting.

"What do you mean?" said Sonny.

"Well, we're really not at liberty to discuss what goes on in a board meeting, you know," said Deerfield.

"But boys, we're all shareholders here," said Sonny, "and I did introduce you to the bank."

"Yeah," said Shem.

Then Lasman spoke up, "Well, you've seen it all before, Sonny. It was her paranoia. She was crazy. She acted out like a cornered dog."

Shem chuckled and puffed on his cigar. "Gotta love her, that Fran."

"That crazy bitch," said Deerfield.

"What happened?" asked Sonny, as if he did not already know the answer.

"Well...well, first the meeting didn't start on time," Hunting said with a gay, dramatic flair, "then *she* came in like a crazy woman, throwing booklets around. And the way she looked, oh, the way she looked. My God, she is no prize, but she was filthy, sweaty, and her hair, well, she looked as if she had slept in her clothes."

"I have never and could never imagine that the president of a bank would look the way she did and conduct herself in that manner," said Deerfield.

Shem was giggling and puffing smoke as the story unfolded. The more Hunting spoke, the more Deerfield added. When a hesitation in the story came, Lasman moved it right along. Sonny was guiding the conversation. He knew just how to say "really" or clear his throat, give a glance or a look, a grunt or sip from his glass just at the right time. Sonny was great at the game. He was the puppet master.

The story unfolded and Sonny heard what he wanted. He heard of her paranoia, which he would exploit to his advantage. Shem drank and smoked, farted occasionally, and dealt cards. Sonny could visualize the weakling on the board one day. With Shem in place, Sonny could unfold his master plan. That day was coming soon. He just had to wait as the calendar moved on throughout the year.

CHAPTER FIFTY-THREE

The balance of the year featured monthly independent director meetings preceding each official board meeting. Fran became more paranoid each day. Her new board chairman created committees to look into various aspects and practices of the bank. The audit committee reviewed expenditures. The compensation committee reviewed the Chicago area mean for compensation and reviewed the goals that Fran herself had set forth for her and her staff. The loan committee expanded and began to review loan files to make sure that everything was in order.

Fran became more uncontrollable and her behavior more unpredictable than ever. She lobbied board members by taking them to lunch and conducting meetings in her office. She called Sonny more frequently. She cried to him and conveyed more and more that he was the only person she could trust. Sonny never found these calls a bother. In fact, she was playing right into his hands. Every call, every whine, and every insult to someone on the board proved his plan was working. Sonny would spend hours in the evening listening and pretending to empathize with her and just at the right time he would reinforce her paranoia by presenting new possibilities of losing her job.

That was the last thing Sonny wanted. She was his moneylender and she was the key to his financial castle. No, Sonny did not want Fran lose her job unless…well, just unless he was in the right place at the right time. Then, screw the bitch!

Stock in such a small, non-public bank had no liquidity. There was no trading market for the stock. Later on, as investors got older and when they were thoughtful about their estate, the stock they held in an entity like Sunrise Bank would be offered for sale to existing shareholders. One of the bank officers became, as is often the case, the "go to guy" when shareholders had stock to sell. His job was to offer the stock to those who had indicated an interest in purchasing more stock and let the existing shareholders negotiate a price with the seller.

In a market that is closed (one that does not exist openly), if there is one buyer with a motivated seller then that buyer can drive the deal. Fran knew that Sonny wanted to buy and certainly could buy additional stock. She directed the bank officer responsible for pairing sellers and buyers that she was to know when any shares were offered for sale. There was a precedent for a price per share based on the last sale. The sellers always wanted to know this price. What the sellers did not know was that the prior sale information was almost always made to Sonny or a member of his family. Sonny drove the price down. The trading quantities were not large, so over time Sonny was buying stock at prices below the initial offering price and adding slowly to his holdings.

The more stock Sonny bought, the more confident Fran became in her ability to feel secure in her position. She trusted him completely. He was her mentor, her friend, and a shoulder to cry on. Even Sonny Jr. was a confidant, someone to get a hug from on a tough day. Junior, a little Sonny clone, knew what to do and say at the right time. He was learning from the master.

Sonny, a "good friend," always took her calls. However, he hated Fran and knew that the more she believed in him, the more his influence would encourage her to comply with his requests and directions.

CHAPTER
FIFTY-FOUR

Headline: Chicago newspapers

Political Power Broker Found Dead on Michigan Beach
Police Suspect Suicide

The community of New Buffalo, Michigan, was a summer extension of Chicago. Less than two hours east of the city, Chicagoans
could transport themselves into the country and stay on the lakefront in Michigan. Large estate homes had been renovated, expanded,
or were torn down and rebuilt. Other than fighting for a parking space
at the local Safeway and women facing off in SUVs, nothing exciting
went on in New Buffalo, Michigan. That's one of the reasons it was so
popular.

The sub-headline read, "Everett Miller, political protégé and godfather to the head of the Illinois Senate and member of the board of
Sunrise Bank, found dead at fifty." The story in part read, "Miller was
found dead near his summer home on the shores of Lake Michigan. In
his hand, pointed into his mouth and upward toward his brain, was a
.22 caliber revolver. In his brain a bullet, on the sand a large pool of
blood. There were no witnesses."

To the police in this quaint community it was obvious Everett Miller
had come to his summer home alone mid-week for this one purpose.
The Chicago reporters who wrote of his death had just days before
been made aware of an FBI probe of alleged kickbacks from politically

connected minority firms with banking relationships to Sunrise Bank. Their connections to Miller were being explored. Two days before his death Miller was seen in Las Vegas with his lawyer and FBI agents as they entered the Las Vegas Federal Building. Sources close to the FBI substantiated the event, but the reporters were sitting on the story, waiting to break it with substantial information that would back up the headlines. The reporters were scooped by the alleged suicide. Now they could include anything they knew to make the front-page banner.

The two stories were similar and addressed the suicide as it may have related to the FBI probe. Perfect tabloid reporting. Just what sold papers. The public loved the schadenfreude, taking pleasure in the misery of others. This meant unneeded publicity for Sunrise Bank. The loan committee and Fran were interviewed by the FBI, as were the employees who had direct contact with Miller and the minority firms in question.

No one associated with the bank knew of the alleged kickbacks to Miller. The money was likely in a vault somewhere. Minority customers interviewed confirmed that part of the deal to borrow money from Sunrise Bank involved Miller directly. He had told them they would not be approved for state contracts without paying him his due. They agreed as this was the way firms did business with the state, through a paid-off powerbroker. It's business as usual. What's the big deal? It is no big deal—unless you get caught.

What seemed to be a solid connection with the FBI probe and the suicide was Miller revising his will seventy-two hours before he "offed" himself. This information was exposed in a follow-up article later in the week, leaked by a paralegal with Miller's attorney's firm who received $500 cash for inside confidential information about their late client.

Everett Miller had served his purpose as a bank board member. He had helped the bank's bottom line by bringing in borrowers. What shareholders did not know was that he was stuffing his pockets with cash from those borrowers. Fran did not care. She had never liked Miller anyway and did not like the way Farin had pushed him onto the board. To Fran it just meant that another board seat had opened up. She immediately appointed her brother Ray to replace Miller.

She called the board members she knew she could manipulate and then called the remaining members telling them directly that a majority had already been polled and that she simply was contacting the other members to see if they were unanimous. Adam Berg was her last call. He suggested it would be a more honest method to conduct a formal nomination and hold an official vote at the next holding company board meeting. He suggested this out of respect to the board and the late Everett Miller. Ramming down a telephone vote before the wake and funeral was at best inappropriate. But Berg was the final call and he was already in the minority. She just didn't care what he said. Ray Kontopolus, the fishmonger and private headhunter, was now on the board of Sunrise Bank.

CHAPTER
FIFTY-FIVE

In an instant snow could cover Chicago like a thick blanket. Outsiders thought of Chicago as the Windy City, but Chicagoans always had affection for the massive billowy layer they often woke to.

Fran was home and it was Saturday morning. She lifted her right leg to get herself out of bed. The blinds in her bedroom were open from the night before, as she had dozed off while watching the city lights. During the night the city was covered with snow due to dense a storm that began when she was sleeping. She could see the snow plows on most streets creating large mounds of snow against the curb. Although she could not hear the salt hitting the streets, she could see the spinning dispenser on the rear of the truck spitting out the large granules.

She watched in a daze without worrying what time it was. It was unusual that she could stand still for that long just staring without an agenda or a distraction. Her mind was at rest.

She felt better now with her brother Ray on the board. She had not slept this well for quite some time. A relaxed quality that she rarely experienced comforted her and for the first time the paranoid president did not feel as if someone was watching her. She entered the bathroom and performed her morning rituals then wandered into the kitchen to prepare a pot of coffee. This was an unusual day for Fran. The soft, deep blanket of snow added to her sense of well-being. When one looked out a window while in a cozy warm apartment, snow had a soothing effect.

Today she enjoyed the feeling of the thick carpeting beneath her feet as the smell of coffee filled the apartment.

She took a moment and began to think back, almost in a time line, to when she first had the idea to begin a bank. She recalled the genuine enthusiasm that she had felt a few years earlier, remembering the fantasy of sitting in a fancy office in a bank building with a staff waiting on her needs. Fran wanted the recognition of being a famous and prominent woman banker in the city. This achievement was in the works. Her father must be proud.

Fran's thoughts continued in this realm as she rose and entered the kitchen to fill her cup with black coffee. With the cup in her hands, she turned and walked into the living room, sat down, and gazed out the window looking at the frozen Lake Michigan. Gusts of wind blew snow across the surface as a baker might blow sugar off a large sheet cake. Fran turned and looked at the city again. She could not see the bank building from her window, so she pretended to have x-ray vision peering northwest, imaging in her mind a laser-like beam that pierced through the downtown office buildings, until she could see the image of her bank building. It did not matter that the sky was gray and the snow was falling. She could see the bank building with her third eye. Returning to reality, she began thinking about the current state of affairs at the bank.

Yes, her brother was now on the board. This was a smart move, but she worried about his health. His newfound prosperity as a high-end corporate headhunter demanding top fees for finding employees had changed his lifestyle. He worked less in the store, he was night clubbing, and his defense of his cocaine use when reprimanded by his sister was that it was the power drug for the "new generation" of powerbrokers. This drove her crazy. Fran had never used drugs. Pot had made her fall asleep once and she did not like the feeling produced by anything other than alcohol, which she did not consider a drug.

Ray did not fit the professional image she wanted for the board, but loyalty to ensure her control was needed more than anything. She had the votes, but Drury's inquires were getting too near the truth for her to handle. And now the FBI?

She began counting and recounting in her head the board members she could count on to vote her way. With Ray on the board, one more vote was in her pocket. Where did Hunting and Deerfield, the newer members, stand? Were they loyal? She did not have to rely on Sonny to persuade them to vote her way. They seemed okay, but she had to be sure. Although she thought of calling Sonny right then, she decided he needn't be bothered this weekend.

As she walked back to the kitchen to grab a Krispy Kreme donut, she made a deal with herself to get through the weekend without calling Sonny. She grabbed her phone and called Ma to spend the day shopping for shoes. Nordstrom's was having a sale.

CHAPTER
FIFTY-SIX

A day of shopping was just what Fran needed to relax. She returned home with six new pairs of shoes and an adorable pair of snow boots with fur trim at the top for added warmth and brass zippers on the inside legs for style. The color, of course, was black. She liked these boots so much and they felt so snug and cozy that she wore them out of the store. The boots she wore when she left the house she carried home in one of the multiple bags from Nordstrom's. Of course, new shoes required new hose, a dozen pair to be precise. The makeup department was on the same floor as the shoe department so how could she leave without a makeover in the aisle? The selections were all that more pleasurable because they were business expenses, at least according to Fran's definition and a pliant accounting department.

Ma watched and thought she should purchase a palette of color when choosing makeup and accessories, so she purchased a new set of lipstick, eye shadow, new fake lashes, and a few barrettes. The jewelry counters were in the next area and there was a wristwatch, a Tag Heuer with a diamond surround, which Fran just loved. Before the day was over Fran spent more than $10,000 on herself and her mother. They had not had a day like this for a while.

She and Ma enjoyed a late lunch at the café at the Four Seasons Hotel, which was charged on her corporate American Express Card and logged as "lunch with new client" on the receipt. The bill was $85. Fran had been charging her mother's telephone bill to the bank as a miscella-neous expense since the bank opened. She had the phone company send a copy of Ma's telephone bill to her home and used the same AMEX card to pay the bill. The amount was approximately $40 per month. It was small enough for her to pass by the auditor. When traveling she pur-chased a second ticket so Ma could travel with her as a traveling com-panion and she charged their food and expenses to the bank. This was second nature to Fran and now, years later, spending the bank's money on Ma or her family was not worth a thought. This was her bank.

When she returned home, Fran opened a new bottle of champagne, took a flute from the cabinet, and poured herself a glass. While the bub-bles were popping, she tried on all of her new shoes and walked around the apartment like a queen. This was indeed a wonderful day. She drank from the flute and filled it once more. She began to play a game. She finished a flute of champagne between each new pair of shoes. By the time she was through trying on the shoes she was rather tired. She sat down on the large white sofa in her living room and flopped back on the fluffy pillows. She was barefoot as she looked out the floor-to-ceiling windows once again. The city with a pitch-black sky was beautifully lit up with the lights from the downtown and business district. Fran gazed upon the city, her city, and slowly closed her eyes.

The cell phone rang and spoiled the reverie. The phone was in her purse. She got off the sofa, walked to her handbag, opened the compart-ment where she always kept her razor phone, and opened it. The caller ID light indicated that it was Lasman calling from his cell. She immedi-ately pressed the green receive button.

"Hello."

"Hi, Fran. Are you busy now? What are you doing?"

"Shopping. Bank business. I arrived home just a little while ago, why?" She tried to hide the curiosity that infected her voice. The old paranoia was showing up.

"Well, I was leaving the health club and with my wife out of town I was wondering if you wanted to have dinner with me tonight?"

"Sure," said Fran without missing a beat.

"Great. How long will it take for you to be ready? I'll pick you up."

"I wasn't expecting this and it'll take me a few moments to pre-pare, so can you have a drink somewhere and pick me up in forty-five minutes?"

She could hear Lasman clearing his throat. He was always in a hurry and she did not want to upset him. Fran spoke again. "On second thought, why don't you go to the International Club at the Drake Hotel? The bank has a charge account there and the food is the best in town. I'll call ahead and make a reservation. They always have a table for me. Have a martini and I'll be there in one hour. Valet your car and I'll sign for that as well. Is that okay?"

"Sure, that sounds great, Fran. See you in a few." And with that Lasman hung up.

Fran was blushing as she looked in the mirror at herself. Her heart was beating. She had thought that she would be alone tonight, and having a dinner date on top of the wonderful day that already took place, she could not believe her luck. She could not wait. She undressed quickly and got into the shower. When she got out she began blow-drying her hair. Her thoughts were childlike. She was as happy as she could be. She was not thinking about the menu, as was often her reaction to going out to dinner. In her mind she began to have a conversation with her father.

While she dressed in a dreamlike state she listened to her father's voice tell her how proud he was of her and her accomplishments. He told her that he could see from upon high what a success she had become and how everyone in the business community respected her. He told her that she had a responsibility to take care of the family and, as the oldest, it was up to her to preserve, protect, and defend the Kontopolus name. As she placed her new watch on her wrist, she was ready. Fran had not had this light, fancy, free feeling since she was a small child. Hearing her father's voice was soothing too and she felt powerful, almost immortal. She glanced at herself in the mirror. She thought she looked beautiful and used one of the new lipstick colors her mother had insisted she buy.

She sat down on a chair to put on the new boots. It was difficult as always to bend over to reach the zipper, but with a deep breath she did it and zipped up the boots. Grabbing her fur coat that hung over a chair in the dining room, she placed it over one arm as she lifted the flute of champagne and drank the remaining liquid in a single gulp. She bounded out the door of her apartment and walked to the elevator. Once in the lobby Fran asked the doorman to hail a taxi.

The doorman walked outside the building and blew his taxi whistle. He came back and with his hand motioned to indicate the cab should pull up to the building. She handed him her coat to assist her. He held it for her. Then he spun the revolving door so she could exit the building and walk to the cab. The doorman walked behind her and raced around her to open the door to the taxi.

"Where to, Ms. Kontopolus?"

"The Drake," Fran responded as she handed him a five-dollar bill.

"The Drake, please, and drive carefully," the doorman said to the driver. Off drove the cab west then north on Michigan Avenue. The hotel was less than ten minutes from her apartment, and it was early enough in the evening that the downtown streets were not yet crowded with the suburbanites who came to the city for dinner and entertainment on Saturday night. The doorman at the hotel opened the door of the cab and Fran entered.

The Drake Hotel was one of Chicago's landmark elegant older hotels, opening its doors early in the twentieth century. The Drake is where heads of state, presidents, Princess Diana, and other members of royalty have stayed. It is located on East Lake Shore Drive, an exclusive address that rivals any of the world's great streets such as Park Avenue in New York. The Cape Cod Room, Coq D' Or, International Club, the Ball Room, the Bar are landmarks in Chicago's circle of the rich and famous.

And then there are the famous hotel rooms, of course. The Beverly Hills Hotel, the Waldorf Astoria, the Breakers are all classy, classy places. The rooms and suites are known for their detail and luxury. The Drake matched or exceeded the best of them.

As Fran entered the International Club, a private dining area overlooking the magnificent mile of Michigan Avenue, the maitre d' welcomed her with a kiss on the hand. He helped her off with her coat and escorted her to the table where Lasman sat with a sifter of martini. He had taken her advice and ordered his drink. The martinis were the best in Chicago, maybe the best in the world.

Lasman rose and the maitre d' pulled out Fran's chair as she plopped down. Lasman asked for another martini glass and another snifter of martini. They arrived quickly with the olives stuffed with blue cheese, just the way Fran liked them. He poured the martinis and they toasted. They both drank swiftly and drained their glasses. As a surprise Lasman had ordered their meal before she arrived. He had ordered the Chateaubriand. He knew this dish was one of Fran's favorites; his too. That was

Lasman. He took care of others, but always managed to take care of his own needs or desires at the same time.

The meal was just as they expected, wonderful. The meat was tender and cooked medium rare. The wait staff sliced the meat very thin. The mashed potatoes, squeezed through a pastry frosting mitt, were shaped with a frosting look and had buttery texture. During the meal they chatted about everything and nothing. Bank business was not the topic of conversation. She told him of her day of shopping. He told her how beautiful she looked, and she blushed. He loved her new watch. She was proud. The martinis continued to flow.

They wanted to order dessert, but the chef had prepared a special flambé for them to share. It was eleven o'clock when the meal ended. Lasman rose and pulled out her chair. Fran rose. They walked to the coat check when Fran said, "You don't have to take me home. I'll take a cab."

Lasman responded, "I decided to stay here tonight and save myself a trip back to the suburbs. They told me when I arrived that they have a suite available for the price of a room. Let's go up and see what it's like."

Fran placed her coat over her arm as Lasman held her under her other arm. They exited the dining club together and walked to the elevators. He reached in his jacket pocket and took out the envelope with the room key. The number of the suite was 2000. They entered the elevator and Lasman pressed twenty. The elevator took off gently. They could not feel the acceleration as it rose through the building. When the elevator arrived on the twentieth floor, the door opened gently. They stepped out and proceeded down the hall.

The suite was at the west end of the building with a double door at the entry. He attempted to slide the magnetic key into the opening, taking three tries before getting it right. "Damn good martinis," he said. Fran giggled. The green light on the door lit up, he turned the doorknob, and held the door for her to enter. The dim lights gave a golden romantic glow to the rich fall colors of the room's vintage restoration. There were golden fabric wall coverings with a stuffing that added a padding or soft feel to the space. The curtains had a burnt wine color to their velvet fabric. The oil paintings in the room added more deep reds, yellows, blues, greens, and purples. The lamps had lovely shades with fabric covers. The furniture was stained oak with a variety of fabric patterns and colors. Fran laid her fur over one of the chairs upon entering the suite.

They were both speechless, simply taking in the beauty of the living area of the suite. The doors were of deeply stained old oak. The hardware was brass and vintage in appearance, consistent with decor found in the 1920s building.

Fran entered the bedroom first. "Wow. Look at this room. And the comforter on the bed is unbelievable."

Lasman followed as Fran ran her hands over the bedspread. "This is wonderful material," she said.

He reached over and took Fran's other hand by surprise. She turned quickly as he held it. Their eyes met. She was taller in her heels, but it did not matter. They just stared at one another. Her breath was taken away for a moment. She sighed deeply. His free hand reached for hers. They caressed each other's hands gently but firmly. The touch spoke volumes and the certain excitement of romance leapt between them.

Could this be happening? Fran thought to herself.

She bent her knee slightly. Her thigh pressed against his groin and she could feel his hardness grow while she pulled him to her. He did not resist. She brought his arms up and let go of his right hand, placing her arm around him. He grabbed her and they held each other as she kissed his neck. Fran was in heaven. Her juices flowed and she could feel herself getting wet with excitement. These damn boots, she thought, wishing she could slip out of them like a pair of her shoes. They kissed and held the kiss for a while. Their lips acted as fingers feeling their way around each other's mouth. Fran was inexperienced in romance and tried to be gentle. She wanted him to be with her. Gentle and firm. The embrace broke and they again stared at one another. Words were not needed. This night was suddenly magical.

Lasman spoke, "Sit on the bed and I'll unzip your boots."

She sat, slowly and ladylike. She lifted her right leg, and he unzipped the boot and pulled it from her foot. She lifted the left leg and he unzipped that too. He pulled the boot from her foot, but did not let go of her as he placed the boot gently on the floor. With his hand he massaged her foot. His other hand joined in. She fell back on the bed. How romantic, how exciting. She was really getting turned on.

Other than Olga, the woman at the nail salon where she had her pedicure, she had never had a foot massage. She always felt Olga was massaging her feet reluctantly, but this was new. A man, even a mid-fifty-year-old balding man, massaging her feet with such care and attention was nothing she could have imagined. Priceless! Fran had never felt this way before. Even when she called an escort service to send someone to her home, they never treated her this way. This was serious affection and she needed affection. She paused for a moment and thoughts flashed through her mind and heart of how she longed for it. And now this, Lasman, oh dear!

His hands massaged above the ankle then up her calf. She moaned. She felt orgasmic. The moment was coming and she knew it. He massaged one leg then the other. Her dress was above her knee as he continued. He reached over for the table lamp. He turned the knob. The click turned off the only light in the room and the glow from the living area created a silhouette on the wall. An imagined haze filled the room as if a light cloud had floated in from the heavens. Maybe it was the champagne and martinis. Maybe it was her loneliness. She didn't care. The moment was magical.

She heard the zip of his pants and unbuckling of his belt then the sound of his pants being flung to a chair next to the bed. She closed her eyes and let the night unfold. Feeling him on top of her, having him breathe on her skin, being touched where she touched herself at night was exquisite. She moaned, she groaned, she was in ecstasy. The lovemaking was unlike the quick humps with male escorts. This was real, she thought. Fran climaxed again and again. She scratched his back, her nails dug into his skin. He said nothing as she gripped him tightly inside of her.

She heard barking, the barking of a dog. She heard the barking and yipping of what she took to be a small dog. It was annoying as the noise got closer and closer. She opened her eyes quickly as her concentration was broken. She jumped up suddenly in a sweat. The barking came from Bo, the dog of her neighbor Lillian. Fran was on her couch, in her apartment. Lillian must have taken Bo for a late night walk.

The new boots were at her side. She had been dreaming. She caught her breath and lay on the pillows once more. The dream had been so powerful, so moving, that she began to relive it. She closed her eyes for a moment then got off the sofa. As she rose she saw the opened bottle of champagne and realized that this was the recurring dream she always had after drinking the expensive stuff. That damned, or blessed, champagne.

She walked to the bathroom. She had to pee badly. She pulled down her hose and lifted her dress and sat down. When she finished she opened the medicine cabinet and took out the new prescription bottle of Ambien. It was 1:00 a.m. She would never get to sleep without sleeping pills. As she walked to the bedroom she realized that she felt satisfied sexually. Something good had happened that day from the moment she woke up to the time she was putting herself to bed. What would tomorrow bring? She thought fondly of Lasman as she dozed off. She was satisfied.

This same night at approximately 1:15 a.m., Lasman woke with a cold sweat in the bed of his suburban Highland Park home. He felt nauseated. The room was spinning. He had a bad taste in his mouth from a belch, which he felt woke him. He walked into the bathroom to urinate and grabbed the mouthwash to rid himself of the terrible taste. He felt sick. In a weird way he began to realize he had had a nightmare about having sex with Fran Kontopolus. When he looked over the toilet bowl he vomited. He felt better and crawled back into his bed.

CHAPTER
FIFTY-SEVEN

At the next board meeting, and thereafter, Fran placed the bank board book with Lasman's name next to her seat. She even calmed down a little more at the meetings. She had the votes now. Just seeing her smiling brother Ray sitting at the board table gave her a secure feeling. But things were changing and changing too fast to feel too confident. First the economy and the real estate market were tightening up. Home sales were slowing as the price of gasoline and transportation costs, food, and related items began to rise. For the first time in years, banks began to feel an explosion in foreclosures.

When a bank lent money, it knew when a loan was getting in trouble. For a commercial loan or mortgages, it happened when payments began arriving late or in increments or not at all. In construction lending things started going south when the interest reserve, the amount of money the lender lends the borrower to pay his interest payments, ran out and the project skewed out of balance.

Sunrise Bank was beginning to experience trouble in both areas. They were not making many residential loans. The delinquent payments from businesses and investment and commercial real estate were beginning to run late or not at all. In the construction arena, development properties were not being sold fast enough to pay the loan and the interest was adding up. Projects required time extensions when the eighteen or twenty-four months of the loan term was expiring. Without the loan paying off, if the interest reserve remained in the budget, the time extension would be approved.

Sunrise Bank had one particular customer who was an immigrant from Rumania, Adrian Rovin. Rovin abandoned his developments, three in all, and fled back to his native land with his pockets lined with cash he had fraudulently taken as development fees. He had started as a contractor for Sonny in the late 1970s. He told everyone he knew that he owed his success to "Mr. Sonny" for helping him get started as a builder in Chicago. Now he owed $4 million from construction loans he would never repay.

When the interest reserve was running out, there was nothing to do but request that the borrower pay out of his own pocket the monthly interest payment. This was something that developers were not accustomed to doing. Most did not want to pay or could not pay out of their pockets.

Fran began to receive the delinquency list each day. Some of the names on the list were minority borrowers with political connections to Everett Miller, but most were clients Sonny had referred. One of the parties was Sonny's boy Kent Shem. Fran did not know what to do. The delinquencies could be masked for some period of time, but not forever. They would have to be disclosed to the bank board. But she did not want to deal with a volatile situation that would or could influence the elder statesmen with banking experience to judge her as a liability.

She thought of her father's words from that Saturday evening in her dream. She had the responsibility to her family. In addition to the economic worries, she had received multiple late night calls from the Chicago Police Department. The car she had leased through the bank on behalf of her brother was being frequently towed and impounded for excessive parking tickets and obstructing traffic.

Ray was arrested for drunk driving and was once found carrying cocaine. Fortunately the security personal at the bank, off-duty police officers, were from in the same police district where he was arrested. She slipped them a "C" note to get Ray out of jail without a record. But she did not like this behavior, not at all. Ma didn't know of Ray's drug use and Fran knew that she would not know how to react, so she kept his drug and behavior problems her secret. Ray did not listen to her repeated warnings and continued with his reckless lifestyle.

As the year went on Ray began to come to board meetings late. The loan delinquency list became larger. Customers were complaining about lack of service. Fran had many balls to juggle. Early on in the process of discovery, Fran decided she would identify the smaller commercial loan problems to the board.

Small business loans and inner city real estate loans to minority businesses that were part of Everett Miller's referrals could be blamed on the dead man. She could easily bury the responsibility for these loans with his corpse. There was plenty of evidence and rumor for her to create a ruckus about while she tried to work out the real estate loans from her clients and Sonny's friends. Even a rehab construction loan to a partner of Lasman that had been a vacant shell of a building for more than a year was in trouble. She had to cover that for now.

She could not be a hard ass with her board any longer. She needed every vote she could get. This was a time for planning and diplomacy. The Dragon Lady had to step aside, temporarily at least. As the proverbial clock kept ticking and the loan problems kept adding up, Fran paced the floors at night. She approached Sonny about his people and asked when they could become current with their millions of dollars outstanding. Fran suggested that Sonny tell them to refinance with other Chicago banks. He agreed and offered a shoulder to cry on, but he never spoke to any of his friends about bringing the loans current or re-financing. He knew that Fran would not create a paper trail of notices and that most of the loans were without recourse. His people had no personal liability. So Sonny listened, kept telling her he would help, and did nothing.

Shona Cohen, a religious Jewish woman, oversaw the loan processing for the bank. She was knowledgeable and followed the loan process closely. She met with Fran each day to apprise her of any delinquency problems and any progress in resolving them. She rarely brought good news. As the real estate market softened, a few things were happening simultaneously. The loans were not paying off, which meant that money loaned out was not coming back. There was no new business to replace deposits that were being withdrawn, and the soft market made the bank look more closely at borrowers' requests. Customers like Sonny, who had millions in the bank, had their money in high yielding certificates of deposits or money market accounts. The bank was obliged to pay out high levels of interest rates. The problems Sunrise Bank was experiencing were exacerbated by high overhead and high interest payments for borrowed capital. This was an equation for failure.

Cohen disclosed everything to Fran in a timely fashion, as was her job. She expected Fran to give her the approval to proceed in a conventional sense, sending written notifications to defaulted borrowers, beginning foreclosure proceedings, placing a receiver to oversee the property, but nothing happened.

This bothered her beyond distraction. It took courage to confront Fran. It took courage to tell Fran the truth, but she had a conscience. She had purchased stock in the bank during her years of employment with her 401K money. Although it was a relatively small amount, the investment meant a lot to her. This was her bank, her money, she felt her job held great responsibility and she decided to ask Fran in a professional manner why on earth she had not directed her to proceed in a conventional way.

Cohen entered Fran's office on Friday morning. She thought that expressing things politely and seriously on a Friday would give Fran the time to think over the weekend so Monday morning they could begin the process of loan collection. She dressed in a businesslike manner each day but this Friday she wore a business suit and rehearsed over and over what she would say and how she would say it to get respect from her employer in this difficult situation. Memories of Fran's past behavior were in her mind as she prepared for the meeting. She was not afraid of Fran, but she was very aware of the delicate nature of the meeting.

Contrary to what she expected, Fran listened calmly. She actually asked how Cohen would like to proceed the following week. She had prepared a written timeline and discussed this with Fran point by point. The meeting took about an hour and both women shook hands as she left Fran's office. Since it was Friday, Cohen prepared to leave the bank at 1:00 p.m. as the Sabbath started at sundown.

She felt good about the meeting and Fran's response. As she stopped at the kosher butcher shop to buy her meat for the Sabbath meal, she felt she could concentrate on her family and get to work in good spirit Monday. Fran's lack of action on serious matters threatening the bank had bothered her for many months. It seemed that this terrible problem was about to be solved.

It was Saturday, the Sabbath, and one of the security guards from the bank, a Chicago police officer who worked there off duty, arrived at

Cohen's home. He rang the doorbell. She had just returned from Sabbath services with her family. They were having their afternoon lunch together. Her youngest answered the door.

"Mama, Mama, there's a policeman here asking for you," he cried.

"Bill, what are you doing here?" Cohen spoke to the guard through the storm door.

"Well, Shona, after you left yesterday, I was told to empty your desk and place all of your items in this here box and deliver it to your home. Your final paycheck is here in this envelope. If you'll open the door I can place the box down."

Cohen's heart dropped. She had expected problems or challenges, but she had never expected to be fired for doing her job. The guard placed the box down and said goodbye. It was obvious he felt badly about being the messenger. As she closed the door Cohen begin to cry. Her family looked at her sadly.

"What's wrong, Mama?" asked her small son. "What's wrong?"

"I was fired today," she said gently.

"On Shabbos?"

She bent down on her knee and said, "On Shabbos."

She hugged him tightly.

CHAPTER
FIFTY-EIGHT

Rush Street had always been a happening place in Chicago with nightclubs and the trendy restaurants lined up one after the other. As generations changed so did the places. In the 1930s, '40s, and '50s Rush Street had dinner clubs. Mr. Kelly's and Fritzel's featured entertainers like Louis Armstrong, Frank Sinatra, Ella Fitzgerald, Dean Martin, and Red Skelton. In the 1970s, sports bars and discos opened. Some would feature wet t-shirt contests and female Jell-O wrestling. Following this were the openings of private clubs like Mothers and Faces with lighted dance floors where cocaine flowed and more people got high in the restrooms than at the bar.

In the mid-1980s, the tenor of the place changed and the tide of change moved upscale again. Popular restaurants were Gibson's, Carmines, Hugo's, and the Lux Bar. The streets were teeming with Rolls Royces, Mercedes, and BMWs. Conventioneers, businessmen, divorcees, and wealthy tourists once again walked Rush Street.

A small triangular park that met Rush Street with State Street became known as the Viagra Triangle. One block west from Michigan Avenue, the area was filled with restaurants, clubs, and bars. Every concierge knew how to give directions. It was a Chicago landmark.

Gibson's was the cornerstone where the politicians ate for free and businessmen transacted multi-million dollar deals over $100 lunches. At night the bar was packed with gray-haired divorced men from the apparel industry and forty-year-old hookers practicing the world's oldest profession.

"It's a scene, man, the place to be," Ray would tell his friends.

Ray Kontopolus found his home at the bar at Gibson's. Most weekday evenings while his younger brother was closing the fish store, Ray was at the bar sipping a vodka gimlet and flirting with girls whose eyes were on his wallet. Ray was always friendly and had a generous spirit. He made many friends from the regulars. He knew every waiter and waitress, every busboy and bartender, and every dealer. He would tip generously and his generosity was accompanied by his cheerfulness. He was a welcomed customer.

Ray loved his newfound life. He knew he was smarter than his brother and did not miss the fish store one bit. He could dress well, have his nails done, and his hair dyed. He could always impress business people with his stories and he loved to have people laugh with him. He knew the people he was interacting with were better educated and more worldly, but he could entertain them and they liked him.

This new emergence was what Ray had been waiting for his entire life. It did not bother him that Fran had handed it to him like a gift, that the job and the prosperity were unearned. He accepted it and liked who he had become. He was not a big drinker, just a steady drinker. He generally had no more than two drinks on his nights out and he would nurse them carefully. But he did enjoy his cocaine.

When Ray became a board member, Fran gave him a leased Mercedes 3 series to drive, a cell phone, and an American Express credit card tied into her account. From a practical and legal standpoint Ray was not entitled to these perks; he was not an employee of the bank. But he was her brother and she had to take care of family.

He met a new friend, Rocco, at Gibson's. Rocco always had some blow for Ray to purchase. He arrived each night at 7:00. You could count on his arrival like clockwork. Rocco never paid attention to the names of his customers. When he saw Ray he would always say something like, "Hello, Captain," or "Hey, Senator." But for $150 cash, Ray could buy a snoot full of coke every day.

Ray saw Rocco enter the bar and say hello to everyone. He was Mr. Popular at Gibson's. Ray's stomach was racing with butterflies as he anticipated the drugs he bought from his new friend. The dealer knew Ray was an easy mark and had promised him that for $200 cash he could have super red Peruvian rock cocaine. Ray was excited. Rocco nodded for him to follow and Ray jumped off his barstool, leaving his white silk scarf. He followed up the stairs to the men's room on the second floor.

As expected, the bathroom attendant was present with colognes and hairsprays lined up above the sinks. Small plates had dollar bills on them reminding the customer to leave a tip after washing their hands. The two men said hello to old Joe and walked into the handicapped toilet stall. Old Joe was used to the routine and became very busy wiping down one of the counters. Rocco opened a small plastic bag filled with red rocks that looked like rock candy. They were covered with a light powder flaking from the rocks.

"Senator, this isn't cut shit, man. This is it, straight Peru. It's the best."

"Can't wait, man, can't wait," said Ray. And with that Rocco grabbed a coke spoon from his pocket, dipped it to the bottom of the bag, and scooped a generous amount of dust. Rocco held it under Ray's right nostril, and like a dust buster, Ray sucked the red/pink powder into his fat big nose. Rocco immediately got another scoop and lifted it into Ray's left nostril.

Ray felt the cold rush of the drug hit his brain and colon at the same time. He felt he had to piss like a racehorse. Worse than that, he had a sudden need to crap. Ray begged his buddy to excuse him while he sat on the can to do his business. Ray laughed. His friend left the restroom.

While waiting for Ray in the hallway between the two banquet halls, his dealer buddy felt his cell phone buzzing. Rocco quickly answered. "Hello. Oh, hi, Sonny, yeah, I got the stuff. I don't know how you got this shit into the country, but if you want to share connections..." He let his voice trail off and then paused a second to hear the response. "Yeah, I'm with him. He had a taste, and the baby laxative I threw in is making him take a dump. Yeah, right now. I'm outside the john. No, he'll buy it. In fact, I think I can sell him two. He's a sucker, a nice guy, but a real sucker. Here he comes, yeah, I know, tomorrow's headlines. Bank Director and Ex-fishmonger Arrested for Makin' a Damn Fool of Himself. Yeah, yeah, gotta go." Rocco closed his phone.

Ray walked out of the restroom with a cigarette in his mouth and a glazed look in his eyes. He forgot he could no longer smoke indoors inside a restaurant. Ray was puffing away. He loved to smoke, especially after a toot or two. He dropped the cigarette onto the floor and crushed it with his heel.

"Okay, man, this stuff is great shit. Give me more. You know I got the money."

"Well, ace, there isn't more of this so I think if you like this shit, get me $400 and you'll have plenty over the next few days."

With that Ray opened his wallet and gave Rocco $400. Rocco in turn grabbed the package with the red rocks and opened a small empty plastic bag. He took two rocks with his fingers and placed them into the smaller bag.

"Cool. I love this shit. I'm gonna fly home tonight," said Ray.

"Okay, Coach, good luck, this is the good shit. Use it wisely," said the dealer.

Ray walked back into the bathroom, entered the toilet stall again, and broke off a small piece of the rock cocaine. He popped it in his mouth. He rolled it across his lips and then around his gums. It numbed his mouth. Ray unlocked the stall and walked out, down the stairs and back into the bar. His barstool was occupied by an attractive woman in a low-cut dress. Ray had left his white silk scarf on the chair and she was sitting on it. Lucky scarf, thought Ray. He was getting woozy and feeling great. The scarf was a great excuse for beginning a conversation.

"Excuse me," Ray said in a suave tone. She turned her head slowly and looked into his fat face. A brief glance and she turned back to her drink.

"Excuse me," Ray repeated. The smell of her perfume was a turn on. He could see the back of her long neck. She was wearing pearls.

"Yes, what is it?" the woman responded coldly. Her response was one that gave the impression that she was bothered by his attention.

"You're in my seat," Ray said.

She looked at him for a while and said, "I'm in *your* seat? Do you know the serial number?"

Ray chuckled his typical chuckle as he prepared to speak, "No, no, I didn't mean you should get up and give me the seat. I should have said it differently. I was sitting here and now you're sitting here. That's all."

"And?" The woman looked puzzled, but she remained aloof. Ray chuckled again. The cocaine was working its magic on his brain. "No, no, I mean you're sitting on my scarf." And he lifted a portion of the scarf to show her that in fact his scarf was there.

"Oh, I am so sorry," the woman said and gently got off the barstool. She picked up the scarf, opened it lengthwise, and put it over Ray's head patting it gently down the lapels on his jacket. Ray's heart was pounding with the drug and the sexual arousal that came with it.

She stared into his rich brown eyes. "What's your name?"

"Ray, Ray Kontopolus."

"Well, Ray-Ray Kontopolus, this scarf feels very good in my hands. Does it feel good rubbing the back of your neck?" She picked up the scarf and threw it over his head. She rubbed the scarf back and forth on his fat neck. Her glance was penetrating.

"Yes, it does feel good. What's your name?"

"My name is Jessica." Her cold voice was changing, becoming seductive.

Ray was almost numb. The cocaine was taking over his mind and he was looking at her as if there was a spotlight on her face. The rest of the room was a blur. Ray felt seduced, cunning, and invincible. He spoke the first thing that came to his mind.

"Would you like a little coke?"

"I already have a drink," she said.

Ray began to giggle again. "No, no, not the coke you drink." Ray leaned over and whispered in her ear, "Cocaine, cocaine, I have some great fresh rock cocaine."

"Well, Ray-Ray, I've been known to enjoy a taste of that once in a while. Just how great is 'great'?"

Ray giggled again, and then he leaned over and whispered back into her ear, "I can't get enough of this stuff." He looked around the bar. It was getting noisier and was quite loud. He felt the desire for another hit. "It's really great. It's the best."

She played with the scarf around his neck again. "I'm quite particular. I have very good taste."

"I can see that," said Ray; the yearning for more coke was disturbing, he was beginning to become fidgety.

"Do you have some with you?" she asked him slowly, breathing gently into his ear.

"Yes, I do."

"Really?" she said.

"Yes, really." He began to giggle after his reply.

She looked at him as if to say, "Okay, now what?" He picked up on the look.

"We should go back to my place and have a little fun," he said.

She began to gently rub the sides of his fat belly. She ran her hands down the side of his jacket then inside the jacket and down the sides of his hips in a seductive fashion. She whispered in his ear. "Ray-Ray, is this the stuff I feel in your right pants pocket next to this long, hard item?"

Ray was quite fidgety. The hit he had in the restroom was wearing off and he was getting excited about this woman and his need to consume more coke. "Yes it is, and we should leave soon so we can enjoy a long evening."

Then like a flash of lightening, she took his right wrist in a Judo hold and turned his massive, pudgy body to the bar. She still had her hand on his as she grabbed his other wrist with her other hand. Next to her and unnoticed the entire time of this encounter was a tall, thin, bald-headed man. He had a pair of handcuffs and he quickly cuffed Ray, squeezing the cuffs tightly onto his wrists.

"You are under arrest for possession of narcotics," said the woman. She reached in his pocket and pulled out the bag of cocaine rocks. "You have the right to remain silent." She read him the Miranda rights.

A silence fell over the crowded bar as every head turned to see Ray Kontopolus arrested.

The bald-headed officer grabbed his portable radio and called for a paddy wagon. Sirens could be heard as the vehicle came closer and closer to the restaurant. Ray began shivering as his need for more cocaine was taking over his soul. He was only semi-conscious, almost in shock, as this was going down. He had to pee badly and he began to wet his pants.

The detectives pushed him through the crowd. They could not have parted to create a passage if they wanted to. The police pushed him through the revolving door and out into the street. The uniformed officers opened the back to the cold, dark, and smelly paddy wagon and shoved Ray inside. They bolted the door and drove away. His legs were cold from the wet pants.

Down the block through the window of his Mercedes Sonny stared at the scene. He watched as the wagon turned left, heading west down

Division Street toward the new police station in the middle of a neighborhood he had developed. How appropriate, he thought.

Back at the bar, the bar tender turned to one of the cocktail waitresses who knew Ray quite well. "Ya know, if I didn't know any better, I would think Ray was just set up!"

"Do you think so?" she responded innocently.

"Yep, I do." Then he turned to a customer who had just walked in and said, "Mr. Vulich, nice to see you tonight, can I get you a drink?"

"Yes," said Sonny. "Just a Diet Coke. And you can bring it to me at my regular table. I'm having dinner with Judge Nebbish."

CHAPTER
FIFTY-NINE

To the working public Fran Kontopolus was a hard, thick-skinned business professional. To her family and friends she was a loving daughter and sister and devoted member of the church. She grew up attending Sunday school at the Lady in Waiting Greek Orthodox Church in the Budlong Woods neighborhood on Chicago's north side. Fran loved the church and she attended services with Ma most every Sunday. She was a generous contributor. She also made a substantial contribution, from the bank, of course, to name a classroom after her father.

She made sure that Dimitri Kontopolus' name was the largest of any in her church. Each Sunday Fran and her mother would arrive and walk down the aisle to the family seats in the front pew. The family had occupied these seats since joining the church almost thirty-five years earlier. The church was where Fran learned ballroom dancing as a teenager while participating in the youth group. She took singing lessons for children's chorus. This was where family celebrations and memorials took place for the community. Fran never ceased being an active member of the church. She participated on the community service committee bringing food and clothing to the elderly Greek families in need, the career mentoring committee, and others. Unlike her banking life, her activities at the church weren't just for show.

When her life was challenged or she was disappointed, she sought solace in the church. The priest always respected Fran and saw her commitment to the church and her family as sincere. Many congregants admired the way she took care of her mother and helped her brothers. These days found Fran visiting the church a little more than before. She had many things to pray for.

By Monday morning everyone in the Chicago business community had heard of the arrest of Ray Kontopolus. Guilty or innocent, the news was simply too much additional negative publicity for Sunrise Bank. Fran knew what had to be done even before she received the call from Stephen Drury and, of course, Sonny. Ray had to be replaced as a board member.

Sonny called Stephen Drury the next morning to discuss the ramifications of Ray's arrest. Sonny told him that, in his opinion as the largest depositor and largest borrower, the board should rid the board of Ray Kontopolus. Sonny was adamant and claimed that an out-of-control drug freak did not deserve the trust, honor, and esteem of being a board member of Sunrise Bank.

After reading the article online Drury called Fran on her cell phone. She was on her way home from church with Ma in the car. Calmly he told her, in the strongest terms possible, that Ray had to resign immediately. This was not debatable. Fran agreed quietly and compliantly as she knew he was right.

Shortly after returning to her apartment at approximately 2:30 in the afternoon, she received a call from Sonny telling her how sad he was at hearing about her brother. He asked her what she thought she needed to do about Ray's arrest, as it certainly did not look good for the bank. Sonny already knew her answer, and he listened quietly as she told him Ray would have to resign. Sonny gloated hearing the words come from her.

"Well, Fran, we need a new board member we can trust, one that you can direct to do what's right. A man we know and feel comfortable with." He paused, as if thinking and then continued with his well-planned speech. "You know who comes to mind, Fran? Kent Shem. You know Kent from the homebuilders club. He follows my footsteps and does anything I tell him to do. Great guy, a great guy. That's the kind of board member that will always do what you want for this board."

"But, Sonny, Shem has a loan delinquency outstanding. That will look bad to the remaining directors who have to elect him." Fran's voice betrayed her concern.

"I've spoken to Kent and he'll pay off the loan. He's attempting to get his property refinanced with M & I bank. Should have a commitment by the end of the week." Sonny's voice was full of confidence.

"Well, that makes me feel much better," said Fran. "Much better."

"Fran, let's put this incident with Ray past us, we have a new day tomorrow. Let's concentrate on the business of the bank."

"You're right, Sonny. I should have never added my brother to the board. Call Kent Shem, and if he's willing, have him call me."

"I'll have him call you in ten minutes or less."

Sonny had what he wanted, another board member loyal to him. With Shem added to the board he almost had a majority. The board members he could count on were Sonny Jr., Lasman, Hunting, Deerfield, and Shem. That made five in total. He needed two more members to move his plan forward.

CHAPTER SIXTY

Fran's humbling call to the board members sharing the news of Ray's resignation "for personal reasons" was well received. Everyone knew of his behavior. They resented his board position as he never paid attention to bank business and they were happy to see him go.

In the case of Kent Shem as a new addition to the board, most members did not know him. Fran presented his resume with a comment that he was a referral from Sonny Vulich. In short order Shem was interviewed in an emergency session. The members found him affable, and they liked him professionally and personally.

During the following months independent directors meetings preceded board meetings. Drury made it clear that the independent directors meetings were not optional. His feeling was that meeting independently allowed board members to speak their piece and review the bank's status without bias. Some of the directors resented having to actually work, but no one spoke up. They still wanted the status and that monthly stipend. *Rock the boat and you're likely to fall overboard,* thought Lasman.

Since the suicide of Everett Miller, the loan losses relating to the minority companies currently undergoing FBI investigations for fraud and kickbacks had become quite disturbing. Federal and state bank regulators were coming to the bank to review each and every file. Even more disturbing was a letter sent to each independent director from Shona Cohen. The letter caused an emergency meeting of the independent directors.

251

Cohen's letter was written in standard business format. It was not emotional in nature and she didn't whine or complain. The letter told of her meeting with Fran and how she was fired without notice after leaving the bank that day. She emphasized that she was not writing to get her job back but writing as a shareholder with real concerns about the financial stability of the bank. The factual and unemotional tenor of the letter added to its power.

She began by describing the many daily meetings that she had with Fran and the frustration with the lack of conventional protocol. The letter described the standard procedure of sending out letters of collection, the process of attempting to work out the loan, appointing a third-party receiver to control and manage the property as well as other steps that were never administered because Fran had stopped the process. The letter noted that too many of the bank's loans were non-recourse, or unsecured credit lines with no collateral. In her opinion, the bank was not acting appropriately or conventionally. In summary she concluded that this unconventionality would lead to significant problems.

After reviewing her letter, the board was quite angry. This was proof that Fran had been hiding loan problems from them, many of them serious problems. This verified a theory among some members that there was a long trail of deception from the president's office. Upon receiving the letter, Drury called the vice president of loans and demanded a spreadsheet of the loan delinquencies and losses faxed to him within the hour.

When the fax arrived he was stunned. The aggregate of problem loans exceeded $60 million. Any bank would be upset and concerned, but this was a $300 million bank and $60 million was 20 percent of all deposits. The amount of problem loans was way out of balance. This equaled years of profits and was an outrageous situation for an entity the size of Sunrise Bank. The board needed more information about the pipeline of all loans. Drury requested this next. The report indicated that more than twenty loans, all exceeding $1.5 million, had various stages of problems. The details included half-built construction projects, land that had no improvements, vintage apartment buildings that were to be converted to condos where no work was completed and the interest reserve had run out. This news was not good. Even the more recent board members knew it.

The question was what the board was going to do to get a handle on this. There were penalties for a president who was deceptive to the shareholders and the board. A discussion ensued about firing Fran and replacing her with an honest and capable bank president. The idea was to appoint an interim president, maybe one of the retired bankers who sat on the board.

This was a bitter discussion, one they did not want to have, a meeting they had been putting off for months. They were at a tipping point and there was only one real option. They had to get rid of Fran Kontopolus or watch the bank fail. Cause for termination was in their hands. Of course, knowing what to do and actually doing it are two different things.

The following day was a meeting of both boards where there were to be nominations for board members whose terms were expiring. The board wanted to see if Fran would present the true state of the bank, thus bringing forth the loan problems they knew existed. It was her duty as president to keep them informed. The elder members wanted to give Fran the opportunity, the benefit of the doubt and all. The others did not confirm or disagree with their idea. Some felt she would not disclose a thing, and after the conclusion of the meeting, another independent director meeting could be conducted to approach options and consequences on the severity of her behavior. They discussed change and the upcoming annual shareholder meeting. The board members whose seats were up for reelection were Berg, Lasman, and the oldest remaining member of the organizers, Friendly. The election, after board nomination, was to be conducted at the shareholder meeting scheduled to take place in the next thirty days. The board elections were a matter of protocol, as most had been.

Although this last year was a year of friction between Fran and the board, Drury made an agreement with her to support the re-slating of existing board members and not to bother the status quo at this time.

She agreed, but it was not her intention to comply. Since her meeting with Sonny at Café De Marco almost two years earlier, Fran knew that this was the time to unleash his idea. Since the last shareholder meeting that cold day in December she had been preparing silently and quietly in her mind how things would unfold.

An Irish developer named Cochran, with close ties to Fran and an investor with Sonny, had a "shick yingle," a Yiddish expression for a "go-for" on his staff. Gene Stone had a youthful freckle face and a pleasant manner. He was a man in his late fifties. Stone was a puppet for Cochran and having him on the board would be the same as having Cochran, who, like Sonny, did not want to spend the time at board meetings. In fact, Cochran was himself having real estate problems and was busy just trying to stay in business.

As she had in the past Fran held off preparation for the next shareholder meeting and expected low attendance. Although the board was aware of the loan troubles, her deception, and the potential regulatory problems that would require a swift and thoughtful response on their behalf, they decided any major decisions, such as firing Fran and a restructuring the management of the bank, should take place after the elections and shareholder meeting.

Lasman had informed Fran that the board had received the letter from Cohen and would be watching her every move. So she would attend the joint directors meet the next day without stating specifically the depth of the real estate loan problems. She would disclose that problems were present and would require attention. That would be enough to satisfy some board members that she was approaching an honest road of thoughtful disclosure.

The shareholder meeting started as expected with a greeting from Chairman Drury and his introduction of Fran. Drury was less than enthusiastic. She presented the state of the bank in general terms and the meeting moved on to the next order of business, the elections. The slate of nominees was read. The board members re-nominated to the board were seated in the front row of the room. They did not pay serious attention to a group of shareholders filling the room behind them as the meeting began. Each member rose as his name was called, faced the front of the room, and identified himself to the chairman. After the introductions a hand arose; a shareholder in attendance raised his hand and was called upon. It was Sonny, standing in the back of the room.

In his typically condescending voice Sonny said, "I want to thank those who worked so hard to create and make this bank what it is today, but you know, it's time to change the board and rid ourselves of those without the experience needed to bring us into the future. I want to nominate Gene Stone as a candidate for the board."

Berg and the others turned and looked around the room. They knew some of the shareholders, but did not recognize some of the others. Drury, who was chairing the meeting, was shocked with this nomination. There was an agreement with Fran not to change the board. Drury paused the meeting and asked Fran to step outside the room for a moment. She exited the room and Belker, the bank's attorney, joined her.

"I don't like this one bit," said Drury. "What's going on here?"

"There are shareholders who want to replace board members. They are entitled to nominate new people."

"That's right," the attorney joined in. "In fact, we have enough votes tendered as proxies to elect Gene Stone." And with that, Belker opened a briefcase filled with neatly stacked, bound ballots.

"Where did those ballots come from?" asked Drury.

"They were sent to shareholders weeks ago and they all felt the same way, my way." Fran couldn't resist rubbing her power in Drury's face.

"Well, I didn't receive one and neither did my mother or my sister. I can assure you that the board members didn't either." Drury was red in the face and seething when the words left his lips.

"Well, the mail, you know, the mail can never be counted on." She knew she had him over a barrel.

"I'll stop the meeting right now," said Drury. He resisted the feeling to jump up, reach for her throat, and choke the living daylights out of her.

"No, you can't cancel the meeting, Mr. Drury," replied Belker. "We have the votes and the meeting has already begun; you must call for the vote and move this forward."

Drury, being an attorney and familiar with Robert's Rules of Order, knew they had him. He walked back into the shareholder meeting looking dejected. He was angry, embarrassed, and sad all at the same time. He knew they had all been taken advantage of. As he entered he could see the puzzled faces of the board, but many shareholders in attendance were not puzzled. They were the friendly faces of Fran's family and intimate friends. They knew what was coming.

When the vote was over Berg, the man who had raised more money and worked harder than any other organizer, was replaced by another of Sonny's lackeys, Gene Stone. The board lost an independent board member and an important shareholder ally.

Fran said a condescending goodbye to Berg with a look on her face that said don't let the door hit your ass on the way out.

Berg was humiliated and trying to overcome the shock of what had taken place in the last few minutes. He had been set up. He could not catch his breath. In his heart he had felt this coming from the time he had had the meeting with Fran in her office years ago. Berg got in his car and entered the highway, driving fast and zipping between cars in traffic. He drove north on the highway endlessly for what seemed like hours, entering Wisconsin without seeing anything on the road. He was in a daze. This was unusual behavior as he did not like to drive long distances.

After seeing the sign on the highway "Entering Wisconsin," he pulled into a gas station for a fill up. The brisk winter Wisconsin wind hit him in the face. It was a strong, freezing wind, but it felt good as he was still burning with anger and animosity for being so stupid about his expectations of Fran Kontopolus. He was to blame, just him. He would have to live with it. He was greedy too. He had leaped into bed with the devil.

The new board convened their first official board meeting after the shareholder meeting concluded. As they paraded into the conference room Sonny, who was "in the shadows" in a corner of the room like a patient predator, took a card out of his breast pocket and began writing names. He added up the statistics. He controlled six board members: Junior, Lasman, Deerfield, Hunting, Shem, Stone, and Friendly, who had been informed earlier in the day that he could keep his seat if he supported the purging of Berg. Friendly needed the board stipend and committed to the Sonny camp with a trembling handshake. The old man knew better than to fight. These men would do whatever Sonny wanted them to do.

Fran began to feel confident that this new board would leave her business practices alone. She hated Berg and had wanted him off the board for years. She had finally gotten her way. She knew that Drury's tenure as chairman was limited to the next election. He would be the next one purged. Like shooting ducks in an arcade, she was pickin' off anyone and everyone in her way. Sonny would continue to help and provide the necessary guidance. He could be trusted, as the saying goes, "All The Way to The Bank."

CHAPTER
SIXTY-ONE

The massage table did wonders for Sonny. While undergoing a deep treatment he could really relax and think. He experienced a hypnotic trance. As the masseuse worked on the muscles in his back he entered something like a hypnotic or meditative state of bliss. He was breathing deeply and it came to him. He knew just what to do next. He could visualize the next steps, baby steps, to make them effective, but he knew just how to get where he wanted to go. He smiled inside. When the treatment was over, he showered and dressed, exited and walked to his car and made the call by pressing number one on the speed dial of his cell phone.

"Hello, Sonny, I could see it was you from the caller ID." It was Fran, of course.

"Hello, dear, can we have dinner tonight? I'll pick you up in twenty minutes."

"Sure, Sonny, I'll be in my office. Call me when you're a block away."

"Okay," and Sonny clicked his phone shut.

He picked her up and drove west to Western Avenue then south to Twenty-fourth Street to the old Little Italy in Chicago. He turned east to Oakley and gave his car to the valet that serviced all of the small storefront restaurants. They walked into Bruna's. It was quiet and they could talk confidentially. Fran asked the hostess for directions to the ladies room.

After they ordered dinner, Sonny got right to the point. "Fran, I want to make a suggestion and tell me if I'm wrong. I had my lawyer read the by-laws of the bank. We had a copy from the original offering memorandum circulated when raising money for the initial organization. The bank has eleven board members currently, but the board can have more. Up to fifteen, I think."

"Yes, that's true." Fran nodded as she chomped on her Caesar salad, savoring the croutons with every bite.

"I've been thinking, with this new arrangement and the makeup of your current bank board, you have one more loyal person, one more vote that you can count on to follow your lead. But I think you need insurance. You need another board member, maybe two, who can give you the peace of mind you need. One never knows what may happen and you have to be sure."

"You're right, Sonny, I never thought of that."

"Fran, I'll get right to the point. I want you to add a board seat as soon as you can and place my younger son in it. His name is Ted. He will be loyal to you, you know that. And he'll do what you need," Sonny suggested.

"You're right, Sonny, I sure could use him." She enthusiastically embraced his suggestion.

"At the next board meeting have Ted added to the board, Fran. I don't think you should waste any time. Remember, some of these guys are for sale. You need a solid majority of the votes to do what you want to do."

"Yes, and I'll propose increasing the board under new business. Can you get me a copy of his resume?"

"Sure, you'll have one in forty-eight hours," Sonny said.

They finished their meal. On the drive back to the bank Fran said, "I need to renew my key man life insurance policy, Sonny. I don't know anything about life insurance. My contract with the bank states that I need to purchase key man life insurance with the bank as beneficiary. Belker said this was a typical contract clause. It forces the president of the company to take care of herself, physically, I mean. If anything happens to me then the bank has to replace my position. Drury wants me to maintain $5 million, but I don't know."

Sonny drove for a while then said, "Fran, as a gesture to the new board, why don't you surprise them with your generosity and purchase $10 million worth of life insurance. You'll be purchasing term insurance and it's not incrementally that much more money. I'll have my insurance agent call you tomorrow to make the arrangements."

"Ok, Sonny, I think that's a great idea. I'll show them my good intent. Who can argue with that?" She was up for anything that would keep the board quiet and strengthen her position.

Sonny drove Fran back to her car, which was parked in the bank's parking lot. Sonny waited for her to get in and drive out of the lot. He watched as she drove in front of him. When her car was clearly out of sight, Sonny pulled over to the curb. He took a business card from his wallet and opened his cell phone. He dialed a number and listened for the ringing. After three rings the phone was answered.

"Hello."

"Hello, Drury. This is Sonny Vulich calling."

"Yes?" Drury sounded a bit confused by the call.

"I know it's late and you probably didn't expect a call from me, but I'm concerned about Fran."

"Go on."

"I need to speak to you. In fact, I really would like to meet with you. Can we have an early breakfast tomorrow?" Sonny did not want any time. Drury might make a few calls of his own. He was a careful man who liked to have all the facts and figures at his fingertips.

"You mean tomorrow?" Drury was beginning to become a little more attentive to the call.

"Yes, at the East Bank Club. I'll meet you in the lobby at 7:15."

"OK, see you then," said Drury. "Can you give me hint as to what this is about?"

"Well, I'm concerned, very concerned. It's something we should discuss face-to-face. We'll talk tomorrow. Goodnight. And thanks."

"Goodnight." Drury hung up the phone.

Sonny smiled to himself as he pulled away from the curb and back into traffic for the ride home. Everything was falling into place just perfectly.

CHAPTER
SIXTY-TWO

onny liked to get to the health club early and swim. He knew
many of the politicians, judges, and celebrities who frequented
the East Bank Club and he made a point of knowing and being
known. The locker room was a powerful place in Chicago.

Sonny arrived at 5:30 a.m. when the club opened, swam for forty-
five minutes, and dressed after he showered and shaved. He had lost
weight recently and thought he looked much more suave in the same
suits that he wore when he was twelve pounds heavier. After dressing
and admiring himself in the mirror for an extra moment, Sonny grabbed
his gym bag and walked to the rear of a restaurant called "The Grill"
located just outside the locker room.

In the rear of The Grill were large booths that were rarely used in the
morning. Most members did their workout and dashed off to work. You
could tell the level of power by the way they left. A quick cup of coffee
to go, a light breakfast at the counter, or leisurely dining with comrades
spoke volumes about who was who in the club. The particular booth he
wanted was one that would camouflage his meeting with Drury. They
would be seen by very few members and that is what Sonny wanted,
anonymity. There was a lot of talk on the street about Sunrise Bank and
he didn't want to add to the chatter.

Sonny placed his gym bag into the booth then walked down the
circular stairway to the first floor lobby. He could see Drury sitting on

a bench waiting for him near the pro shop. Sonny walked through the turnstile that allowed the members to exit.

Drury rose as he saw Sonny approaching and extended his right hand. They shook hands and exchanged a civil nod. Drury knew the process for entering the club. He followed Sonny to the registration desk where he asked for a "grill pass" to bring a guest into the club. The receptionist completed the pass, tore off a copy for her files, and handed one to Sonny. With the pass in hand, they entered the members' only part of the club. Sonny led Drury past the elevators, the catering office, and the salon to a rear entry to The Grill. They walked in discreetly and Sonny led his guest to the booth in which he had placed his belongings.

They slid into the circular booth. They stared at each other. Sonny spoke first. "Thanks for agreeing to meet me. I know it was a late call but I think it's important to talk."

"I'm confused," said Drury.

"Things have changed at the bank. Fran has been quite nervous lately. We have to keep things stress free for her; her health is at stake."

"You may not be aware of certain improprieties that have surfaced and have been brought to the board's attention," Drury said. "As a shareholder, a rather large shareholder and depositor, you must know that she has created a potentially volatile situation for you and the other shareholders."

"I have heard rumblings," said Sonny. He had to act cool, Lasman was his fly on the wall and had informed Sonny through regular briefings what was being disclosed and uncovered in the board meetings. With the information he was being fed from Fran and Lasman, it was likely that Sonny knew more than Drury about the truth.

Sonny continued, "Look, Drury, she has her faults. She's like a caged tiger, we know that. She is not one of my favorite people, but Fran is Fran. I've known her for years. I know her faults." Sonny shrugged his shoulders. "You don't know what she's going to do."

"Okay," said Drury, "I still don't know why you asked me here."

Sonny spoke in a slow, scripted, and condescending way. "Here are my thoughts. I have an idea. She clearly has a majority of the board votes now. Anything that you try to do is likely to get stalled. I would like to suggest a buyout."

"A buyout?"

"Yes, a buyout. But on certain conditions. First, we agree on a price per share, not just for you, but also for the other board members on your side of the fence. If we can agree on a price per share then we can move forward." Drury had a serious look on his face. He was considering all the angles of the proposal. Unfortunately, he didn't have all the angles to examine.

"It would have to be at a premium for us to exit respectfully," said Drury.

"Yes, of course, a generous premium," Sonny said. He knew what a buyout would entail. He had spent the night reading the list of shareholders and calculated what percentage of stock the board owned.

"This must include Adam Berg and his family too," said Drury.

"Of course." Sonny had been anticipating this suggestion as well. He did not want Berg to remain as a shareholder.

Drury stated his conditions. "And the buyout must include all of the investors I brought in as well as the other board members' friends and families."

Sonny had not anticipated this. He needed time to figure out the cost of this additional group. But as a seasoned negotiator, Sonny knew what to say next. "I suggest a couple of things. If you're interested please get back to me with a share price you think would make you happy, and secondarily, get me a list of people you want to include in the buyout and their total aggregate shares. But before we go on, I must insist that you keep this between us. Until this deal is put together, no one must know of it."

"You have my word," said Drury. "I'll get back to you in a couple of days." Drury got up and left the club. Sonny stayed and ordered breakfast. As he sipped his coffee his mind wandered. He knew his goal. The only question left unanswered was to determine the steps remaining to getting there.

CHAPTER
SIXTY-THREE

A week passed. Sonny did not hear from Drury, and he was beginning to wonder what was going on. He knew that if he called Drury the man would see it as a sign of weakness that would put him in a weaker negotiating situation. It was 3:00 p.m. about ten days after the meeting when Sonny's secretary rang from her private office. He pressed the speaker phone button. "Yes, Matilda."

"I have a Mr. Drury on the phone."

"Okay, thanks. I'll take it."

Sonny looked at the flashing light on the phone. He knew which line to pick up. He liked to be thoughtful before picking up a call. He paused, took a breath, and picked up the phone. "Hello."

"This is Drury, Stephen Drury."

"Yes, yes," said Sonny. "How are you?"

"Fine, thanks. Am I interrupting you or can we speak for a moment?"

"If you don't mind, let me finish the call I'm on. Can you wait a moment?"

"Sure."

Sonny pressed the hold button, but he did not have another call. He used this technique to gather his thoughts and put the other party off for a moment. Sonny took a notebook out of his desk and a pen from his pocket. He kept a book to take notes in his multiple meetings and he wanted to write down Drury's comments so he could recall items later as necessary.

He picked up the phone again and spoke, "Hello, thanks for waiting. Have you thought about our meeting?"

Drury spoke with confidence and without hesitation. "Yes I have. I think, all things considered, it's a welcomed opportunity. If we can agree on a price. I took my time to trace the sales of stock, and I was surprised, or maybe not so surprised, to learn you've been the lead purchaser of stock over the past few years. Now I don't have a problem with that, but I must say that the prices you've paid are low relative to value. Again, that's fine, you are entitled to purchase stock at anytime at any price, but if you want to buy us out than we want $30 per share, which is two times book value with a premium of twenty percent."

Book value meant a value of the company assets on a balance sheet. Banks sold at a multiplier of book value. Two times book value was not unreasonable if the entire bank was being sold, but this was a portion of the stock, not the entire bank. Sonny was not surprised. He had anticipated a request for a premium. Since their meeting he had developed a strategy. He had anticipated a generous offer and anticipated those shareholders who would be included in the buyout for control. He was prepared.

"Okay, Drury, do you have list of shareholders to include in this offer, provided a price is agreed on?"

"First, Sonny, I want you to know this is a non-negotiable price per share. Non-negotiable. Don't even come back with a penny less than $30 per share. And yes, I have the list and will e-mail it to you. I trust you'll keep it confidential. And each and every party on this list must be included too. No one is to be left off. I've spent a thorough amount of time determining those to be included and have kept this confidential as I said I would. I must have unanimous approval from the board members involved in this transaction before it can go forward. Now, let me say one more thing. If we are going to go forward with this sale, I want agreements drawn up and executed in sixty days. This will take a big effort on the part of all of us and I don't want a lot of time to pass by. Is this understood?"

"Yes, I understand. I don't think sixty days is unreasonable, but I need to sell this deal too. I'll get back to you soon. Goodbye." Sonny hung up the phone. He looked at his computer, and the e-mail arrived promptly as Drury indicated. Sonny opened the e-mail. An excel spread sheet was attached. As he read the list, he saw that it had all of the names he thought would be included. He had not been far off. At the bottom of the column was the aggregate number of shares: 312,500 x \$30 = \$9,375,000. That is what would be needed to buy out the opposition.

Sonny's next step was to sell Fran on the idea. That would be easy. She hated Drury and would do anything for full control of the bank. He could imagine their meeting. He was right when he called Fran the next day and met with her in her office. She was elated that Sonny was showing his true friendship by thinking up this plan. He suggested that the bank borrow the money from a larger bank and make interest payments on the money. He knew that Fran had so much ego invested in the bank that she would not consider the cost of the interest, how it would affect the bottom line or the ability to repay the loan. She played right into his hands.

She promised to keep the matter confidential until Sonny put it together. She gave him the go ahead. Fran felt she could finally be the master of her domain. The bank would borrow the money and own the shares of stock. She could run the bank with the board of her choosing and never have to worry again. Sonny had really come through for her. When he left, she bent to one knee, crossed herself, and said a prayer to God. She knew this was the right decision.

Meanwhile Sonny had other things on his mind. He had one more item to discuss with Drury, one more important item that needed to be part of the deal. They needed a gentleman's agreement, nothing in writing. This was as important as anything. How to do it was what Sonny was contemplating. Just how to do it.

CHAPTER
SIXTY-FOUR

In a small office on the twenty-fifth floor of the Dickson Federal Building on Dearborn and Adams in downtown Chicago, the FBI regional department head of the Bank Fraud Division was conducting a meeting. Madison Perry looked like a bookkeeper. He was a tall, slim man with horn-rimmed glasses. Perry came from an East Coast family who had a history of domestic and foreign service to the government. He had majored in criminal psychology at Columbia in New York then attended graduate school at Boston University Law School. After law school he joined the FBI and began in the fraud division. The government paid for one more advanced degree for Perry, forensic accounting.

As the FDIC was investigating Sunrise Bank, Perry was receiving updates with more frequency. The investigation was getting deeper and deeper and more and more dirty laundry was showing up. Perry knew that it was important to have a case well coordinated before filing charges and then slapping the bank with a "Cease and Desist" order.

He was listening to his subordinates as they reviewed their findings to date. He stood with his back to them as he looked out the window of his office. The gray sky that seemed ever present in Chicago during the winter months was depressing. Each day waking to gray and going home in the dark was enough to depress anyone. He turned back to his staff and tuned in as they were reading a list of the directors and depositors who had borrowed money with unusual or preferential terms and conditions from Sunrise Bank.

Perry knew that patience in his business was always required. Filings could be made at any time; there was never a rush. The best target for an investigation was one with a big ego who thought his or her behavior was flawless, someone who felt invincible. He had read about Fran Kontopolus and Sunrise Bank. He had seen the ads in the business journals and newspapers. The ad was always the same. Her face was as big and bold as Franklin's was on the one hundred dollar bill. But rather than a serious, contemplative look, she had a cunning grin, looking like Sylvester the cat with Tweety Bird in his mouth. The copy in the ad was very small and one had to read carefully to see what was being advertised. It was a socio-gram for who she was. When a person thinks she is the institution that spells trouble for the institution, he thought.

The attitudes of Leona Helmsley when she said publicly that taxes were for the "little people" and Marie Antoinette said "Let them eat cake" were shared by Fran Kontopolus, who was following this same path to ruination. Although this investigation began in a stepped-up fashion after the death of Everett Miller, the FBI had been watching Sunrise Bank through FDIC and state regulatory reports for some time.

As Madison Perry continued listening, he noticed something unusual on the floor and wall of the office. It did not strike him at first but then it grasped him, it grasped him so strongly that he turned quickly to look out the window once more.

He noticed his shadow. The sky was now bright blue. This was the first time he had seen the sun in days. It was an uplifting moment as he listened to the case. It was coming together in his mind. The case for conspiracy to defraud, filed on behalf of the depositors and shareholders of Sunrise Bank, was finally coming to light.

CHAPTER
SIXTY-FIVE

Sonny accomplished what he had set out to do. The agreement to pay Drury and his group the price requested and in a timely fashion was accepted.

On behalf of the bank, Lasman was assigned the task of preparing the written agreement between the board members and the investors. Drury had been assigned power of attorney to accept the offer on behalf of all of the selling parties. The agreement stated that upon its execution by both parties, Sunrise Bank and Drury, pending the payout, the named board members would sell their stock and resign their seats. New board members would be appointed by Fran with Sonny's approval or recommendation.

Sonny had Drury agree to have Ted Vulich placed on the board in the eleventh board seat without opposition as soon as possible. Drury insisted that a non-refundable deposit of $250,000 be placed in an escrow account on behalf of all sellers while Lasman was completing the purchase agreement. Drury knew the final draft of the document would take some time to read, review, and finally accept. Drury's demand was accepted and the $250,000 was deposited at American Bank.

Sonny had one last condition and demand for Drury. At the final meeting Drury would chair, and as his final act before handing the gavel to a new board chairman, Sonny wanted Drury's promise to fire Fran and have her immediately escorted out of the building. He said that the seven members he controlled would support this action. After her firing, Drury and his people could resign with a clear conscience. This is what they wanted, wasn't it? Drury had made clear that he felt Fran's behavior was unprofessional and an embarrassment. This way Drury and his people could leave the board feeling that they had accomplished something for themselves and the remaining shareholders.

Sonny's final request was one that weighed heavily on Drury. He had become less and less favorable to Fran as the years passed. He knew that he too had been seduced by her when he had raised money and brought investors to the bank. But he had worked very hard swimming upstream to keep Sunrise Bank afloat and genuinely protect his money and that of the shareholders. He told Sonny that he would have to think about this last request as he awaited Lasman's first draft of the purchase agreement.

Drury did not sleep at all that night. He returned to his office and sat at his desk with a legal pad of paper writing his thoughts. He wrote the pros and cons of firing Fran. As the clock ticked past the hours and the sun began to rise, Drury had made his decision and agreed to go along with Sonny's request.

It took the entire spring and most of the summer to finally receive an acceptable purchase agreement from Lasman. During these months, board meetings were held with no productive business being conducted. The multiple drafts Lasman submitted to Fran were returned with her comments, then revised and sent to Drury.

Many drafts were intentionally written in error, so that Lasman would be able to charge the bank more money in legal fees for his work. When the final document was presented and accepted by Drury on behalf of the shareholders, it was mid-October. This was the last board meeting for Drury and the remaining directors loyal to the shareholders. Although the buyout was strictly confidential to both the public and the bank's employees, the entire board knew what had been discussed and negotiated as to the price per share and who was participating in the buyout. Just to be fair to everyone on the board, Drury insisted that any member who wanted to be bought out, even those loyal to Fran and Sonny, have the same opportunity if they so chose. Those loyal to Sonny chose to stay.

The replacement board members waited in the bank's dining room. They were called into the conference room to hear Drury's final comments then assume the seats of those board members departing.

"Gentlemen," Drury began, "and lady, I was an enthusiastic participant as an organizer of this bank almost ten years ago. I met with Fran and believed, and still believe, in Sunrise Bank. It is not a secret that I haven't liked the way leadership has been conducted on behalf of this board and the shareholders. I think that for those of you remaining on the board you must remember it was the shareholders who financed this bank. The shareholders put up the money and the shareholders are owed the duty and responsibility of the management of this bank.

"Thus," he continued, "I must say I am sad today as I walk out of this board room and this bank for the last time. Very sad. I wish everyone the best of luck and wish you all well." He paused. Obviously something even more serious was on his mind. "I am still the board chairman, right?"

Everyone nodded or said yes. "In that case I have one more piece of business." He looked at Fran. "I've done everything I could to create value in this bank and have had a hard time over my tenure as board chairman. Sonny Jr., you are going to replace me as acting chairman until after the shareholder meeting in December. Before I hand you the gavel and dismiss the exiting board members I want to ask the present board if anyone wants to add anything under new business."

A hand went up. It was the hand of the eleventh board member, Ted Vulich. "I would like to make a motion. I move that we fire Fran Kontopolus, effective immediately, and in her place appoint Earl Lasman as temporary president."

Fran almost fainted and she began to tremble. Before she could catch her breath, she heard Drury call for a second to the motion. The motion was seconded by Pischer. The last words she remembered were "All in favor say aye." The vote was unanimous.

With that Drury banged the gavel. "Motion passed, thank you. Sonny Jr., here is your gavel. Goodbye, everyone."

Drury and his group of former board members left the room without looking at Fran or any of the remaining members. They weren't rats deserting a sinking ship, far from it. The rats were the ones staying onboard. Fran's head was spinning. What just happened? No sooner did the men leave and the new board members sit down, then all faces looked at Sonny Jr. Fran watched, sitting limp in her chair.

"Board members," Sonny Jr. began, "I appreciate everyone's confidence in my leadership, but I don't deserve the honor and responsibility of this position. For that reason I want to suggest that my father, an honorable and knowledgeable businessman who has been an advisor and active participant of this bank as depositor and shareholder, take my place. Do I hear a motion?"

"So moved," said Lasman.

Fran gasped.

"Seconded," said Stone.

"All in favor say aye."

"Aye," they said in unison.

Sonny Jr. opened his phone and texted something. A moment later Sonny appeared with a security guard. The guard had been briefed as to what to do.

"Hello, everyone, and thanks for your confidence. Guard, could you escort Ms. Kontopolus directly out of the bank, please. Be sure she does not enter her office or take the leased automobile that she has used during her employment. Get the keys now. She is to walk down the stairs privately and without incident through the rear of the building. Once she is gone, her office will be purged of her belongings and delivered to her apartment. Thank you."

And with that the guard walked to Fran, placed his hand under her arm, and lifted gently but firmly. Fran rose with his gesture. She was dazed and confused as she exited the bank. *Her* bank.

A homeless man was walking by as she stumbled down the street. She knocked him, and his package of cigarettes fell to the sidewalk. As she got to the corner she eyed a Seven-Eleven. She entered and purchased a package of cigarettes. She opened the package, lit one, and smoked it, deeply pulling the thick smoke into her lungs. The cigarette almost made her pass out. She felt light-headed. She hailed a cab and went home. She sat at her window and smoked and drank until the sky was dark. She was in a coma of sorts.

The pain began in her chest. She was belching an acidic liquid followed by more pressure and pain. Fran had never experienced this feeling before. These symptoms would not end. She felt she was having a heart attack. She could not breathe. What was she to do? She could not move and her chest felt heavy. She was dying.

She tried to scream for help but she had no voice. She was panicking. Fran was sweating. Her head was damp, her underarms soaked. She saw her purse on the chair in the dining room on the table. Her phone was in the purse. Until now she had been sitting and thinking over and over about what she would do to retaliate and get her position and status back. She thought she would sue the bank board on behalf of the shareholders for insubordination.

Now she had to stop thinking about anything other than surviving. She needed the phone to call 9-1-1 and she began to stand up. She staggered, holding on to one chair and leaning on another until she made it to the dining room. She fell to her knees, grabbed and opened the purse. She fell to the floor and landed on her back gasping for breath and rummaging through her purse for the phone. She finally felt the zipper compartment on the inside wall and opened it. Her hands were shaking. She opened the phone and began to press the buttons. Nothing was happening, the phone was dead. The bank had terminated her phone service. Sonny had thought of everything.

She instantly looked at the telephone on the wall in the kitchen. She repeated the motions of getting up from the floor to her knees and supporting herself to get there. It was not easy but she made it and dialed 9-1-1. She heard the voice on the other end of the phone. She told the operator she was having a heart attack and needed help; she gave her address and told the operator to hurry.

Fran collapsed on the floor. The next thing she knew was that firemen were breaking down the door to her apartment. She had an army of medics over her, some were taking her blood pressure and others were putting an oxygen mask over her face. She was lifted onto a gurney and rolled to the elevator then down to the ambulance. She was taken to Northwestern Hospital and spent the night in the cardiac care unit.

Fran did not have a heart attack, but she was kept in the hospital under observation and sedated with anti-anxiety drugs. For forty-eight hours Fran remained under sedation at the hospital. During these long hours she began to take it all in. Her bank was gone. She had lost her bank. All the stock options in her contract gone, her car gone, her phone gone, her office gone, her prestige gone. She had always wanted her face in the paper but not like this.

Sonny had deceived her. All of her friends had deceived her. Lasman, Stone, Deerfield, Shem, and Jr. all had stabbed her in the back. *How could they do this to me? I don't deserve this. I've always been so good to everyone. So good.* Her thoughts turned from shock and sadness to revenge.

Fran began to plan her lawsuit and how she was going to get back at Sonny and his gang. She knew how to make life miserable for people and she wanted her bank back. The two days in the hospital helped her become composed and, once at home, she began to contact attorneys to represent her case.

CHAPTER
SIXTY-SIX

The calling became frustrating; Fran found no one would take her calls. The word on the street was that Fran Kontopolus was now powerless. There was no one willing to go to bat for her. She had no leverage anymore. Fran was leaving messages all over town, yet no one was calling her back. The legal community in Chicago was shut down to her. Sonny had clearly let it be known that anyone who dealt with Fran on any level would be eliminated from representing him, Sunrise Bank, or any of the related companies he controlled or influenced.

Sonny got regular reports on Fran and her efforts to find legal representation. She wasn't giving up and this would not do. Sonny had to shut this down himself. Some lawyer or legal firm would break down and someone would eventually take her case. He knew that he would have to be the messenger and that he would have to convey the right message.

It was almost a week since the firing and the new board was scheduled to meet for the first time in a few days. His sources told him that Fran never left her home except to go out for cigarettes and alcohol. He received a copy of the medical report from her hospital stay. He had loyal people all over town. He could imagine her manic behavior as he chuckled to himself. Fran was a real pain in the ass, perhaps the worst in his career. But he could and would handle her. "*Levarse na petra de la,* my butt," he said.

His position as chairman was a perk. He enjoyed the letters of con-
gratulations arriving from the business and political community. He had
the finest decorators and carpenters redecorate his new office. It was
gutted to the studs within twenty-four hours of Fran's departure and
crews worked around the clock getting it ready. All traces of Fran Kontopolus were eliminated. He wanted the office perfect for him when he
arrived the morning of the first board meeting.

The checks were being cut for the shareholder sale and the chief
financial officer of the bank was readying them for distribution. Drury
was coming himself to read each one and make sure they were written
properly. He was glad to have this over. The loan to fund the buyout
from American Bank was stalled. To accelerate the payout, Sonny deposited his own money, close to $10 million, in the escrow account to
fund the stock sale. He knew Sunrise Bank would repay him within the
next few weeks. He was the chairman of the board. He could charge the
bank interest on his loan. As long as he was making money, he did not
care about anything else.

It did not faze him that the FDIC and state regulators had increased
their presence at the bank and additional personnel were reviewing
files. So what? These men and women reserved the conference room
with their staff reading and reviewing every loan document and lending
agreement in the files. Big deal. The FDIC "smelled blood in the water"
and was determined to be as thorough as humanly possible. Sonny never
paid attention to the auditors, He was too busy patting himself on the
back.

The shareholders of Drury's group received their checks. *Thank
goodness they're gone,* Sonny thought. One more piece of baggage was
out of his way.

Sonny began reviewing the by-laws of the bank with his personal
attorney to prepare amendments to change certain rules that would favor
him and his group now that he was in charge. But first he needed to quiet
Fran. It was noon on Sunday, the first day of the end of Daylight Savings Time, the night before the clocks fell back increasing darkness by
one hour. In the cab ride to Fran's apartment Sonny's thoughts began to
fester on Fran's vulnerability. He realized that someone in a weakened
emotional state, especially an alcohol and drug abuser, might be ma-
neuvered into walking in front of the moving train. Her lack of control

was her paranoia. *Just how far can I push this bitch?* he wondered. The ideas of how he could torment her were coming fast and furiously. He couldn't stop them. Then something occurred to him. If she killed herself, there would be no fingerprints on the smoking gun.

Sonny chuckled.

He waited until noon to arrive at Fran's building and slide the doorman fifty bucks to open the door to the resident's entrance. Sonny entered the elevator and pressed the button. When it reached her floor, Sonny stepped out and walked toward her apartment. The hallway reeked of cigarette smoke. Sonny found the odor offensive. He knew that when he departed he would have to go home, change clothes, and have everything he was wearing sent to the dry cleaners.

A knock at her door was unexpected. Ma or her brothers might come to visit her, but she always knew when they were coming and they all possessed a key to her apartment. She thought the knock was the maintenance man. She heard the knock again, this time more forcefully.

She looked like a mess. She rarely dressed these days and her old makeup was running down her face. Her hair was flat on her head. She opened the door without asking who was there.

Sonny stuck his foot in the door as a mobster would collecting a delinquent loan. The real bully had arrived. He pushed the door open and she reacted by stepping backwards. She began to tremble. It was him, the devil himself. She could not garner the strength to say anything.

He walked into her smelly apartment and grimaced. He circled her living room once and then spoke, "Fran, Fran, Fran. You have certainly looked better." He saw the empty liquor bottles and ashtrays filled with cigarettes. "Full ashtrays and empty bottles. Not much of a lifestyle, girl."

He looked around for a place to sit as his plan unfolded, but the fine layer of gray ash over virtually everything changed his mind. "Franny dear, I want you to know something. Your phone calls are getting you nowhere in the legal community. I've cut you off. You're boxed in." He paused to let that sink in as he gazed out the window at the Navy Pier Ferris wheel lighting up the night sky. "Now I'm not here to gloat. I want to make a deal with you. You shut up and accept your medicine like a good girl or I'm reporting you to the IRS."

"IRS?" she repeated.

"Yes, the I-R-fucking-S."

"What are you talking about?" He could tell by her tone that he had pushed a button in her and that she was gaining strength to attack. God only knew what she might do. She might physically attack him or push him out of a window. After all, she was angry and really upset. This was a woman one would put nothing past. He carefully walked around the dining room table so a wedge was placed between them.

"I am going to say this once, Fran, and only once. I have a record of your spending the bank's money for your possessions, thus the share-holders money, on yourself. Your shopping, dining, and travel expenses for your family and even your mother's utility bills were charged to Sunrise Bank. Not only is that illegal, it's income to all the members of your family who benefited by these illegal expenses. It's all taxable. Have you paid taxes on your supplementary income, Fran?"

He grinned, already knowing the answer. "In fact, your actions are subject to severe penalties since you or they never reported it as income. Think about that as I'm leaving. Should I hear from one more source that you're contacting lawyers I'm going right to the IRS! Do you hear me? As chairman of the bank, I have a duty to the shareholders. You'll still have your pension and your health insurance will remain in place until COBRA rolls in at 180 days. Don't do anything foolish as the key man life insurance covering your life doesn't expire for another year. In fact, do something foolish and we can all gain by it." There, he had said it. He thought to himself, *Go ahead. Pull the trigger, bitch.*

Sonny gave her an evil look, left the apartment, and exited the building. Fran was furious. She was still trembling as she reached for her bottle of vodka on the dining room table. It was room temperature, but she poured it into a standing glass still dirty from the day before and gulped down a mouthful.

It was not yet 2:00 p.m. on this dreary November day and she could see the lights of the Ferris Wheel at Navy Pier as the wheel turned ever so slowly. She chugged down another gulp of vodka and coughed as the burning hit her throat.

She was hungry and began to think of what she could eat. She opened the refrigerator, grabbed three eggs, and tossed their contents into a mixing bowl. She beat the eggs as hard as she could for a while, wishing she was pummeling Sonny's face. She paused to gulp more vodka. She grabbed a frying pan, threw in some butter, and poured in the eggs.

As they began to sizzle, she lit a cigarette. She stood over the eggs with the cigarette dangling precipitously from her lips as she finished cooking. Ashes fell into the pan. She threw the cigarette into her sink and ate the eggs directly out of the frying pan. She poured more vodka, this time adding orange juice, and topping it off with some ice cubes from the freezer.

She looked at the row of expensive knives on the counter. *I should have stabbed the son of a bitch. Right in his heart,* she thought. What did it matter what happened to her now? Jail, a life sentence; she had had enough. She wanted him dead.

Fran was feeling nervous and went to the bathroom. She opened the medicine cabinet and looked for some drugs to take the edge off. She grabbed several medicine bottles. Many were empty, she saw as she lifted them then threw them violently. Her anger increased.

The telephone in the apartment rang. It was now 4:30 p.m. and getting dark quickly. She stumbled back in the kitchen. She lifted the receiver. "Hello."

"Hello, Fran, this is Ma. What's wrong?"

"Sonny, Sonny, he was here. The devil, he was in my apartment." Fran gave a whale of a scream.

"That son of a bitch," said Ma. "That son of a bitch, I'll be right over. You need me, baby."

"Okay, Ma. Come quick." After she hung up the phone, Fran saw her bottle of Ambien by the sink in the kitchen. A nap, that's what she needed. The pills would help. She could sleep for a while, Ma would let herself in, and they could have a good cry followed by a real "bitch session."

Fran opened the bottle of sleeping pills, took a couple, popped them into her mouth, filled a glass with water, and drank it as she swallowed. She poured vodka into a glass, filling it to the top. She lit a cigarette with an old Zippo lighter that she found in a drawer. She clicked the lid shut to extinguish the flame as she began pacing the apartment. As she paced, the drug and alcohol combination began to make her dizzy. She needed another cigarette and stumbled back into the kitchen to get one. She did not notice that she had bumped into the stove and ignited a burner. She turned again and her arm sloshed a good bit of vodka onto the stove, dowsing the burner and the pilot light. The particular smell of natural gas began to slowly flood the apartment.

281

Fran found her way into her bedroom even after falling to her knees on the way. But she was so out of it the smell of the gas never registered. It was just one of many foul odors in the apartment. With the cigarette burning in her hand, she fell into her bed and into a deep sleep. The cigarette fell and burned into the mattress. The room filled with smoke as the mattress smoldered. The combination of cooking gas, smoke, and fire was deadly.

CHAPTER
SIXTY-SEVEN

Within ninety days of Sonny's first board meeting, the FDIC placed their "Cease and Desist Order" on Sunrise Bank. FDIC officials dismissed all management and board members and appointed their staff to run the bank. What had been uncovered during their investigation was that the bank not only had become insolvent, but that the officers and directors had violated a banking regulation referred to as "Regulation O."

"Reg O" came into effect during the Savings and Loan crises of the late 1980s and early 1990s. It prohibited the preferential treatment of officers and directors of a bank when borrowing or lending money was concerned. Violators were subject to strong criminal and financial penalties. Sonny Vulich, Earl Lasman, Kent Shem, Stone, and others had been treated preferentially by Sunrise Bank, way above and beyond the norm. As the people or related parties such as sons and partners were overseeing the approval of such moneys, there was conspiracy of fraud in the charges. Madison Perry and his FBI team were even busier than the FDIC boys.

Lasman lost his law license and Shem and Stone lost their real estate state licenses to revocation. All members of the board of Sunrise Bank were charged with tax evasion, fined severely, and prohibited from entering the banking industry again. There was quite a bit of turmoil for the employees as well. Many who knew of these dealings were fired and prohibited from entering banking again also.

When the government found insolvency, Sunrise Bank was closed and the assets, deposits, and liabilities were offered to another institution. The money did not just disappear. It was just put into capable hands.

Sonny, who had much more than the FDIC-protected $250,000 in his account, lost millions in the shutdown. He never received a reimbursement for the money he loaned the bank to pay off the existing shareholders. As careful as he was, he never had a note signed by Lasman as acting president placing responsibility for the loan to Sunrise Bank. Sonny had been counting on the payoff from the key man life insurance, but that payoff never arrived until after the FDIC intervention. The insurance became an asset that would be transferred to the new institution that would absorb the assets and liabilities of the insolvent institution. When the bank became insolvent, like any company, the stock lost all of its value. The stock deflated like a balloon. Sonny's stock was worthless as was the stock of the remaining shareholders. In all, Sonny lost close to $15 million in bank stock.

CHAPTER
SIXTY-EIGHT

After sorting things out and stabilizing the balance sheet of Sunrise Bank, the determination was made and the bank assets and liabilities were assigned to another Chicago bank.

"Well, who would have thought we would be adding this to our locations?" Tom Steiner said to one of his clones.

"I like the location of the new sign. Roosevelt Bank needed a presence in this neighborhood," responded his vice president in charge of marketing.

"Yes, so do I," said Steiner.

"I like it too."

"Thanks, Adam," said Steiner.

"This will be a great location for you guys," said Berg.

"You mean for us, don't you Adam? As a board member, you're an important person here." Steiner was genuinely enthusiastic.

"It's been fun, Tom, I know the bank will do well with this location, and I want to see the bank effective in this community," said Berg.

The crane was moving away as the workmen completed the electrical sign installation. It was turned on and it glowed brilliantly, THE ROOSEVELT BANK. The sign represented an institution that was prominent, distinguished, and untainted by scandal.

As the workmen moved on they began to unscrew the plaque that was attached to the building listing the founders of Sunrise Bank.

"Tom, may I keep that plaque?" said Berg.

"I don't see why not. Take it, Adam."

Berg walked to his car and told the workers to place the plaque in his trunk. When they complied, he spoke to himself. "Enough is enough" and he closed the trunk and symbolically closed the lid on the last remnant of the bank of deception and its sordid, squalid history.

END

About The Author

Mark B. Weiss, CCIM founder of Mark B. Weiss Real Estate, is a graduate of DePaul University and one of the country's foremost real estate authorities. His expertise results in frequent interviews on local, regional, and national radio and television programs, and he is quoted regularly in such publications as *Time, Money,* the *Chicago Tribune,* CNN, FOX NEWS and CBS MarketWatch.Com. Weiss is a former president of the exclusive Lincoln Park Builder's Club and served as a member of the Chicago Association of Realtors Board of Directors and chairman of the association's Commercial Committee. Weiss is a CCIM, Certified Commercial Member of the National Association of Realtors. Weiss was an organizer and Holding Company Director of the New Century Bank in Chicago. Weiss is the author of five books on real estate whose total sales have reached more than 100,000 copies.